THE LADY'S CHOICE
QUEENMAKERS SAGA II

BY
BERNADETTE ROWLEY

Acknowledgements

To Louise Cusack for her inspiration and advice over the last nine years.

To MG for being there to bounce ideas off.

To Romance Writers Australia (RWA) and Queensland Writers Centre for assisting writers, especially in regional areas.

To my husband, Michael, and my sons for their unending love and support and for sharing in the disappointments and triumphs of a writing life.

Titles by Bernadette Rowley

(in suggested reading order)

DEDICATION

Dedicated to my mother, Patricia Garton, my first teacher.

Table of Contents

CHAPTER 1

BENAE smiled to herself as her maid fussed with the tiara that adorned her dark hair. *Finally, something in my life is going to plan.* In moments, she would descend the grand central staircase to meet her host, Prince Jiseve Zialni, next in line to the throne of Thorius, Lord and Master of Brightcastle. If her scheme worked, she need not be all alone in the world. Being solely responsible for the five hundred citizens on her estate wore her down. Despite being surrounded by people, with her parents and brother gone, hers was a solitary existence.

She shook her head and dragged her thoughts back to the present. Now was not the time to be dwelling on difficulties. Her project was well in hand. Tonight, at dinner, she would shine in comparison to the princesses.

She didn't deceive herself that it would be simple to win the hand of the prince. The other contenders had arrived some time ago while Benae had been delayed by the myriad problems that accompanied the running of her estate. Now she was in residence and determined to make it impossible for Prince Zialni to resist her. Benae met Merel's eyes in the mirror.

"You are lovelier than I've ever seen you before, My Lady," Merel said. "That emerald silk makes you look a princess. His Highness won't be able to take his eyes from you."

"You're kind to say so."

"Everyone agrees you're the greatest beauty in all the land. Now that I've traveled outside Tylevia, I think they must be right. I've seen no other to rival you."

"It is said that the prince is rather vain, so I am hoping he prizes beauty over royalty," Benae said, spraying jasmine perfume on her neck and wrists. "I have no title or fortune to offer, as the other ladies have, but I can give him what he desperately seeks - a son." She smiled at Merel. "I must go. Don't wait up for me."

Merel bobbed a curtsy and withdrew. Benae checked her reflection one last time, sending a silent plea to the Goddess to watch over her that evening. She gathered her skirts and was preparing to leave the chamber when a commotion drew her to the window.

Below, in the castle forecourt, two men argued. She recognized the lieutenant who had welcomed her on her arrival. Vorasava was tall, thin and dark with tilted eyes in a rakish face, but it was the other man who held her attention. He was immaculately turned out, his dark-blue tunic snug across shoulders and hips, his cream breeches accentuating the powerful muscles of his backside and thighs. Long blond hair was tied at his nape and he had an air of calm control. As he stabbed his hand toward the stables, the blond god's blue eyes found Benae's and her heart stuttered. *Oh my!* Whatever he had been saying was lost, for the lieutenant also turned her way. Vorasava snapped a comment and strode off through the front gates.

The blond man broke eye contact and headed toward the castle entry. It was only then that Benae noticed the sword at his hip and the cat-like grace with which he walked. He was soon gone from view, but it took Benae's heart much longer to cease its pounding. There was something about the man that resonated with her, drew her, compelled her. He was about her age or perhaps a little younger and he obviously held a position of importance. She couldn't wait to make his acquaintance. This visit might be more than just a chance to claim the prince as husband. Perhaps there was other fun to be had, but for now, it was time to meet Prince Zialni and her rivals. *Time to see the competition.*

As Benae turned from shutting her chamber door, she almost ran into a tall, fair-haired woman in an exquisite pale-green gown. The woman's gray eyes held no warmth but Benae smiled anyway. "Hello."

"You must be Lady Benae Branasar," the woman said, unblinking.

Benae couldn't help the tension that entered her shoulders. *Talk about a welcoming committee.* "That's right…and you are?"

"Princess Avalin of Tylevia, of course."

Benae made a small curtsy as befit her rank. "I'm pleased to meet you, Princess Avalin. You must call me Benae. Have you been in Brightcastle long?" Benae took in the frown lines that were already etched into Avalin's face even though she looked to be similar in age, a mere twenty-six years old. Her straight, almost-white hair was pulled into a severe bun, held by a silver tiara studded with pale-green gems. Avalin's face was too long to be pretty and the picture she presented was, all in all, one lacking color.

"It's two weeks since I arrived. The prince and I have spent many moments together and I've become quite fond of him. This is a magical place and Jiseve is truly a wonderful man. He needs a woman who will bring a cool and practical head to the union."

"He is of fiery temperament then?" Benae asked, a ripple of interest coursing through her. Fiery she could appreciate. She had hoped and prayed the prince would not be a cold fish of a man.

"Oh yes, he has a temper at times." Avalin turned to walk along the hall to the staircase and Benae had to hurry to match the stride of the taller woman.

"Has he lost his temper with you?" Benae said.

"No, but I stick to safe topics." Avalin looked down her nose at Benae.

"Such as?"

"He loves to talk about his family, and he is very proud of this marvelous castle." Avalin looked Benae up and down. "I suppose you and he would have horses in common."

Benae smiled, thinking of her stallion, Flaire, and sent the horse a message of love. In answer, a picture of them galloping over a grassy meadow appeared in her head. *How can he be bored already when we've been here a mere few hours?* She realized Avalin was waiting for her outside a gilded door inlaid with quartz.

"Are you well, Lady Benae?"

"Of course, sorry."

A page opened the door and Avalin swept through ahead of Benae who stopped to thank the boy. She crossed the threshold of the room and paused as two richly dressed young women turned to her.

The woman with red locks and pale-blue eyes was the first to speak. "I am the Princess Lella of Brevisten, Lady Benae," she said, giggling. "Might I say you have the most glorious green eyes? I so wish I had *your* coloring." She sighed and stepped aside so that Benae could meet the last princess.

"And I'm Marey of Issia," the blonde girl with rich, brown eyes said. She couldn't have been more than eighteen years old. Benae wondered at her parents sending their daughter to be a candidate in an arranged marriage with someone old enough to be her father.

"I'm pleased to make your acquaintance, Princess Lella and Princess Marey." Benae bobbed a brief curtsy. These two girls would be no competition for her in the prince's affection, though if he wanted an heir, it paid to select a young woman.

Benae cast her gaze around the room. It was a small parlor with crackling fireplaces at each end and wall hangings depicting horses, dogs and huntsmen. The floor rugs were woven in rose and pale blue. "What a lovely chamber," she murmured.

"Yes, decorated by Prince Zialni's daughter Alecia, I believe," Avalin said. "Not to my taste. I'd pull those ghastly hangings down and raise portraits and paintings instead. Surely there must be local artists whose work would be polished enough to grace these walls?"

"You've been here some time, Princess Avalin," Benae said, "what do you know of Princess Alecia and her disappearance?"

"You should really ask Prince Zialni about his daughter, Lady Benae," Avalin said, the intensity of her gaze sending a warning tingle down Benae's spine. "I do so hate gossip."

"Well, I don't," Princess Lella said. "I heard from the servants that Alecia and her father had a falling out. He chose some old lord as her fiancé and she couldn't bear the thought of it. Then about a month ago, the prince had Alecia locked up in this very castle and no one knows why. Fancy a father locking up his grown daughter!"

The thought of Prince Zialni incarcerating his daughter rang an alarm within Benae. It didn't seem possible and yet Lella was convinced. "What of the kidnapping?"

"Oh, yes, Lady Benae," Lella continued, her blue eyes wide, "the official word is that Alecia was abducted by her protector, Captain Vard Anton, but my sources say she went willingly and that it was more rescue than abduction."

"That indeed is an intriguing and disturbing tale," Benae said, beginning to wonder about the true state of affairs in Brightcastle.

"*If* you believe the gossip," Avalin said. "I've not seen or heard a word that convinces me our host is anything but a loving father. His dealings with the common folk, however, are said to be harsh. Mind you, it's my experience that the *peasants* will always complain about their betters. It's their nature."

"Indeed, Princess Avalin," a deep, masculine voice said from the door.

Benae turned to see a strikingly handsome man in his middle years. He had dark wavy hair, a sensuous mouth and thick eyelashes framing sharp, blue eyes. He walked toward her with the grace of a swordsman and reached for her hand.

"The Lady Benae Branasar, I presume," he said, his voice like warm honey. "I am Jiseve Zialni and I am delighted that you would visit me in my humble home." He raised her hand for a kiss.

Benae smiled and curtsied, dipping low and in no hurry to rise. Let him believe he was all that mattered in that moment. "Your Highness, you honor me by inviting me to your court."

"It is I who am honored, Lady," Jiseve Zialni said. Warm his voice might be, but his smile was wintry, his features cloaked in sadness; understandable when his daughter had been kidnapped. Having lost his wife to consumption some time past, the prince was all alone in the world. Would Benae be the one to return sunny days to this battered man?

Jiseve was stunningly handsome and vital for an older man. It wouldn't be such a bad thing for her to devote her life to him, even if she couldn't love him. There were things more important than love. Benae tried not to dwell on what her sainted father would think of an arranged union. She had to believe he would at least understand her need to secure the estate, both financially and from the threat of the dark elves.

The prince turned and pulled on a rope beside the door. A bell echoed in the halls of the castle and, in moments, the blond god Benae had seen earlier slipped through the door into the chamber.

"Lady Benae, I want you to meet Squire Ramón. He will oversee your care while you are here."

The squire had changed into breeches and tunic of midnight blue and he wore a ruffled white shirt. His shoulders and arms strained at the fabric that encased them, as if he had recently come into his size. His golden hair glowed like none she had ever seen, and was tied back from his clean-shaven face, but his deep blue eyes were what drew her attention; they showed the heart of this man and Benae suspected that heart was pure gold.

He bowed over her hand and rose, his sweet citrus cologne swirling around her.

"Ramón Zorba at your service, Lady Benae," the squire said, his polished tones sliding down her spine. "I trust you had a pleasant journey."

Benae gazed at his mouth as he spoke and imagined those lips on her skin. A sigh escaped her and she became aware that silence had fallen. All eyes were upon her. What had he asked her?

"Yes, Squire, a very pleasant journey indeed." Benae turned to the prince who wore a frown. If she didn't take care, she would spoil her chances with Jiseve before her bid began. She gave herself a mental shake. *You're here to win Jiseve's hand, not make eyes at his squire. Remember your people. Their future depends on you.*

Benae gazed up into the shadowy eyes of the prince. "I know I'll enjoy my stay here."

Jiseve smiled. "I will ensure that you do, Lady." He looped his arm through hers. "Now let us adjourn to the dining room. Squire, see to the other ladies."

Jiseve guided Benae out the door and down a wood-paneled passage. The princesses and the squire followed.

"I hear you are an excellent horsewoman," the prince said. "Your mount is a fine creature; such a perfect dappled gray."

Benae just managed to control her gasp of surprise. Just how much did this man already know of her? Not too much, she hoped. It was wise to keep some mystery. "Yes indeed. I love to ride and Flaire is one of the deepest joys of my life. I trained him, you see."

Jiseve smiled. "I will show you my horses tomorrow, Lady —"

His words were interrupted by a ripping sound and Benae felt her skirt snag at the back. She gasped and swung around to find Princess Avalin's slippered foot resting on the delicate emerald lace bordering her gown. The skirt pulled away, exposing her underskirt.

"Oh dear, Lady Benae," Avalin gasped. "I'm so sorry about your dress." She stepped back and Benae gathered the sagging fabric, trying to hold it in place. Anger replaced shock as Avalin's lips curved in a tiny smile. *So this is how it is to be!*

"You must go to your room and change, Lady Benae," Avalin said, stepping past Benae and grasping the Jiseve's hand. "We'll wait for you in the dining room."

The prince, who had been silent, frowned as Avalin took over. "Yes, My Lady, it will take only moments to change. I will save you a seat next to mine." His voice purred with a subtle appeal that was not lost on Avalin, whose mouth twisted in a grimace. Benae was sure Avalin would take full advantage of her absence to woo Jiseve, but the

Tylevian princess had already had two weeks with him. If he wasn't convinced of her suitability yet, then he never would be. *I still have a chance to win this race.*

The prince turned to Ramón. "Show my guest to her chambers, Squire, so she can change, and then escort her back to the dining room."

Jiseve's words brought Benae's gaze to Ramón. A muscle tightened along the squire's jaw. Seemingly, the handsome squire was not best pleased to be escorting Benae to her room. Since when did a man not seek her company? *Since never!* Benae determined that the delectable Ramón Zorba would not be the first.

* * *

Ramón walked in silence beside the beautiful, dark-haired woman who was the latest of the candidates for his master's arranged marriage. *Has she no shame?* For a moment, Lady Branasar's sparkling, emerald eyes and commanding demeanor had spoken of a different type of woman to the three princesses who had arrived before her. But she was just like the rest. Willing to prostitute herself for the sake of money. Where was love? Where was the sanctity of a union between two souls who spoke to each other?

The thought of love drew his mind to Princess Alecia, though it had been one way with her: *his* love and admiration against her worship of Vard Anton. The two times they had kissed stood large in his memory. Alecia could have loved Ramón in the right circumstances. She had professed to love the previous squire, Jorge, but he had been killed by mercenaries. Ramón now had his suspicions that the murderers had been hired by Prince Zialni. Alecia had her own way of dealing with the killers, tracking them down one by one and dispatching them.

Awe inspiring! No wonder I love her. And here am I, cooped up in this damned castle while Anton makes free with the woman who should be mine! If only he had stopped them from escaping when he had the power; instead, he had allowed Alecia's pleading lilac eyes to sway him. Now it was too late. *No! It wasn't.* Somehow, he would shake off the duty that kept him tied to Brightcastle, and by then his sword skills would be equal to the infamous Captain Vard Anton. Calm descended upon him as he imagined the kidnapper breathing his gurgling last.

* * *

"Are you well, Squire?" Benae asked of the man who escorted her. He had made no attempt to converse and the silence grew wearying.

"Yes, Lady, I'm quite all right." He frowned. "I must apologize for Princess Avalin's behavior. The damage to your dress was deliberate."

"Of that I am well aware, but you're not responsible for her actions."

"Still, you're under my care."

"At least I know what I can expect from her now."

The squire's jaw tensed. *What ate at him?*

"Forgive me if I pry, Squire Ramón, but you seem out of sorts. Have I done something to offend you?"

"No Lady." He averted his gaze but there had been something, a flash of shadow that told her he hid deep feelings about something. It would be fun getting inside his head.

They reached the base of the central staircase and he grasped her elbow to help her up the stairs. The touch sent a thrill through her and she covered her gasp with a cough, concentrating on her breathing to bring her emotions back under control. This was all wrong. She was usually the cause of these feelings not the sufferer; and this man seemed completely unaffected by her.

When they reached her room, Ramón opened the door. "I'll wait here, Lady," he said, closing the door on her after she had stepped through.

Benae stared at the barrier, unable to believe he had all but shut the door in her face. He could not have expressed more eloquently his lack of desire for her company. But who could blame him? She was here to win the hand of Ramón's master, not to have a fling with the delectable squire. A shiver ran from the base of her skull to her core at the thought of those strong hands, those sensuous lips, on her body.

"Lady Benae," her maid said, as she came through from her quarters that adjoined Benae's sleeping room. "Why are you returned so early?

Oh…" Merel came forward to examine the damage to the back of Benae's dress. "Your favorite gown! I'll help you into a new one and mend this right away. How would the black satin with the golden lace suit? You can still wear the emerald choker and tiara."

"That would do well, Merel." Benae could have kissed the woman for not asking how the damage had been done to her gown. Her young maid would hold her own in any of the royal courts.

In moments, Benae was attired in the new gown, golden lace over black satin, which left her shoulders bare and displayed a tempting amount of cleavage. *Let's see how that chit Avalin deals with* this *dress. Not to mention the squire.* Benae shook her head. *Really.* She should be beyond such silly thoughts. She was twenty-six, a woman of the world and head of her own estate, though the reason she was leader there still caused her endless sadness.

She pulled her thoughts from the past and squared her shoulders. "Thank you, Merel. That will be all for tonight." Benae opened the door and stepped into the hall.

* * *

Ramón straightened from where he had been leaning against the balustrade. He struggled to control the lust that swept through him at the sight of the breathtaking woman who had just stepped from her room. Flickering candles in the wall sconces leant her an air of mystery. He clamped the urges back where they belonged – shut away. He had no right eyeing her this way.

She paused and her gaze speared him though it was too dark to see her eyes. He would need to be made of stone not to be affected by her; so petite yet fiery enough to handle the million-and-one details an estate owner must tackle. He knew only too well what it took to care for property and people.

"Let us hasten to the dining room, Lady," Ramón said, guiding her toward the stairs. "They'll be waiting for us."

She touched his hand. "What has you so irritable, Squire?"

"You misinterpret my mood, Lady."

"I do not."

Ramón drew a deep breath. *Very well, she has asked the question.* "I don't understand why you would put yourself in the position of competing with others for the prince's hand." *There, it's out, done.*

"Oh, really?" Lady Benae's fiery emerald eyes made him rethink his words. *Did she never wonder how her actions would appear to others?*

"Yes, My Lady. You have your own estate and I can see you are intelligent. Why would you stoop...?" Ramón stopped, realizing he might have gone too far.

"I don't believe my motivations should be a matter for public speculation."

"No, Lady, forgive me."

They continued to the dining hall in silence. The sooner he was out of Brightcastle and on the road to finding Alecia the better.

* * *

The impact Benae made on entering the dining room was nothing short of satisfying. Avalin's jaw dropped and Jiseve immediately leapt up, walked to Benae and drew her to the seat on his right. It made up for how annoyed she was by Ramón's judgement.

Benae hoped she might be free of Ramón's company at dinner. He was far too distracting. However, there were six places set at the candlelit table. The squire sat between Avalin and Lella on the opposite side. If Ramón had been beside her, she might have been able to keep her eyes from him. *He's not for you.* She steeled herself to ignore him while she was with Jiseve.

Once Benae and the squire were seated, Prince Zialni rose. Glass of ruby wine in hand, he gazed at each of his guests in turn. *Oh, how he loves the spotlight!* Perhaps there was not so much sadness after all. Perhaps he was coldly seeking to fill his bed with a warm woman. If that was the case, why had he not advertised for a wife sooner? His wife had been dead four years and it was said that he had never been seen with another woman since Princess Iona breathed her last. Until now.

"With the arrival of Lady Benae, our party is complete," the prince said. "I will not hide my delight at having you all here under my roof, but there is a serious reason underlying your visits."

Benae cast a surreptitious glance at the squire. His eyes were downcast and jaw tense. From where did his disapproval stem? He clearly believed this contest for the prince's hand to be beneath her and the other ladies. *Why?* For some reason, his disapproval unsettled her. She shook the thought away and returned her attention to the prince.

"I find myself without an heir when I had thought my plans set." Now it was Jiseve Zialni's jaw that clenched. "You all know how important that heir will be to this kingdom. My brother cannot rule forever and has no children. I am next in line for the throne but only a son, not a daughter, can be heir. I had thought perhaps a grandson would solve the problem, but it is not to be. And so, I come to the reason for your collective visit. From amongst you I will choose my bride. She will bear me a son, or sons, to ensure Thorius remains in Zialni hands. My nephew Piotr —" The prince bit his lower lip as though he had nearly said too much. Benae guessed there was no love lost between the two.

"My decision will be made in all haste for I have already let too many years slip by since the death of my beloved Iona. So raise your glasses." Everyone at the table followed his words with action. "To your very good health, my beautiful guests."

As Benae toasted the others, her gaze fell upon Avalin. If looks could kill, Benae would be lying dead at the ice princess's feet. Oh yes, Avalin had identified her main competition. Before Benae's arrival, the Tylevian princess must have thought her position secure, though why she would discount the younger women, Benae could not say.

The kitchen staff arrived to serve the first course: pheasant, served in a broth with fresh white bread.

"Please give praise, Squire Ramón," Jiseve said.

Ramón stood and Benae closed her eyes to concentrate on his deep voice as he spoke the blessing. His love of the Goddess was apparent in the heartfelt way he said the prayer. These seemed not just empty platitudes for Ramón, but a core part of his being. It struck a chord within Benae who had been raised to worship all that was the Goddess.

Their eyes met as Ramón resumed his seat. He didn't return her smile but turned and engaged Lella in conversation. Nothing could have better reminded her of her earlier resolve. Jiseve was the reason she was here, not Ramón, as delectable as the blond squire was, with his azure gaze she could so easily lose herself in. She turned to the equally compelling sapphire eyes of the prince.

Jiseve reached for her hand and squeezed it. "Please go ahead and begin, Lady. The pheasant was freshly killed this morning."

He watched as she sliced a piece from the bird in front of her and placed it in her mouth. The meat had a strong, gamey taste, but was tender and delicious. She licked the salty broth from her lips. The prince's throat moved in a sudden spasm, his pupils dilated, his breathing quickened. *He is enjoying my little game!* She raised her glass.

"Your good health, Highness," she said, tapping her glass against his, the musical note of the crystal ringing around the table. This was almost too easy.

Avalin went on the attack.

"Lady Branasar, how many people live on your *little* estate?"

"Five hundred, give or take," Benae said. "Surely you would know that, as your father is my king."

Avalin's pale cheeks flushed. "Oh…you are of the Tylevian Branasars. I should have realized." Avalin flushed a deeper shade of red as she fell from one blunder into another.

"What of Tylevia, Princess Avalin?" Benae said, pinning Avalin with her interrogator's stare. "What are your responsibilities there?"

Avalin turned her gaze on Jiseve who appeared to be enjoying the rivalry between the ladies. "I have a myriad of responsibilities. Suffice to say I am aware of the duties of the head of a household," then looking to Benae, "*Lady* Benae."

Benae narrowed her eyes at Avalin. She wasn't sure where this was heading but she suspected a change of topic was wise.

Just then, Princess Lella piped up. "I've been schooled by my tutors from a young age to run a kingdom," she said, "even though I have four brothers who will rule before I ever do. We still have ruling queens in Brevisten, you see. My mother and father are joint rulers."

Prince Zialni seemed not best pleased to be reminded of the differences between kingdoms. "I don't believe any wife of mine will be called upon to undertake the duties of a ruler. Iona was content to run our household and care for myself and our daughter. That is all I would ask."

Avalin seemed content, while Lella's pale-blue eyes were troubled. Marey sat across from the squire and seemed lost in contemplation of him. As for Benae, she resolutely kept her gaze on the prince, well, mostly.

"Prince Zialni —" Benae said.

"Please, call me Jiseve."

"Jiseve, surely there are other traits, other skills you would seek in a wife?"

Avalin sniggered but Benae ignored her.

"My wife must have grace and beauty, she must be young enough to bear children and she must have good taste and discretion."

Well, that left Marey out of the race. The Issian princess was still gazing at the squire. For all Benae knew, the girl was probably playing footsies under the table with Ramón. She tried to ignore the spike of jealousy that thought provoked.

"Jiseve, surely you wish your wife to have a mind of her own," Benae said, "to be able to converse and to be a stimulating companion."

Avalin sniggered again. "I'm sure Jiseve has found me to be a most 'stimulating' companion over the past two weeks."

Jiseve smiled indulgently at Avalin.

Benae's eyebrows climbed her forehead. Of all the words she would have used to describe Avalin, saucy wouldn't have been one of them. Perhaps she needed to reappraise the title of "ice princess". Had Avalin already slept with Jiseve? *What* is *the true state of affairs here?*

Jiseve turned to Benae. His eyes burned into hers, creating a private moment between them. Benae's stomach tightened and desire trickled through her belly. *Oh my, he's seducing me in front of Avalin!*

"I'm sure you have all the attributes I could possibly want in a companion," he murmured, catching her hand and kissing her fingers.

A chair scraped across the floor and they turned to find Ramón standing at his place. "If you'll excuse me, Your Highness, ladies, I'll take my leave."

"You will stay," Prince Zialni said, "and help me attend to the needs of these fine ladies."

Ramón frowned.

"Do you have a problem with that, Squire?" Jiseve's voice held an undercurrent of menace.

The implied threat brought the previous conversation about Jiseve's harsh treatment of his daughter, and the common folk, back to Benae. Perhaps there really was a dark underside to life in this castle. *Or maybe I should concentrate on my plan and stop looking for problems.* After all, the situation on Benae's estate was desperate and Jiseve could offer a solution that would benefit both.

Ramón shook his head. "No, Your Highness." He resumed his seat as the main meal was delivered.

Benae sent a smoldering look to her prince. She could almost taste victory. Soon she would be mistress of Brightcastle, and her people could embrace a future free of starvation and the dark elven menace.

* * *

Ramón watched as the prince swept Benae from the table and onto the small wooden dance floor. *Will this evening never end?* He had other things in mind for tonight, like meeting up with one of his mercenary spies, but what did the whim of Ramón Zorba matter beside the desires of the prince. And "desires" was the right word. As the two lute players plucked out a sedate court tune, the prince steered Benae around the small dance floor, her body held close to his, his lips moving as though he whispered endearments. Even Ramón could see that his employer was different with Benae than he was with the rest of the candidates. He was smitten, and no wonder. She was enchanting, with her flashing green eyes, full sensuous lips and perfect form. *Any man would kill just to have her in his arms*. He almost choked on his wine. Where had that thought come from?

He scraped his chair back and asked Marey to dance. The youngest princess giggled her response and he swept her onto the dance floor. Benae had her eyes closed as she was guided around the floor. Perhaps the attraction was mutual, and the lady had fallen under Zialni's spell. He was handsome for an older man and he had wealth and power. These seemed important to Benae.

Anger welled up within him and he crushed Marey to his body without knowing what he did. She squeaked and he gazed down upon her. Marey was young, perhaps eighteen. She could not have any experience with men and here she was being offered up to Prince Zialni as a brood mare.

He shook his head. "What are you doing here, Princess?"

Her wide, brown eyes gazed back at him. "What do you mean? You know the purpose of my visit."

"You should be safe in your palace, entertaining the young men of your court, not here vying for the hand of a man old enough to be your father."

Marey's saucy smile shocked Ramón to his core. "Are you jealous that the 'old' prince receives all the attention? Perhaps you and I could meet later, so you can attend to my 'needs'. The prince has asked you to do so. Did you not take note?"

Ramón choked as breath rushed into his chest. Not so innocent then, or she was playing a damned convincing game. He coughed and pushed her back from his body, completing the dance at arm's length. They returned to their seats and Prince Zialni began dancing with Princess Lella.

Ramón's eyes met Benae's across the table. "Please join me in a dance, Lady." Before Marey could raise her blonde brows, Ramón was beside Benae and pulling her into his arms for a lively court dance that soon became a waltz. She was tiny, barely reaching his shoulder, but her body was formed of hard muscle from her horse-riding. It was a heady mix of soft feminine curves and toned flesh, but he shouldn't be thinking like this. He took a deep breath.

"What's amiss, Ramón? You're quite pale." Her lovely eyes shone up at him and he was seized by a strong urge to kiss her full lips.

"Princess Marey propositioned me," he said.

Benae laughed. "The Issians are a precocious people. Their girls are first bedded at fifteen, so by Marey's age they are experienced in the ways of the bedroom."

Ramón stared. When would he ever understand women? Why did they not save themselves so that the giving of their virginity meant something? He had been saving himself for Alecia since he had first seen her, the evening of her debut at Wildecoast. And Alecia had chosen Anton, a man so unworthy of her it took his breath away.

After a month on the road with Vard, Alecia's good name was surely ruined, but Ramón didn't care about any of that. Alecia would be his first and only partner. His manhood stirred at the thought. It had nothing to do with the lovely woman in his arms.

"Now you're blushing, Ramón. I'd give much to know your thoughts."

He frowned. "I was thinking of Princess Alecia."

"So, that's the reason you're holding me so close I can feel your arousal."

Ramón sprang back and Benae laughed out loud. All eyes were upon them.

"I'll escort you to your place, Lady."

Ramón excused himself and left the dining room, his mind and body roiling with frustration and disgust. Instead of returning to his room, he fled the castle, exiting the grounds via the park gate.

He craved release from his inner turmoil, needed to run off the frustration of the last few weeks when his job had changed to minding women who would sell themselves to the prince. He sought to forget, for a moment, his aching desire to have Alecia in his arms; to banish his body of the angry impotence that Vard Anton had placed there.

He broke into a jog and was soon running into the forest.

26

CHAPTER 2

THAT was a magical night, Benae thought. The dinner with Jiseve and the princesses had ended well. The prince seemed reluctant to leave her side, but had been called to attend to another matter. She left straight after, although Avalin was still at the table, drink in hand. Well, that was what the woman deserved for trying to spoil Benae's efforts to impress Jiseve. It had backfired on her, thank the Goddess.

As Benae reached for her doorknob, a low moaning drew her attention. The sound came again, drifting over from the east wing. Though it was none of her business, Benae couldn't ignore suffering. She followed the noise until she stood before a door. Yes, the poor soul was within this room.

Benae opened the door silently and entered, closing it behind her. As she crossed the sitting room and peered into the bedchamber, the stench of rotting tissue hit her like a physical blow.

Ramón bent over a skeletal form on the bed, bathing the face of the victim while he murmured words Benae could not hear. The patient moved his head from side to side and the covers over the man's abdomen were stained with blood.

Stomach churning, Benae joined Ramón at the bedside. "Let me tend him."

"What the hell are you doing here, Lady?"

She met his anxious gaze. "I could ask you the same. Who is he and why is he here?"

"It's none of your concern."

"Who is he?"

"Lord Giornan Finus, Princess Alecia's betrothed and Prince Zialni's advisor. He tried to stop Vard Anton from taking Princess Alecia. This wound is the result. He has lain here this last month, dying."

Benae placed her right hand on the man's forehead and closed her eyes. There was almost nothing left of him. She sank through the layers, delving deep into his body and spirit, questing for the hurts and the hope. She found none of the latter. The delving left her chilled and she shuddered.

"His wound is taken over with foul humors. It won't be long before he leaves this world and continues his journey." Benae closed her eyes again and wove a net of peace then let it fall. Finus settled and seemed to sleep.

"Another of Anton's legacies," Ramón said, "though I never had much time for Lord Finus. At least he is calm now."

Benae withdrew her hand, but the filth had seeped into her very soul. She turned from the patient to find Ramón's intense gaze upon her.

"Are you well, Lady?"

"I can never abide suffering and death and there has been so much lately." She turned away and rested her forehead on the bedpost. The wood was cool against her skin. Several deep breaths had her emotions back under control.

There was a sound from Lord Finus, and his breathing became a gasping struggle. As they both beheld the skeletal form on the bed, the lord gave one last tortured breath and lay still. Benae's chest tightened and a sob rose to her throat.

Ramón grasped her hand. "His passing has upset you."

Benae struggled to meet his gaze. *What's happening to me?* Why couldn't she conduct herself with her usual aplomb? "I lost my brother recently and before that, my parents. His death reminds me of them and of how they suffered." *And I could do nothing.*

"You're on your own in the world?"

"I am."

"That's the reason you entertain this 'arrangement' with the prince?"

Again, she felt Ramón's disapproval of her quest for marriage. Well, he could keep his opinions to himself. "That's none of your business." Had her voice ever sounded so cold?

She turned to the corpse. "We must take steps to prepare him for burial."

"Return to your suite, Lady Branasar. I will summon a woman who will wash the body and dress the lord in his ceremonial robes. Tomorrow he will begin the journey back to his family estate where he will be buried."

Benae stared at Ramón. He could be so commanding when he desired. There was a wealth of authority hidden deep within this man and, when that power broke free, it would be like a butterfly emerging from a cocoon. She nodded at him, took one last look at Lord Finus and swept from the room.

* * *

Ramón left Lord Finus's body with the woman who would wash and dress it and returned to his chambers. Benae Branasar was not his concern and neither were her motivations. Why should he care if she offered herself to the prince? To Ramón's mind she was little better than the prostitutes who sold their wares on the street. He had thought that loneliness was her motivator, but, judging by her reaction, she was embarrassed about the situation. Did she feel that her reasons wouldn't stand up to his scrutiny? Did she even care what he thought of her?

Of course, she doesn't care. What was wrong with him anyway? He would seek his rest and to hell with Lord Finus and Lady Benae Branasar. It had been the longest day with the arrival of more guests, his sword practice, forest run and then the bedside vigil. He didn't regret it though and hoped that someone would sit with him when it came time for him to pass to the other life.

29

CHAPTER 3

BENAE rose early, hoping to catch Jiseve at breakfast. Her heart did a girlish jig when she walked into the breakfast room and her host was still at table. The young maid attending him curtsied and scampered from the room, cheeks wet with tears.

"Lady Benae," he said, placing his tea cup on the table, "you are truly unique among women. None of the other ladies are awake yet." He crossed to her and kissed both her hands. "I hope you slept well?"

"Oh, yes, quite well, Jiseve. I was just eager to see you." Benae glanced to where the girl had disappeared. "Your serving maid seemed upset."

Jiseve waved a bejeweled hand in dismissal. "She cannot pour tea the way I like it, but she will learn."

Benae stiffened. For a moment, Jiseve's words had again sounded threatening but she must be mistaken. A servant couldn't truly be in trouble over tea, could they?

"Is there anything in particular you wish to discuss, Benae?"

Her name on his lips was a caress. She must have mistaken the threat of a moment ago. Yes, she could see herself falling for this handsome prince – in time. "Do you suppose we could go for a ride after breakfast? Flaire is already restless."

Jiseve smiled his sad smile. "I'm afraid Princess Avalin has the pleasure of my company on a ride this morning. Tomorrow, you and I will ride together. I thought a picnic?"

"That sounds wonderful," Benae said, even though she ground her teeth at the thought of Avalin having her way with Jiseve. Hadn't the woman monopolized the prince enough? By the Goddess, she'd been in Brightcastle two weeks! She had so much of a head start.

Jiseve drew her forward to the table and she tried to put aside her disappointment and enjoy his company. He asked her about her trip and recounted stories of his travels in his youth.

"Why did you journey so far to the north, Jiseve?" Benae asked, as she buttered a piece of bread and spread it with honey.

"I was sent by my father, then king, to lead a campaign against a faction of the dark elves, some two decades ago. There was an elven prince called Faenwelar who had some notion of conquering Thorius. We drove them far back into their mountain homes and secured an understanding with the elven king, that he would control this unruly faction. I thought never again to be plagued by them, at least in my lifetime. And now you tell me your kingdom has been troubled."

"Something must be done. Tylevia has already lost too many men, young and old." Benae took a sip of tea, thinking of the brother she had buried only two months ago.

"It's a little early to assume this is more than isolated tribes reaching for power," Jiseve said.

"I hope you're right." Benae didn't think Jiseve knew the full extent of the trouble. On her own estate, dwellings were locked up tight when dark came on and so were livestock. Still they lost people and animals to the elves.

"I am, my dear."

With that, Jiseve changed the subject. Throughout breakfast, he gently probed for more information from Benae. His knowledge of her was surprisingly accurate and detailed. All went well until the subject turned to family.

"I am saddened to hear of the loss of your parents and brother, Lady Benae," he said, sympathy thick in his gaze. He reached across the table and grasped her hand. It was strong and warm.

Pain and loss, never far from Benae these days, rose up, threatening to split her heart open. What could she tell him of life after her parents and brother, Alvan, were so tragically ripped from it? "Thank you, Jiseve. It has been a difficult time, but you know only too well of the sadness of such events."

His face clouded more than she could ever have predicted. "I lost my dear wife, the catalyst for this project of mine, over four years ago. She was my soul mate." His voice trailed to a whisper and Benae's heart broke for him.

"What of your daughter? I hear she is absent too?"

His gaze snapped to her face. "Alecia was taken by a scoundrel and I will move heaven and earth to retrieve her. She is all I have left."

"She's in love with this captain?"

Jiseve surged to his feet; the chair crashed backward, and cutlery fell from the table. Benae gazed up at him, heart pounding.

"I bid you good day, Lady. If you wish to go riding, Squire Ramón will see to it." He strode from the room and Benae was left frozen in her seat. The servant waiting just inside the door smiled at her and averted his eyes. Well, the subject of Princess Alecia was definitely off limits. Why had she listened to Avalin? Family was a "safe topic" indeed. It seemed Avalin had struck a blow without even being present and Benae feared all her good work had been undone.

Benae left the breakfast room, deep in thought. She might have had a set back with Jiseve, but she wouldn't believe all was lost. One silly question couldn't spell disaster for her future with Jiseve, surely? She couldn't dispel the seed of fear that settled in her gut.

"Oh!" she said, coming to an abrupt halt against a broad chest. She found herself staring into the deep, blue eyes of the delectable Ramón Zorba. "Squire," she murmured, holding his gaze longer than she should. Perhaps he would prove a timely distraction?

"Lady Branasar," the squire said, his features flushing a deep red as his eyes dipped to her hands on his chest.

There was something about this one, something special. She would dearly love to explore the possibility that they could be friends, perhaps more than friends, but that wasn't the reason for her visit. She had to remember that.

"I trust you slept well." He frowned, as if his comment brought unwelcome memories. Did the shadows beneath his eyes tell the tale of a restless night? He was so complex, intriguing, beguiling. Suddenly mischief filled her heart.

"I slept well, thank you." She fixed him with a long, assessing look. "And the scenery is so spectacular here, I believe I'll enjoy my stay." Benae ran her gaze slowly over him, from top to tail.

He tensed under her scrutiny. "I'm glad you approve, Lady Branasar. Now, if you'll excuse me."

"No," she said.

The squire had moved to walk past but paused, a frown marring his brow. He would be so much fun to toy with, to manipulate, to do other things with...

"I beg your pardon, My Lady?"

"You're not excused. I require you to accompany me to the stables to inspect Flaire."

Ramón's eyes widened and then flicked to the side as if he struggled for a reason to deny her. *He really doesn't wish to spend time with me!* A hot blast of anger almost made her gasp out loud.

He smiled but it never reached his eyes. "I would be happy to accompany you, Lady Branasar." He offered his arm and they walked together out the front door and across to the stables.

"Did the body of Lord Finus leave this morning for his estate?" she asked, distracted by the texture of his hard muscles beneath her hand.

Ramón cleared his throat. "It did, My Lady."

"You seem preoccupied."

"I apologize if I'm less than attentive."

"You have other matters on your mind." Out of the corner of her eye, Benae saw him glance at her.

"I have much to concern me at this time, but you are a part of my duties. I wouldn't have you think you're not my priority."

Benae turned to face him. "Your duties! Are those duties so odious? Keeping the company of beautiful women and seeing to their comfort seems hardly difficult to me."

His eyebrows shot up into his blond forelock. "I've angered you," he said quietly. "I apologize. I could ask someone else to see to your needs."

Despite her irritation, Benae smirked at his choice of words. "See to her needs" indeed. If only he knew what she "needed" at that precise moment. She took a deep breath and swallowed the passion that made her heart race. "I asked you to accompany me and you I shall have."

He nodded and they continued toward the stables. Flaire was munching hay in his spacious stall, his dappled gray coat gleaming from a recent brush. Benae reached over the stable door to give her mount a pat on his forehead. He nickered softly. He was such a gentle horse and they shared a bond she had never imagined. He read her intentions, her very mood. When she was tranquil, he carried her at a sedate pace, and when her spirit was troubled, he would gallop recklessly, imbuing her with an exhilaration she had found nowhere else.

Flaire hung his head over the edge of the door and Benae rested her forehead on his. They stood thus, breathing each other's breath, listening to each other's heartbeat. Benae felt her racing heart slow to match Flaire's steady beat.

"You beautiful thing," she said. "We'll ride together tomorrow." She sent the horse a mind picture of them galloping together through a meadow and he tossed his head, a sure sign of joy.

The squire cleared his throat. "You must have great affection for him."

Benae wrenched her mind from Flaire's and turned. The horse stamped his foot. He could be a jealous friend. "I raised him from a foal. Everything he knows, I taught him. He has been my only companion since I lost my family." Her voice caught on the last words and she strode past Ramón and out of the stable. He wouldn't see her cry!

Ramón was soon at her side. "Lady, I seem to make a habit of upsetting you. I'm sorry."

His azure eyes were so earnest; she knew his words were sincere. A powerful urge to kiss him overtook her, but that would be forward, even for her. Instead she smiled. "Please call me Benae."

"It's not proper."

"I insist," she said quietly, holding his gaze.

Ramón nodded. "But not in public. The prince would definitely not approve."

Benae smiled. He was so stiff. She would like to turn his rigid control on its head, and she could, given the opportunity.

"Shall we return to the castle?" Ramón asked, offering his arm.

Benae was not ready to return to the confines of the keep where all she would do was worry about her mistake with Jiseve. "I should like to see the small castle park. Could you show me?"

Ramón inclined his head but frowned. *Oh, I must change that!* All she was to him was a job. He seemed not to have the slightest interest in her as a woman. Her stomach lurched as an abhorrent thought occurred. Could Ramón be attracted to men? No, she just wouldn't believe that the female population could be denied so beautiful a specimen.

He led her among the trees and Benae spied a bench under a huge old oak. She sat on it, patting the bench beside her. Ramón sat stiffly, his eyes scanning the nearby foliage, his right hand resting on his sword hilt.

"You suspect danger even here, Ramón?"

"Yes...Benae, even this close to the palace. After the events surrounding the disappearance of Princess Alecia, we realized extra vigilance was required." Again, a cloud dimmed his magnificent eyes.

"Forgive me for being blunt, but I notice you're particularly affected when you mention the princess. Why is that? Do you hold yourself responsible for her loss?" *Oh, that was blunt, perhaps too blunt?*

He rose and strode around the small clearing, eyes everywhere; everywhere but upon her. "I do hold myself responsible for Princess Alecia's kidnapping." He stopped and faced her, his gaze wild.

Benae stared. She didn't understand. "Why would you feel responsible? Were you in charge of security?"

Ramón turned away. "No."

"Then how?" She gasped as an idea occurred to her. "You're in love with her?"

Ramón spun back. His mouth opened and closed several times before he spoke. "This really is none of your business, Lady."

"That's it, isn't it? You love Princess Alecia. What will you do?"

His jaw tensed and he frowned. "I'm doing all I can to find her but it's difficult when Prince Zialni has forbidden me to be part of the search."

Benae stood and reached for his hands, her fingers brushing the calluses on his palms. "I'm sorry. That must be difficult for you. How long have you loved her?"

He pulled his hands away. "Does it matter?"

"Tell me," Benae said, trying to get as much information from him as she could before he shut the door on his feelings.

"Ever since I first saw her, back in Wildecoast, before I ever came to Brightcastle. She's beautiful, but more than that, she's brave and stands up for what she believes. She didn't go meekly to Lord Finus as her father willed but fought as best she could. And I allowed it all to happen. All of it." The last was said in a whisper, as if he had forgotten Benae was there.

"Ramón." His eyes again met hers and the pain in them speared her heart. He put on a brave face but inside he was hurting and angry. It was burning him up. "None of this is your fault."

"You don't know anything!" He pulled his hand from hers and stepped backward.

"You did all you could."

"I didn't, but I won't make that mistake again. Alecia was smitten by Vard Anton. She left willingly but even so, I could have prevented it —" Ramón's mouth snapped shut. "I shouldn't be speaking of this."

Benae pushed back the angry words that threatened to leap from her tongue. She didn't know him well enough to push this, not yet. She had all the information she needed for now. Ramón distanced himself because he was in love with another woman. It made perfect sense. "Let's return to the castle."

"As you wish, Lady."

"I 'wish' for you to call me Benae. Please do so."

He hesitated, his sensual, kissable lips pursed, but he nodded.

Benae gave her head a small shake. He was stubborn, this man; perhaps more so than she. At least she knew the reason for his distance now. He held a torch for Alecia and that was his choice, but Benae would do her best to make him see that his love for the princess would never be returned. The niggling question of why she wanted to do that, Benae pushed aside.

* * *

Ramón ground his teeth as he watched the Princesses Avalin and Lella and Lady Benae play *bonzer* in the formal castle garden. The word "discontent" was too mild for his mental state. He wanted information on Alecia. He wanted to be told she had been found. He wanted to be the man to kill Vard; except that "want" was too mild a word as well. Need would be better, burning need even more so. *Obsession?* He snorted with wry amusement. Now he was getting close.

His feelings burned, made him impatient with duty. Lady Benae was right; his behavior toward her had been abhorrent this morning. She was his responsibility as were the other women who contended for Prince Zialni's hand in marriage. But Benae saw things that most people didn't. She had perceived his love for Alecia. She was most definitely dangerous. He had observed what could only be described as a predatory gleam in her eye when she beheld him. Even now, she flashed a smile at him whenever their eyes met. Had she no shame? A tinkling laugh filled the garden, and he looked up to see Benae hit the winning shot in the game, her ball flying through the last hoop, much to the disgust of Princess Avalin. Ramón momentarily lost his train of thought at the sight of captivating Benae, her long dark hair swinging against the gold fabric of her gown, brilliant green eyes shining with delight at her victory. She stirred his blood, robbed his mouth of spit and made his manhood hard. He wouldn't act on his desires for there were too many barriers between them: Alecia, the prince, his contempt for Benae's choices. All were enough reason on their own for him to remain aloof from this enchanting woman.

Benae spied him watching her and flashed him a smile that set his heart racing. He allowed none of it to show on his face, or so he hoped. Down that road was ruin. She was here for a much greater purpose than a dalliance with the prince's squire. He would do well to remind himself of that often. Greed and self-interest motivated Benae, and perhaps a healthy interest in men too, if the rumors were to be believed.

Princess Avalin stormed past him. "I require to be escorted back to my chambers, Squire." She didn't wait for him, disappearing through the door into the castle ballroom, which adjoined the garden. Ramón hurriedly followed, flicking a signal to the page, who was apprenticed to him, to attend to the two ladies remaining. The sooner these demanding women were out of Brightcastle and back in their palaces and estates the better.

CHAPTER 4

BENAE laughed at Jiseve's joke as she guided Flaire around a hole in the track. It was a beautiful day and they were on their way to the mountain meadow for a picnic. Four of the prince's guards rode behind at a distance, with two more blazing the trail ahead. She had to admit they were well-trained, for she could forget the men were there for long stretches of time.

"You have the most beautiful laugh, Benae," Jiseve said, his mellow voice sliding over her. He hadn't mentioned the unpleasantness of yesterday and had been his usual charming self. He was striking, with his dark hair, sharp blue eyes and whipcord body. He cut a fine figure in a tunic and his skills with the sword could match all but the blade master. Benae again wondered if her father might have given her scheme his blessing. She frowned at the thought.

"What is amiss?" Jiseve said, pulling his horse up.

Flaire stopped instantly. He was such a champion animal, perfectly trained. *He* was her rock. "I was thinking of my father and wondering if he would accept my being here."

"My Lady, that thought proves to me what an extraordinary woman you are. That you would be concerned about your father and his opinion. You are a treasure beyond value."

Benae smiled at him. Of course he would find that attractive after what Alecia had done to him. The pain in his gaze was echoed in her heart, but she would not mention Princess Alecia again, not unless Jiseve spoke first. "I thank you."

"Let us continue to the meadow. We will feast and talk of the future."

At his words, Benae's heart skipped a beat. Surely it meant Jiseve would ask for her hand in marriage?

On arrival at the meadow, the guards placed a thick rug under a tree and set out the basket, plates and cutlery. Once all was ready, Jiseve dismounted and came around to help Benae down from Flaire. His hands lingered at her waist, his eyes searching hers as if he sought to understand her deepest thoughts. Yes, she could develop feelings for this man if he treated her well; if he could love again.

He led her over to the mat and helped her sit and arrange her skirts. A guard led their horses away. Jiseve poured two goblets of deep red wine and handed them to Benae. He cut thick slabs of bread from the loaf and spread them with butter. He sliced goat's cheese to go with the bread and took his wine from her.

"Here's to us, Benae," he said, raising his wine to her. "To a long and happy association."

Benae's heart sped away. "Is there something you wish to ask me, Jiseve?" It was forward but Benae followed her intuition.

"There is. First, I must do this." He reached for her, his free hand looping around the back of her head and pulling her to him. His lips met hers and she stiffened with shock. He didn't relent. Benae had little choice but to allow the kiss and slowly her body responded as Jiseve's mouth mastered hers. The kiss deepened and he pushed past her lips to devour her mouth. Benae found an answering need deep within her, where she had expected none. Her hand curled up into his hair and she wished she had both hands free to explore his face, his neck, his body.

Jiseve pulled back, his breathing ragged, pupils dilated so that only a slim ring of blue remained. He sucked in a deep breath and ran a hand through his hair. "That was ...wonderful," he said, his words ragged with passion.

Benae smiled. She wouldn't have described it in those words, but it was so much more than she had expected.

"Lady Benae." He took her drink and placed it beside his, then grasped her hands. "Would you accept me as your husband? Would you agree to spend your life with me and have my children? If I should become king, would you sit beside me on the throne?"

Benae paused. He had truly spelt out all her responsibilities if she should agree to this union. This was a monumental step and one from which she could not retreat. It would shelter her people, bringing her estate an alliance that would protect it financially and from the ravages of the dark elves. This was what she had come to Brightcastle for and now her goal was within her reach.

She looked deep into his eyes and saw his fear, uncertainty and hope, revealed. Any man who could show this much of himself couldn't be bad. He had suffered: first losing his wife and then his daughter. Jiseve needed Benae as much as she needed him, only for different reasons. She didn't need love, having had her fill of men and the thrill of bedding them. She hadn't loved deeply, but wasn't creating a family and securing a kingdom of greater importance? This would truly be a reciprocal arrangement and if that kiss was anything to go by, she might come to love Jiseve in time. He was fit and still in his forties. Some might say he was only just past his prime. Benae was not without healing that could help him delay the onset of old age. *A pity I can't do the same for myself.* Yes, this might work out very well and her estate would be secured, her five hundred dependents assured of a safe and prosperous future.

Benae smiled. "I would be honored to become your wife, Jiseve. I will be the mother of your children and sit beside you should you become king."

Jiseve leant forward and kissed her tenderly, his eyes full of wonder. "I did not expect to find a wife as beautiful or kind as you, Benae. I am indeed a lucky man." He handed her back her goblet and they toasted to a long and fruitful union.

* * *

Ramón was wielding the practice sword against four opponents when the prince and Benae returned from their ride. Benae glowed and Prince Zialni wore a smug expression on his tanned face. Ramón was momentarily distracted and missed the sweeping arc of his opponent's wooden sword; that is, until it smashed into his calf. He went down, searing pain taking his breath. Another of the fighters knocked Ramón onto his back and placed the pointed end of a practice sword against his throat.

"A timely lesson, Squire," the weapons master said. "Distraction is death and you must remember it. If this were a real contest, you would be dead."

"If this were real, I wouldn't be so distracted," Ramón said, glaring up at the huge man above him.

"Practice as you mean to perform." The master still had the wooden sword at Ramón's throat. The prince and Benae had stopped to watch.

"Your words are true. Let me rise."

With that, the weapons master stepped away and Ramón sprang to his feet, bowing to his opponents and handing the practice sword back to the master. He collected his sword and belt from his page, fastened them at his waist then strode to the prince.

"Not a very impressive sight to be greeted by, Squire," Prince Zialni said.

Ramón stamped upon the anger and shame the words brought. If he continued like this, the prince would never consider him as a son-in-law when Alecia returned. Correction —when he brought Alecia home. "Indeed, Your Highness, I have learned a valuable lesson today."

Prince Zialni dismounted and drew Ramón away from the horses. "I would like you to gather the princesses. I have made my decision. We will lunch together, and you must be present to escort the unlucky ladies to their rooms and see to their departure from the palace."

"Certainly, Your Highness." Ramón hurried to Benae's side to help her down from Flaire. He waited as she touched her forehead to her horse again. She had the most amazing affinity with the animal. She stepped back and her eyes met Ramón's.

"Lady Benae." His heart constricted at the sight of her. This woman was more beautiful than any he had ever seen, but it wasn't only that. Her eyes held a sadness that spoke of suffering and yet she could still laugh and take part in life. Had Zialni chosen her? If it were his choice, Ramón knew whom he would pick: this petite and fiery woman before him.

"Squire," she said. Her voice, deep and rich, sent excitement swirling from his stomach right down to his groin. "Can you see that Flaire is cared for?"

The reminder of his place in her life blew away desire as completely as a gale blows the autumn leaves from a path. "Certainly, Lady." He bowed and led Flaire over to a stable boy. "See that he is rubbed down and fed, Billy." When Ramón turned back to Benae it was to discover that Prince Zialni had led her to the castle steps. As Ramón watched, they disappeared inside.

He snorted. "Time to do my job," he muttered and hurried into the castle to summon the other contenders for the role of princess of Brightcastle.

CHAPTER 5

THE ladies gathered in the dining room, their faces flushed, finery in place. All no doubt hoped to make a final impression on Jiseve Zialni. Ramón met Benae's gaze across the room and she blushed. Did the roses in her cheeks confirm she had been chosen as the next wife of Prince Zialni? He tramped on the disturbing tremor of unease that thought raised.

A maid served the ladies their drinks and Ramón took one as well. He had a feeling he'd need it before the end of this gathering.

Prince Zialni arrived and the first gaze he met was Benae's. He smiled at her and then at the other women. Princess Avalin watched Benae, her teeth bared in what was more a snarl than a smile.

"Please be seated and we will eat," Jiseve Zialni said. He led Benae and Avalin to places at his right and left as they had been seated that first evening. Ramón escorted Marey and Lella to their seats and sat between Avalin and Lella.

"Will you not tell us your decision now, Your Highness?" Avalin said, her cool, gray eyes demanding acquiescence.

"I know you are impatient, my dear, but please enjoy your repast first."

Avalin sent more venom in Benae's direction but that lady's rapt gaze was fixed on the prince. Hoping to ease the tension that had gripped his shoulders, Ramón engaged Lella and Marey in conversation about their morning pursuits.

"Lieutenant Vorasava kindly took us shopping this morning, Squire," Lella said.

"Oh yes." Marey giggled. "Anyone would think that the Lieutenant escorted ladies on shopping trips every day of the week."

"He was most attentive," Lella said. "He helped me select a handsome gemstone that I'll have made into a broach to remind me of my time here."

Ramón let their conversation wash over him, torn between politeness and a need to watch out for Benae. Avalin sat stiffly, her hands in her lap and eyes on her plate. Two serving girls ladled soup into bowls and deposited small loaves of bread on the table.

By the end of the meal, Ramón's nerves were stretched taut. Benae talked animatedly with Prince Zialni and tried to include Avalin. The prince endeavored to converse with all the ladies, though his eyes were most often upon Benae. It set Ramón's nerves on edge. It shouldn't but it did.

Finally, Prince Zialni stood and cleared his throat. "Ladies, Squire Ramón, I have come to a decision regarding my future wife." He studied each of the candidates starting with Avalin and making his way around the table. Finally, his gaze rested upon Benae and he held his hand out to her. She placed her hand in his and rose. "Lady Benae, will you consent to become my wife?"

Avalin gasped and surged to her feet as Benae curtsied.

"I will gladly take your hand in marriage, Your Highness," Benae said. Prince Zialni raised her hand to his lips and kissed it lingeringly.

Ramón stood and moved behind Avalin's chair.

"I'll not forget or forgive this injustice, Your Highness," Avalin said, her voice rising to a screech. "I'm clearly the most suitable candidate for the position you offered, and you have fallen for this harlot."

There were gasps from the other princesses and Benae went white, whether from horror or anger, Ramón did not know.

"Oh yes, *Lady*," Avalin said. "I've heard the rumors of your affairs and that you're not fussy as to the social standing of the gentleman, and I use the term in its loosest sense."

"Princess Avalin, that is quite enough," Prince Zialni said. "I have made my decision. Your insults do not become you." He raised his eyebrows at Ramón.

"Come, Princess," Ramón said, "I'll escort you to your room where you can compose yourself." He stepped forward and offered his arm.

Avalin seized her goblet and swung it at Ramón. The vessel hit him on the left cheekbone and pain speared into his eye and skull. He grabbed a napkin to staunch the flow of blood, inwardly cursing the temper of princesses and ladies in general. Avalin stalked from the room and Ramón followed, eager to be away from the horrified eyes of the prince, his guests and Benae.

He followed Avalin at a respectful distance, cheek and eye throbbing with each step. The door was closed when he reached her room and she refused to answer. The sound of breaking glass followed but Ramón had learnt his lesson. He wouldn't be sticking his head through that particular door any time soon. Vorasava could deal with her. The sooner Avalin left Brightcastle the better.

* * *

Benae closed the door to her room and leant against it, a delicious glow simmering low down in her belly. Her lips were swollen after an evening of passionate kisses with the prince. *Her betrothed.* It seemed he couldn't get enough of her. His hands had wandered further than she considered appropriate considering the length of their acquaintance. Her cheeks heated at the thought.

Jiseve was still very much in his prime and four years of living by himself had only whetted his sexual appetite. He had carried things to the point where she had thought they might consummate their union this very night, but he had withdrawn, leaving her panting and wanting more. This could work out very well indeed. She might enjoy making babies with her handsome husband-to-be.

In the midst of her joy, Benae remembered Ramón. She had wanted to go to him when he was injured, but Jiseve had ensnared her arm and held her at his side. She had no choice but to spend the rest of the evening in his company and soon she had forgotten her concern for Ramón.

As the glow of Jiseve's passion faded, Benae remembered the ugly scene at dinner. She washed her face and fixed her hair. She touched her lips in wonder. Yes, they did look thoroughly kissed. *Time for daydreaming later.*

Benae left her room and crossed to the east wing. She found Ramón's chamber and knocked quietly on the door. It was some time before the door opened to reveal the squire dressed only in his breeches.

"Lady, you shouldn't be here."

"May I come in? I'm concerned for your health."

"If that's the case, you'll leave immediately," he said. "If your betrothed catches you in here it will be curtains for me."

Benae stared at the golden-haired man before her. He was indeed beautiful; as fair as Jiseve was dark. He was taller and broader of shoulder than the prince and she had always been attracted to blond men. *Why, my first....* Benae pushed the thought away.

"Please may I enter, Ramón?" she asked. "I only wish to check your wound. How could my husband object? After all, you'll be my responsibility in a very short time."

His jaw tensed but he stepped aside and allowed her to pass. She swept by him, lapping up the scent of the citrus cologne he preferred. She seated herself at the small table in front of the fireplace and patted the other chair.

"Please sit and let me see your face."

He frowned, moving forward to perch on the edge of the chair beside her. She ran her eyes over his features, not only the cut and swelling below his left eye, but his broad forehead, high cheekbones and sensuous mouth. She caressed his bruised skin and he flinched. Her eyes met his. A wild urge swept through her but she kept her voice level. "That's nasty. Shall I heal it for you?"

"What do you mean?"

"My dark secret, Ramón. I'm a healer." *Though sometimes my skill deserts me, as it did with my parents.*

His eyes widened. "Do you speak of witchcraft?"

"I'll not harm you," she said. What was he afraid of?

Ramón snorted. "It wasn't *my* safety I was concerned for. You must have heard of the prince's aversion to all things magical? Breathe a word of any association with the dark arts and your betrothal will be but a memory. You'd be lucky to escape with your life."

Benae gasped. "I had decided the rumors must be false."

Ramón shook his head. "I tell you, they're not. He once ordered a witch burned at the stake."

"Then I must be careful," she said, "but I want to heal you."

She held his gaze and the room and castle fell away until all that existed was their connection. She felt it and so did Ramón if his gasp was anything to go by. He did things to her, moved her in a way no one ever had. He called to something deep within, not only sexual. She couldn't explain it, just knew it couldn't be ignored, that it had to be nurtured. It felt like…it *was* like the connection she had with Flaire.

Her shock must have shown in her eyes for Ramón grasped her hand. "Lady, what is amiss?"

The spell broken by his touch, Benae breathed again. "Nothing is wrong." What could this man be to her? What part of him touched the deepest fibers within her, striking a chord, calling to her? She shook her head. She was past these urges, ready to settle down and do her duty for her people, for Jiseve. She must ignore these impulses, they were not becoming of a betrothed lady. The words of Princess Avalin echoed in her mind.

Harlot, harlot, harlot.

Benae hadn't suspected the tales of her behavior had spread so far. Jiseve had dismissed Avalin's words as envy. The truth was she *had* enjoyed herself with men of all walks, common and noble. And… would… not… apologize.

Oh bother, she didn't know whether to be angry or mortified at Avalin's words. She looked up at Ramón. There was puzzlement and discomfort in his eyes.

Benae stood and the squire's eyes widened. He sat back a little in his chair and she seized his head before he could slip out of reach. "Close your eyes."

He frowned.

"Please," she said.

His eyes slid closed and Benae cupped her right hand over his injury while she rubbed her left palm back and forth across the knuckles of the hand below. This couldn't be too complete a healing or Jiseve might ask questions; just a suppression of the swelling, help Ramón's body to remove some of the bruising and take the pain away. This she did, her mind weaving spirit and water in a complex net that she cast through her palm and into the soft flesh of his cheek.

He gasped as the weave hit; his eyes flickered open.

"Hush. Be at ease," she said.

He grasped her wrist and pulled her hand away from his face then strode to the gilt-edged mirror nearby. "Your words were truth. The bruising is mostly gone, the pain vanished."

"It's the least I could do after you incurred the injury on my behalf. Who do you think Avalin would have liked to hit with that goblet?"

He turned back to her, fear and distrust in his gaze. It hurt to see them there. These people of Thorius truly did fear what they couldn't understand.

"What *are* you?" he said.

Benae flinched as though he had struck her. She drew her shoulders back and met his gaze. "I'm a healer."

"That explains nothing. What you did was surely witchcraft. It's forbidden here."

"Report me to the prince then," she said, angered that he couldn't be grateful for her efforts. She stepped closer and stroked her knuckles gently down the side of his injured face. The stubble on his chin was rough against her skin. She stepped even closer until his minty breath caressed her face. She could have this man, if she chose; her body yearned for his, hummed with a riveting, dark intensity whenever he was near. Ramón might object at first, might hold out against her efforts for days, even weeks, but eventually he would succumb.

Benae's eyes dropped to his lips. Oh, to kiss that mouth, to embrace its sensuality against her, everywhere: on her skin, in her hair, touching her secret places. Just the thought made her wet…

Ramón grasped her by the shoulders and gently held her away from him. "Please return to your chambers before someone suspects you of infidelity."

Benae blinked at him. His hands on her, even in such a benign way, were a revelation. Their heat burned through the thin fabric of her gown. Her body responded, muscles tightening deep down in her belly. It had been too long.

"Lady."

Now Ramón sounded distressed, even angry. He dropped his hands from her shoulders and the spell was broken.

"You're right, I'll go." She gazed at the face that had been battered and bruised moments before. Only a small cut remained. "I'm sorry." That made no sense; sorry for what? For his injury? For healing him? For touching him?

Benae turned and left the room, returning to her chamber without a backward glance. She had a lot of sorting out to do.

* * *

Ramón let out a slow breath as Benae closed the door. She was so unexpected. And the magic! He didn't care what she said, it *was* magic, and the prince couldn't discover her secret. Benae didn't know the danger she was in. How could she marry the prince and hide such a talent? One thing was sure: her betrothed would *never* accept it.

Her touch invoked unwelcome desire. He itched to take her in his arms, longed to kiss that delectable mouth, but how could Benae fit into his life? The answer was that she couldn't. Alecia was his future,

50

if he could find her and if Prince Zialni agreed to the union. He must cling to Alecia's memory. Already he had thoughts of another, but the princess need never know. Besides, hadn't she run away with Anton? She could hardly criticize him for a few wanton thoughts about the dark-haired beauty her father was to marry.

His face was almost healed. Maybe he could get some decent sleep tonight. Perhaps he could get his attraction to Benae straight in his head. No! He wouldn't even think of her. He'd do his job, care for her to the best of his abilities and stay away from compromising situations. He could at least do that. Couldn't he?

* * *

Benae woke, disquiet spearing her gut as sleep left her. Why should she be anxious on waking? All was well. She had won the hand of the heir to the throne of the kingdom and together they would ensure prosperity for all. Her people would be saved the cruel fate of starvation that had hung over their heads for the last year. They might even be saved from the dark elven invasion that threatened. Yes, all was well.

Then what did she fear? Ramón's face danced in her memory and instantly she knew. A slow burn began deep in her abdomen at the memory of his hands on her. The way he made her feel was new. The desire wasn't, of course, but the connection…His heart spoke to hers but what did it mean? She had time to test her feelings. The marriage was weeks away and Ramón oversaw her care. It would be easy to see if the reaction he invoked was true or just fleeting desire.

She rose and dressed in snug breeches and an emerald-green satin shirt, then pulled her hair into a twist. She slung her ermine-trimmed, dark-green cloak around her shoulders and left the room. The castle was quiet as was the forecourt. Billy, the boy on duty, squawked with surprise when she appeared at Flaire's stable door. Benae smiled at him.

Flaire poked his head over the stable door and she rested her forehead against his nose as they breathed each other's exhalations. The stallion's mind held a flutter of thoughts: fresh oats, pungent hay, green meadows under cerulean skies and the thunder of flying hooves.

He was happy here. *Such a simple creature.* Benae suddenly wished life were that simple for her.

"Billy, I wish to go for a ride," she said. "Have you seen the squire?"

"It will only take a moment to fetch him, My Lady. If you don't mind my saying, ma'am, Flaire's just had breakfast so he'll need an easy ride, at least for the first leg."

She smiled. The boy showed laudable concern for a horse that had only been in his care for a few days. Flaire was in good hands. "I'll be sure to go easy on him, Billy. Thank you for the warning."

Billy flushed and raced away to find Ramón. Benae leant against the stable door and watched Flaire nose around in his feed bowl, trying to get the last grains from the corners. Footsteps sounded on the stone floor and she turned ready to greet Ramón. Lieutenant Vorasava appeared instead.

"You wished to go riding, My Lady?"

The lieutenant's dark hair and eyes matched his olive complexion. He was fit, tall with slim hips and broad shoulders and a commanding air that said he would go far; that Brightcastle was only a stepping-stone. Benae allowed her gaze to wander over him. She did love to contemplate pretty men and here was one of the prettiest. But where was Ramón?

"Lady Branasar?" he said, a touch of impatience in his tone.

"I didn't want to trouble you, Lieutenant. I sent for the Squire."

"This I know, My Lady. I was with Zorba when the boy appeared. He is attending to an urgent matter and asked that I accompany you on your ride. I trust that meets with your approval." He smirked at her as if assured that she would accept his company.

Benae raised her right brow. She felt like turning him down but Flaire had read her intent in their mind link and he would be sad if he didn't get his ride.

"Yes, Lieutenant, that will be acceptable. I'll wait at the front of the stables." She strode from the building and perched on some bales of straw in the sun. Closing her eyes, she lifted her face to the golden globe that her people had once revered. Not surprising that primitive people had worshipped such celestial might. It felt good on her skin, the warmth, the life… Benae opened her eyes in time to see Ramón hurry across the forecourt toward the entry gate. He lifted his hand to her in greeting then disappeared through the gate.

* * *

Goddess, what a sight! Benae seated on a bale of straw, her glorious face uplifted, the early morning sun glinting off her lustrous hair and thick dark lashes, her breasts pushing against the emerald satin of her blouse.

Ramón grew hard just remembering. Damn, what was happening to him? He deliberately formed a picture of Alecia in his mind – her long fair hair, generous breasts, elegant legs as he had often seen them in breeches, tiny waist, impish smile, the velvet of her lips against his and her curves under his hands. Ah, yes! That was better! He had to keep traitorous thoughts about Benae where they belonged: safely locked away.

Ramón smiled. Benae could manipulate him as much as she liked but he was eminently capable of staying one step ahead of her. He put the alluring lady out of his head and hurried on into the town.

Chapter 6

BENAE sipped her morning cup of tea in the hope that it would dampen her frustration. A whole week had passed since Ramón had sent Vorasava in his stead and still she had not succeeded in spending time with the illusive squire. From her position at the dining room window, she could see the corner of the weapons practice yard. Ramón fought back the assault of five men with practice swords. How did he hope to defeat five men on his own? He was infuriating, and if she could corner him on his own for a moment, she would tell him in no uncertain terms how ridiculous she thought he was!

She knew the reason for his insane behavior. Her husband-to-be had finally noticed Ramón's prowess two days ago and he was to be sent on an expedition to find Princess Alecia. Instead of reducing the need for him to practice, he seemed to be training even harder. Where he had fought four men, now he fought five. Where he had partaken in two sessions a day, he now could be found in the practice yard three times daily. And the running! When Ramón wasn't practicing at weapons, he was either heading off on, or returning from, a run in the forest. It was no wonder she hadn't been able to converse with him!

The past week had dragged. She was used to physical exercise and Ramón had managed to worm his way out of another three rides with her, saying she must ask Jiseve instead. But Jiseve had no time for long trips to the upper meadow. He had wooed his bride and now his mind was on other things. She supposed he might have put many tasks to the side during his search for a wife.

Her betrothal ceremony had come and gone. At the feast afterwards, no matter how hard she tried, she couldn't conceive of a way to get

Ramón on his own long enough to have a conversation. The rest of her week had been taken up with planning her wedding, which would take place in a matter of weeks. It seemed that, after waiting more than four years, Jiseve Zialni was impatient to start life with his new bride.

Even though Jiseve had been too busy to go riding, her prince had been so sweet to her. He had announced a journey to the king's seat at Wildecoast, where she would be fitted for a wedding gown sewn by none other than the royal dressmaker. He brought her something every day, whether a bouquet of flowers or a trinket from his master jeweler. Her engagement ring was stupendous – white gold with rose quartz from the very walls of the castle. Since Benae had been told that magic had been used in the construction of the quartz walls of Brightcastle, surely this was a sign that Jiseve was not as averse to mystic arts as Ramón asserted?

Ramón danced into view with only one opponent following. *My, he looks good!* Each day his muscles became more defined, his clothes pulled even tighter in certain distracting regions. One of those places was across that magnificent backside. Benae fantasized about those buttocks beneath her hands, in fact she fantasized about all of Ramón beneath her hands.

"He fights well."

Benae spun at the quiet words of her betrothed. "Jiseve, I had almost given up hope of your company."

Jiseve stared at her for a long moment and for only the second time in their relationship, Benae felt his disapproval. "He has come a long way in the last month or so. The only greater motivator than love is revenge, and the squire has both."

"Do you speak of your decision to send him in search of the princess?"

"It is all he has hoped for since she vanished, and I see that he is finally worthy of the duty. This last week he has been especially focused. I worry what he might do if I don't grant his wish."

"You depend on him," Benae said, hoping to gain an insight into her husband-to-be.

"More and more. He has grown so much since he arrived in Brightcastle not even four months ago. I hardly recognize him. Sometimes it is so with adversity, but so often it defeats a man. He loves my daughter and seeing him now, sometimes I wish…"

Benae yearned to finish the sentence for him but, after their conversation the first evening, she didn't dare. Instead she grasped his forearm and looked up into his eyes. It was difficult to lose those you loved. "When does he leave?"

"Three days. In the meantime, we have a wedding to organize. Come," Jiseve said, "let us break our fast together and then you can tell me of our big day."

Benae turned her back on the squire and his fighters, ready to bask in the security her future husband offered.

Benae and Jiseve had just completed breakfast when Lieutenant Vorasava stuck his head through the door to the dining room. Jiseve bid him enter, and Benae was again struck by the lieutenant's arrogant presence.

"Your Highness, I'm sorry to interrupt," Vorasava said. "I have word from the north. It involves the dark elves."

Jiseve stood, his eyes meeting Benae's. "I will see you at lunch, my dear."

"I'm anxious to know this news, beloved," Benae said. "My estates—"

"Do not fear. I am now the master of your estates and I will keep your people safe." He lifted her hand to his lips. "Until luncheon, my dear. I may have more information then." He released her hand and left the dining room.

Benae's fist hit the table and the cutlery jingled. She wasn't some little woman to be pushed aside when troubles raised their heads. She was an estate owner. Those lands held people she cared for. Those very same elves had taken her brother from her. Lunch was too far away to wait for information. She swept from the room in search of the one person who might be able to tell her if the sporadic sorties the elves had mounted against her lands had progressed to an invasion.

* * *

Ramón's muscles ached more than they ever had in his life. He had beaten the five warriors but at what cost? If he could make it to his room, he might sleep for two days. He thrust his practice sword in the rack and leant on the wooden structure, sucking deep breaths into his lungs.

"Squire Ramón, I need to speak with you."

Ramón suppressed the groan those words brought. *Not now, please not when I'm close to exhaustion.* He turned to the speaker and bowed, using the movement to disguise the instant reaction his body had to the stunning woman before him. "Lady Benae."

She came close, close enough to smell the evidence of his labors, but her face didn't change. Her emerald gaze bored into his and he knew he had been wise to avoid her over the last week. Goddess, she was exquisite, and it looked as though she would like to take his head off.

"You've been avoiding me. Why?"

"I've merely been busy, Lady. I'm sure your betrothed was only too happy to attend to your needs." Ramón felt heat in his cheeks at his words.

She frowned. "I wished for *your* company, Ramón, and what happened to you calling me Benae?"

"It's not wise for us to become close."

She stepped closer, her breasts rising and falling in her agitation. She was magnificent indeed and at times he was so lonely. It would be easy to give into this attraction, fill the emptiness within. He thought Benae might be willing, but down that road lay guilt, and he had enough of that already.

"I thought we had formed a friendship. I thought I had made it clear that I cared for you. I know you're not unmoved, Ramón, I can see it in your face every time you look at me. You want me!"

"No, Lady," he snapped. "What you speak of isn't friendship. I'm trying to protect us both. You've won the hand of the prince and must be content with that."

Benae stamped her foot. He couldn't believe it. Did she always get what she wanted? *Well, not this time.* "I'm sorry, but it wouldn't be appropriate for us to spend time together. I'll fetch and carry for you. Anything else you must put from your mind."

She reached up and Ramón gasped as she brushed the hair from his eyes. He swallowed to force the lump from his throat. If he listened to his body, he would take her in his arms and give her what she demanded. She might say "friendship", but she meant so much more. He'd done stupid and impulsive things in the past and lived to regret them.

He would *not* risk all he had gained, to assuage this animal attraction he had for Benae. The prince was coming around to his way of thinking and Ramón would set off on this quest and bring Alecia home. He had real reason to believe they would be married.

"You're betrothed, Lady. Are you not content? Your husband is the only man who can give you everything you want and need. Look to him for companionship. I remain your faithful servant only."

Benae's head rose until she gave the impression that she gazed down her nose at him, even though she only reached his shoulder. "Of course, I am content."

She stepped back and Ramón expelled a quiet sigh of relief. *Finally, she might leave him be!*

"There was one other matter," she said.

He ground his teeth. Of course, Benae wouldn't let go so easily.

"What news do you have of the elves?" she asked. "The lieutenant mentioned them, and I'm concerned for my estates."

"There have been raids on some of our outlying farms," Ramón said. "I don't know what is occurring further north."

She stared at him as if assessing the truth of his words then nodded. "Be about your business, Squire. I'm sorry I held you up." She turned on her heel and strode toward the stable, no doubt to check on her stallion.

Ramón hurried from the practice yard, his spirits curiously deflated. It seemed he had convinced her of the unsuitability of any relationship, but Ramón knew she wouldn't be that easy to banish from his thoughts.

Ramón entered the dining room to find Benae pacing up and down. She froze when she saw him.

"What are you doing here?" she said, her big green eyes devouring him.

His body responded in its usual way. Since when could he not leash his manly desires? "Prince Zialni called me to dine with him." He studied her, noting the strain around her eyes and mouth. "What's amiss?"

"I told you. I'm anxious to hear more of the elves and your presence here makes me wonder about the news Jiseve has to deliver." She continued to pace, clearly agitated.

"I don't believe we have an invasion on our hands just yet, Lady," Ramón said, trying to lighten her dark mood. "Best to focus on your wedding."

Benae glared at him, her gaze as dark and stormy as the seas at Wildecoast. "How can I contemplate gowns and weddings when the elven pestilence threatens?"

"Compose yourself, my dear," Jiseve snapped, as he entered the room. "Leave the elven threat for me to deal with. We cannot have panic amongst the people. Our wedding will distract them from more serious concerns. We have a duty to see that life goes on."

Ramón took the moment to really observe the prince and his lady. They made a handsome couple, both dark-haired and attractive. Their children would be blessed in all ways. Would Benae be able to bow to the will of His Highness? Ramón didn't think she was as subtle a manipulator as it was said Zialni's previous wife was. No, with Benae it would all be up front. He could see many arguments looming. Was this to be the first?

"What's the news from the north, Jiseve?" Benae asked, her hands clutched at her bosom. "What news from my estates?"

"As to your estates, I have heard nothing, but our distant farms have been plundered. I fear I must travel north and west; see how I might finish the task I began twenty years ago. I will visit your people and check on my farmers."

"No Jiseve!" Benae snapped. "You can't risk yourself so."

"Who else will go? Vorasava must stay here to defend Brightcastle. I am the only one who can do this chore. I will speak with your estate manager and he will send word to the king of Tylevia. The rider will vouch for the union between our kingdoms and we can open discussions about the dark elves. Perhaps I can take the opportunity to invite your king to our wedding, my dear?"

Zialni reached for Benae and drew her against his chest. She looked the picture of an obedient wife, but Ramón wasn't fooled.

"Who will accompany me to Wildecoast if you are heading north, Jiseve? You said the trip must be soon." She gazed up at her husband-to-be and Ramón felt he was intruding on an intimate moment. They did seem fond of each other. Perhaps this union would be a happy one. But if the lady were set on a happy life with the prince why did she need to reach out to him, Ramón?

"The trip will go ahead," the prince said. "The squire shall escort you, along with a small company of soldiers. We cannot be too careful."

Cold shock ran through Ramón. *No!* That was insanity to the highest degree to send his betrothed off to Wildecoast with another man. Benae flicked a glance at Ramón. She didn't appear half as uncomfortable as he felt. What was this? A test? Or was the prince so certain of Benae's love for him that he didn't fear she would misbehave? After all, he hadn't known her long but if he knew what Ramón knew…

"How will that appear, Your Highness?" Ramón had never changed the prince's mind before, but he had to try.

"You will have a company of soldiers as chaperone, Squire."

"That might be so but Brightcastle can ill afford the soldiers. With the search parties out and you heading north, Vorasava won't have enough to defend the principality."

"That is the beauty of this plan. Most of the search parties will have returned by tomorrow or the next day at the latest, including the mercenaries I have hired. Brightcastle will be well defended."

"You can't postpone the search for Alecia."

"You forget yourself!"

Ramón's face heated. "There has to be another way, Your Highness. I'll go to Tylevia and check on the lady's estates and the dark elves. You know I'm capable of it. And what of my mission to find Alecia? You're not only postponing it but pulling in most of the search parties. Have you given up hope?"

A muscle in Prince Zialni's jaw twitched and Ramón knew he had pushed the prince as far as he could. "I will never give up on Alecia and the searches will resume when I return. In the meantime, I have two operatives on the hunt for my daughter and that vermin, Anton. Perhaps they will succeed where larger groups have failed. Anton may get sloppy if he thinks I have given up."

The prince fell silent, perhaps imagining the eventual capture of his nemesis, then his eyes snapped back to Ramón. "Suffice to say that I believe my presence is needed more to the north than in escorting my lady to Wildecoast. You will follow orders and they are to accompany my betrothed to the coast so that she can be fitted for her wedding gown. I will not delay my marriage or place the kingdom in jeopardy because my willful daughter has run away from home. Is that clear?"

Ramón swallowed the desperation that bubbled up inside him and bowed stiffly to the prince and to Benae. "May I take my leave? I have preparations to make."

The prince frowned deeply at him, but nodded. "You depart tomorrow at first light. I rely on you to keep my lady safe."

Ramón bowed again. "Have no fear, Your Highness. Your lady will be safe with me." He threw Benae a look that said *he* at least could be trusted and swept from the room.

* * *

Benae couldn't sleep. The news that she would travel with Ramón instead of Jiseve made her restless. It was what she wanted, wasn't it? To spend some time with Ramón, get to know him better? Perhaps have one last flirtation before she settled down with Jiseve. She wouldn't let it go too far. Perhaps some passionate kisses in secret or even … She imagined Ramón's hands on her bare skin and groaned. Who was she deceiving? The way she felt about the squire, she wouldn't be able to stop if he were willing. Lucky for her he wasn't. She only hoped he had enough strength for them both.

Why did she feel thus? Her marriage to Jiseve was what she had come to Brightcastle for. He was besotted with her. Tonight, after dinner, he had invited her to his room, and she had thought he meant to take her to his bed. But no. The last night before they would be separated for weeks and he had kissed her to within an inch of her life, had her panting for more, then escorted her back to her room! What was wrong with the man? He had only to begin undressing her and she couldn't have refused him.

Perhaps that was what ailed her. Jiseve had brought her to the edge of longing each night since their betrothal and then walked away. Her body couldn't take much more of this teasing without combusting. She needed release and she needed it now.

She flung herself out of bed and drew her robe over her nightgown. He wouldn't deny her if he saw her in this filmy creation. It left little to the imagination and since she never wore pantaloons to bed, there would be no barrier to deny her betrothed. As she stood in the light of her parlor's flickering fire she hesitated. What if he turned her away again? Desire coiled its way up from her core and she groaned. She must have her release!

She opened the door quietly and slipped into the dark hallway. Leaving her door ajar, she turned in the direction of Jiseve's room only to be halted by a familiar, masculine chest. Hard callused hands gripped her upper arms and the scent of citrus swirled around her.

Her heart leapt and raced away. "Ramón! What are you doing here?" In her aroused state, Benae was intensely aware that his hands had tightened on her arms. She swayed toward him, but he kept her at bay, a stray moonbeam outlining the convulsive movement of his throat.

"Prince Zialni had some late instructions. Are you on your way to bid him goodnight?" He sounded so proper it was like a slap in the face. His glance took in her clothing and Benae was suddenly glad she had pulled her robe over her flimsy nightgown. Her body drove her toward this man, the mischief in her nature made her wonder how he would behave once his passion was unleashed. She wanted to be the one to release that passion, for she suspected that Ramón was a virgin. Could she betray her betrothed and give Ramón a reason to be ashamed? He did so pride himself on his honor.

Benae took a step backwards and Ramón's hands slipped down her arms to her hands, lingering there before falling to his sides. His gaze hadn't left her the entire time. That much she could see in the dimness. Oh Goddess, if only she could pull him into her room and kiss him until he lost his taut reserve, stripped the clothes from her and made mad passionate love to her. How ready she was to accommodate him. Her belly clenched at the thought and she stepped toward him once more, laying her hands on his chest. She leant against him and, yes… felt the bulge in his breeches that told of his susceptibility to her.

Her thin thread of control snapped, and she launched herself at him, wrapping her arms around his neck, assaulting his mouth with a savagery that surprised even her. His lips didn't disappoint – so full and sensuous were they - after a moment's surprise, they moved beneath hers, passion mounting until his tongue forced its way between her lips and began an intimate exploration of her mouth.

Benae groaned and pushed her hips against his. She was ready for him, oh so ready. She was beyond ready. His arms enclosed her, pulling her soft curves closer, until every hard muscle from chest to knee strained against her.

Ramón shoved her door open with his shoulder and pulled her with him into her room. He kicked the door closed, his lips never leaving hers. She breathed in his heady citrus scent, her hands dropping from his neck to explore the muscles of his chest, then his waist, before drifting to the buttocks she had admired for so long. Ramón's hands mimicked hers and he groaned deep in his throat as his fingers kneaded her bottom through her nightgown.

Benae stepped away and allowed her robe to drop from her shoulders, leaving only the sheer nightgown between them. Ramón's eyes darkened as he took in her body and he groaned again. He was close to the edge. All she had to do was give him a nudge. She let him stare, knowing that her darkened nipples were visible. He swallowed repeatedly, his breath coming in quick gasps. Her own chest rose and fell in time with his. Benae's desire peaked as she imagined the moment he would lay her down and push his way inside her.

Slowly, Benae gripped the fabric that barely concealed her and gathered it in her fists. She inched the hem upwards, revealing first her shins and then sliding above her knees. Her eyes never left his face. Ramón licked his lips, his gaze riveted to the hem of her nightgown and what it revealed. Benae's excitement rose closer to fulfilment. She would climax soon even if he didn't touch her. It was so erotic watching his reaction to her seduction. She prepared to raise the gown to her hips, knowing that this would tip him over the edge. Ramón's hand grasped her wrist.

"Stop," he said.

"You want this."

"Of course I do, but it's not mine to want." He pulled her hands from the hem of her gown and adjusted its folds, so they fell to her ankles, then stooped and retrieved her robe. He drew it around her shoulders and held her there, his hands gripping the front of her robe, his eyes dark, troubled. As Benae stared at his torment, his gaze fell to her mouth and he drew her close, his lips claiming hers for a tender kiss. Her heart melted. No one had ever kissed her thus, as if she were the most precious gift in the world. Perhaps he had changed his mind. But as Ramón drew back, his hands dropped to his sides and he took a deep breath.

"One of us must remember your betrothal. Now get yourself to bed. We depart at first light." He turned and left the room without another word or a backwards glance.

How could he resist? She had been virtually naked in front of him, performing a striptease. Although, he had said he wanted her. She frowned. What did that mean? And that last kiss! Goddess, how did he kiss her like that and walk away? That kiss promised more than rapturous abandon. It spoke of a lifetime of love and trust. At least that was how it felt to her. Tender was how the kiss had felt; nothing to do with lust.

Benae shook her head, annoyed that things had slipped beyond her control. If Jiseve hadn't teased her so, she might have been able to resist Ramón's broad shoulders and soft lips. Then again, perhaps not. If she were honest, the squire had been an irresistible force from the very first time she saw him. Now she must spend days traveling in his company, knowing she had offered herself to him and been rejected. Her insides curled in shame. Her heart and mind roiled in confusion. What was she? Dignified court lady or a wanton hussy as Avalin had suggested?

Ramón was right to refuse her. He had kept his head when he should not have been able to resist her. Perhaps he wasn't the virgin she thought him. He didn't kiss like a virgin. Her heart thudded anew at the memory of his kisses. She knew now what she was giving up by marrying Jiseve, knew his kisses, his love would never match Ramón's. No matter how content she might be with Jiseve, it would be Ramón she would crave and Ramón she would never have. How stupid she had been to believe she could make this contract with Jiseve and not pay a price.

Benae must retrieve her dignity as best she could. She would get over Ramón in time; she had to believe that. In Jiseve she had a husband who would protect her estates and her people. A little frustration was a small price to pay.

CHAPTER 7

RAMÓN supervised the loading of the coach that would transport Benae to Wildecoast. Two trunks had been strapped to the back along with Ramón's small chest. The tents were stored on the roof of the carriage, one for himself and four others for the eight soldiers they were taking as a guard. Billy, the stable boy, led Flaire over to the coach and tied him to the rear.

"Thanks Billy," Ramón said, surreptitiously checking the knot. It wouldn't do for the horse to be lost on the trip. He wasn't even sure why Flaire had to come, but it was a battle not worth fighting. The horse was fitted with Benae's saddle, complete with silver adorning pommel, cantle and stirrups. Billy handed Ramón a matching bridle, which he slung on a hook at the back of the carriage. The stallion was tethered by a plain head collar that was much more practical and comfortable than wearing a bridle, especially when he wasn't being ridden.

"I'll miss him, Squire," Billy said, giving the horse a pat on the neck and getting a soft muzzle against his ear in return. The boy was one of those rare individuals who attracted animals. He made them feel comfortable and unafraid but had been in all sorts of trouble since Vard Anton left. Ramón shook his head. As much as he hated Anton, he had taken Billy under his wing and the lad clearly missed the enigmatic captain. Ramón had vowed to look after the boy. After all, it wasn't easy to be torn from your mother's side and expected to do a day's work when you were only thirteen.

"You keep out of trouble while I'm gone, Billy," Ramón said, placing his hand on the boy's shoulder. "If there are good reports when I return,

I'll commence weapons training with you. But only if you have a clean slate."

Billy's eyes widened and his plain face was lit by a huge grin. "Right you are, Squire. I'll make a good warrior, you'll see."

Ramón smiled. Billy reminded him of himself at that age: full of big ideas and mischief. However, Ramón's domain had been the king's castle at Wildecoast where he had been sent at the age of twelve to begin his training.

He could remember getting into trouble, too, playing pranks on the senior squires to embarrass them during visits by dignitaries. He had missed his family just as Billy did. His heart lifted at the thought that he would visit his parents while he was at Wildecoast. His younger sister, Alique, had joined the Queen's ladies-in-waiting at the time Ramón left for Brightcastle. He looked forward to discovering how her new role had changed her.

There was a commotion at the castle entrance and Benae and Prince Zialni appeared. The lady was dressed in a somber green traveling dress with divided skirts, her dark hair pulled back from her face into a bun. She was pale with dark circles under her eyes and avoided his gaze completely as she approached with her betrothed.

"Ah, Squire Ramón," Prince Zialni said. "I see all is in readiness."

Ramón bowed low to hide the sudden flush he knew had crept over his face at Benae's appearance. Had the events of last evening been a dream? He pushed the memories from his head for they would not help to dispel the creeping redness. He rose and met the sharp blue gaze of Prince Zialni. Was the man having second thoughts about sending his betrothed off with another man?

"I am relying on you to convey Lady Benae safely to Wildecoast and back." The prince's voice was cold, almost threatening. "Do not let me down."

"I will defend the lady with my life, Your Highness."

"I trust that will not be necessary. You have an escort and I cannot foresee any danger great enough to threaten you with eight soldiers in your party. All will be well."

"I'm sure you're right, Your Highness. When we reach Wildecoast, I'll send word via pigeon."

"I will not be here to receive them but send them anyway. Give my best to my brother, the King, and tell him I will expect him at my wedding."

"Most certainly I will, Your Highness. May you have a safe journey."

Ramón bowed and stepped back to give the prince and Benae some privacy. They turned to each other and Prince Zialni kissed Benae on both cheeks. She gripped his hands tightly.

"Are you sure this is for the best, beloved?" she asked.

"I know it is, Lady. We will be wed upon your return and we shall be as one."

Tears welled in Benae's eyes. "I wish…"

"What is it?" Prince Zialni said.

The distraught note in Benae's voice drew Ramón's attention. Fear lay in her glorious eyes but who was she scared for? What did she wish?

She swallowed hard, chewing on her bottom lip. "Never mind. It's best not to speak of our fears. May the Goddess protect you, Jiseve. I look forward to our union, more than you can ever know."

Ramón spun away, making one last circuit of the carriage to check the wheels. Benae's words struck a sharp spike of jealousy into his heart that he had no right to feel. Last night she had offered herself to him, Ramón, and now she implied she would miss her betrothed. He had been so close to giving her what she wanted. Her body, barely hidden by that nightgown … Ramón suppressed a groan as he tightened the traces on one of the carriage horses. And now she gazed tenderly at the prince. How could she contemplate marriage when she would bed any male who came along? Anger boiled in him and he thanked the Goddess he had been the one to step away last night. The carriage moved and he glanced up in time to see Benae seat herself. Their eyes met through the window. Ramón's heart ached at the raw, pained look she flashed him. They stared at each other for a beat then he dragged his gaze away. He strode to his black gelding, giving the order to move out as soon as his buttocks hit the saddle. It was going to be a long journey.

* * *

Benae's head pounded with the rocking of the carriage as they wound their way through the strip of forest east of Brightcastle. She had barely slept after Ramón left her room and now, she faced four days and three nights on the road with him. Surely her spirits could sink no further? A small voice told her to be glad she hadn't slept with him, but she couldn't agree. His body beneath her fingers had felt so strong, his arms around her had seemed right. It was not so with Jiseve. He was strong in a wiry way and handsome and his kisses stirred her blood, but Ramón's body moved her on a visceral level. His eyes spoke to her heart, even if he did not know it.

Sweat broke out on her palms and she clenched her hands in her lap so Merel wouldn't see her distress. If only she could push Ramón's image from her mind, but her meditation tricks deserted her and thoughts of him kept pushing back. Since the kiss, her mind had even more fodder for daydreams. Where would it all end? What must he think of her after throwing herself at him?

He rode past the carriage and she groaned. When had she become a slave to her desires? True, she liked the company of men, but she had never felt this driven toward anyone. Again, she wondered if it was just her raging need for fulfilment that drove her toward Ramón. If only Jiseve had made love to her each night for the past several, her arousal might now be dimmed by a budding pregnancy.

Benae's eye fell upon the bed opposite her. Jiseve had commissioned a clever carpenter to modify one of the seats in the coach so that it became a comfortable bed. This was where she would sleep. It was large enough that Merel could share as well.

"Merel, I didn't sleep well last night. I'm going to lie down and close my eyes for a time."

"Surely, My Lady. A rest will do you the world of good. I'll sit here quietly with my knitting." Merel smiled calmly, her serenity a panacea for Benae's turbulent thoughts.

Benae lay down on the bed and closed her eyes. Miraculously, she slept.

Benae was woken by a peal of laughter some time later. The carriage was stationary and Merel absent. She sat up and glanced out the window. They were in a clearing near the road and Merel and most of the soldiers sat around a campfire. Ramón and one of the men stood guard, their backs to the fire. It must be luncheon. Benae's stomach grumbled. She rose and rubbed her face, smoothed her hair and stood to let her skirts straighten.

She opened the carriage door and Ramón was there, ready to hand her down. He was a miracle. How had he known she was awake? She paused as he offered his hand.

"Are you well, Lady?"

Her heart skipped as she stared down into his azure eyes. No wonder he haunted her dreams. *I am bound to Jiseve.* "I'm well." His hand touched hers and she swallowed down the lump that rose to her throat, her breath quickening. "I wish to apologize for my behavior last night," she said quietly. "I will offer no excuses."

Ramón's hand squeezed hers and she was reminded of their last embrace, but then his gaze hardened. "Forget it. I already have."

Benae stumbled as she stepped from the carriage and would have fallen but for his hand on hers. He had already forgotten their kisses? Had they not moved him at all? She shook her head as she found her feet. She had not mistaken the longing in his eyes, the tenderness of his kiss, especially that last, lingering one. Benae frowned up at him. "Thank you…I think."

He glared at her. "I don't understand you. Why would you jeopardize your future with his highness for a fling with me?"

"I thought you had forgotten it," she snapped.

Ramón drew a sharp breath and looked away. When he turned to her, his eyes were troubled, uncertain. "One of us has to act with propriety. You're a betrothed woman and you behave like —" He bit the words off, as if not trusting himself.

"Say it," she hissed. "I act like a village whore."

Ramón's eyes widened. "They weren't the words I sought."

"No matter," Benae said. "You don't approve of me, but you'll have to accept me as I am."

"I don't have to accept anything. You're in my care. It's not for me to judge you."

"And yet you do." She wrenched her hand from his and stalked to the fire.

Luncheon taken, they resumed their journey and were soon through the forest and into the rich farm lands that had helped make Brightcastle principality wealthy. Farm wives waved from their homesteads. Benae was heartened to witness such normality after her days at court. She relaxed against the well-stuffed cushions of the coach and allowed the familiar scenes to soothe her troubled mind. Scents of chicken yards and baking floated to her on the breeze. It was warm for early winter and she hoped the weather would hold until she returned to Brightcastle. She didn't relish the thought of traveling through snow.

Merel sat quietly beside her, knitting a new shawl, and Benae amused herself with thoughts of her wedding, making notes in her diary as ideas occurred to her. Jiseve had said she could plan the festivities. The budget he had given her would have kept her small estate running for the better part of half a year. She shifted uncomfortably at the thought of such waste.

Her betrothed said it was expected, almost required, that she present an image of wealth and abundance. After long months of struggling to feed her people, Benae couldn't quite believe she didn't have to pinch every penny. More importantly, Jiseve had immediately sent funds to tide her estate over until its finances could be settled properly. So much depended on her future husband. She hated that he put himself at risk by traveling north. She was beginning to see that he would do as he saw fit. All she could do was trust and pray that he stayed safe. She had relinquished her freedom to enter this arranged betrothal and she didn't regret it. She did not and she would not.

A deep sigh slipped from her lips as the memory of a certain broad-shouldered, golden-haired squire intruded. He was persistent, she had to say that, or at least his place in her musings seemed set. Usually she wasn't this scatterbrained but lately she couldn't seem to keep her mind where it needed to be.

The carriage slowed and Benae looked up from her jottings, almost upsetting the ink bottle balanced on her diary. The sun had almost dropped below the horizon and they were pulling into another small clearing by the side of the road.

Ramón had set up the camp so the carriage was in the center of the five tents, the horses tethered nearby, except for Flaire whom Benae insisted should be tethered to the carriage. She wrapped her arms around his neck and breathed in his horsey scent. Joyful equine thoughts flooded his mind. He was happy to be moving again, muscles tired after a day's trotting behind the carriage. He pulled against her arms and she released him. Instantly he put his head down to graze on the grass beside the road. It wasn't lush but would seem so to Flaire after days in a stable. Oh, to find joy in such simple things. Benae almost wished she could swap places.

One of the soldiers prepared a humble but tasty meal over the fire with Merel's help and Benae sat upon a large log, her plate balanced in her lap. She didn't mind a modest life. It would be hard to get used to the trappings of wealth and royalty, but she could adapt, with Jiseve's help.

Ramón sat beside her. "My Lady, two of us will keep watch during the night. The risk of ambush is small but there's no point in being careless."

"Jiseve seemed unconcerned."

"I'm sure His Highness is right, but I'll still set the watch." He took a spoonful of venison stew and chewed thoughtfully. "Mmm… this isn't bad. Who would've thought Seve had it in him to create this tasty meal? Perhaps he has missed his calling."

Benae did not know what she could say to this, so she remained silent. She finished in unseemly haste and stood up, placing her plate beside the fire. "Thank you Seve, Merel. Squire, I bid you goodnight." With that, she walked to the carriage, kissed Flaire on the muzzle and climbed into the conveyance.

73

CHAPTER 8

THE next morning, Benae woke at dawn refreshed, despite sharing her bed with Merel. The two women drew the blinds on the carriage, removed their nightgowns and sponged away the dust of the road. They donned their travel dresses that Merel had aired the night before and breakfasted with the soldiers around the fire. Ramón was quiet, dark smudges beneath his eyes. He would have taken his turn on watch. That was the kind of man Ramón was: one who took his responsibilities seriously, not leaving matters to chance.

Benae sighed, her gaze on the squire, even though she hadn't yet caught his eye this morning. Ramón was such a rock. He would make a wonderful husband. The image of a little, blond-haired son and a pretty, dark-haired daughter popped into her mind, but she pushed the picture aside. They were two people on different paths. She was given to another, and Princess Alecia had ensnared Ramón's heart. She would have a good life with Jiseve. Life was about duty; love had to come second to that.

Breakfast over, they broke camp and were soon on the road. Benae's gaze found Ramón whenever he was near, but he was all business; trotting up and down the line, his horse on the move continuously, his eye scanning the countryside. Benae longed for a smile from him but remonstrated with herself for the thought. She wouldn't admire him so if he didn't take his task seriously, if he didn't value her safety and that of all in the convoy.

But she noticed the small details, like how he placed a reassuring hand on his horse's shoulder, the fact that he didn't wear spurs and his gentle words for Alec, the youngest soldier, who was hardly a man at all. Ramón had a respect for people that one didn't often find in the nobility. He truly cared for all under his protection. Benae found herself wanting to find Princess Alecia and give her a piece of her mind. This Vard Anton must have been some man for the princess to spurn Ramón's attentions in favor of the disgraced army captain.

Ramón trotted past again, and a bolt of pure desire stabbed through her. His hips rose and fell in time with his horse's movements. She imagined herself beneath him, the sweat on his skin glistening in the flickering light of candles, her body meeting his —. She snapped her eyes shut to block Ramón's body from her thoughts. It was no good. He was in her mind, in her heart; it felt like he had wormed his way into her very soul. And Ramón? His heart was constrained by duty and loyalty, and what he felt for her couldn't compete with that. The thought blew away her desire as a gust of chill wind hurls autumn leaves across flagstones. She picked up her quill and turned her attention to the wedding plans.

Nearing midday, the convoy spied a farmstead and pulled in at the gate. The horses needed a drink and it was still some miles to the next stream. Benae watched as Ramón spoke to the farmer and then approached the carriage.

He poked his head through the door. "We've been invited for luncheon, Lady," he said. "The men will eat in the yard. I'll escort yourself and Merel to the homestead." His voice was brisk and business-like, but his hand lingered on hers as he helped her down. Benae stomped on her fluttering heart savagely. *Honestly!* She really must get her feelings in hand.

"I will welcome a meal indoors, Squire, and the company of others," she said, as Ramón guided her through the gate and toward the homestead. Merel followed a discreet distance behind.

Ramón frowned. "We've been on the road but a day and a half, Lady, and what is wrong with your current companions?"

"What companions? *You,* Squire, have been avoiding me. I had not thought you a sulky child, but I find I have to revise my opinions."

"There is much to do." His voice dropped so only she could hear. "I'm too busy to sit with you and pander to your every need. That's why Merel is here."

Benae gasped and stepped closer to Ramón. "I can't put what happened out of my mind and I don't believe you can either," she whispered. "You're so distant. It breaks my heart."

"Can't you see this is wrong, Benae?" The torment in Ramón's eyes ensnared her, as did his use of her name. "You made a choice when you became betrothed to the prince. You're his. No matter how I feel, nothing can change that."

Ramón's words startled her. His admission that he harbored feelings for her lit a glow within her heart, made hope blossom. The world slipped away as they stared at each other, wrapped in a realm that Benae had never thought existed.

Ramón was first to shake off the spell. "This is neither the time nor the place. We'll talk later." He took Benae's hand and placed it on his arm, continuing toward the homestead.

Benae doubted they would truly discuss the matter that lay between them; this dangerous attraction they shared. She tried to focus on the farmer who stood before the door of a humble cottage.

"May I present Lady Benae Branasar, the prince's betrothed, Master Orard?" Ramón said, his gentle hand on Benae's back.

Master Orard bowed low then rose slowly, his kind eyes crinkling at the corners. "It's an honor to have you share our table, Lady." He stood to the side so they could pass across the threshold. Benae introduced Merel and then stepped inside. It was cozy indoors, out of the strengthening wind. The farm wife was setting the table and paused as introductions were made.

"It's an honor, Lady, Squire," Mistress Orard said, "we live so far out, I had not heard your joyous news. Perhaps the prince will produce an heir yet?"

"Cana! It's not for us to suggest what might come to pass." He turned to Benae. "I hope she didn't offend, Lady."

"Nonsense, Master Orard," Benae said, placing her hand on the farmer's arm, "I hope we shall be blessed with more than one child. Children are such a joy, don't you agree?"

The faces of the Orards clouded over, striking a pang of fear into Benae's heart. "What's the matter?"

"Our daughter," Mistress Orard said, "she is abed with the fever. I've tried every remedy I know but nothing helps."

Benae froze at her words, remembering two other souls who had died of the fever. It must have shown on her face for Master Orard stepped forward. "We will understand if you don't wish to share a meal with us. You can't risk an illness with your important event so close."

Benae stared at him, wondering if she could take the next step that would expose her to more of the pain she lived with daily; failure and loss.

"Master Orard, my heart breaks for your daughter. I would like to help." The hope in their eyes sharpened her fear. What if she let these good people down? What if she couldn't save their precious child?

Ramón drew her aside. "Proceed with caution," he murmured. "If you use your arts openly, word will spread throughout Thorius of the witch betrothed to the prince. Your life might be in danger."

"I won't stand by if I can help." She turned to Merel. "Fetch my tonics from the carriage, if you please, Merel. Mistress Orard, show me your daughter."

The farm wife scurried to obey, leading Benae into a small adjoining room. At first, darkness prevented Benae from seeing the girl on the bed, but soon her eyes adjusted to the dimness.

"Is there no window in this room?" Benae asked.

"There is, Lady, but Elin can't bear the light."

"She needs to have fresh air if she is to recover. Open the shutters."

Benae expected opposition. Instead, the woman hustled across to the window and pulled on a lever to open the shutters. A cool breeze swirled in from the east to ruffle the girl's long brown hair. Benae crossed to the bed and sat on its edge.

"Elin?" she said gently. "Can you hear me?"

The girl didn't stir. So pale was her face that, for a moment, Benae thought she had passed. The child gave a whimper and her chest rose in a shallow breath.

"She has barely been awake these last two days, Lady."

"How old is she?"

"She has seen ten summers —" Mistress Orard's voice broke in a sob. "I can't lose her, she is all I have left, with her brother having entered the army."

Benae knew how it felt to lose a loved one to the army. She hoped that death wouldn't be the ultimate outcome for their son, as it had been for her brother. Merel entered the room and deposited a wooden box on the bed. She had assisted Benae before and knew her methods, never suspecting the deeper skill beneath her mistress's care. At least, Benae didn't think Merel knew of her gift. The maid circled around to the other side of the bed and together they pulled the covers down. They lifted the child to a sitting position and removed her nightdress, so she wore only her small clothes. Her mother hovered.

Benae looked up. "I'll need hot water and a spoon, Mistress." As the woman left, Benae placed her palm on the girl's fevered brow and closed her eyes. She sent a tendril of spirit into the child, first to the bones of the skull and then into the mind. Yes, the illness had upset the balance of the elements in the girl's body. Fire dominated water, but there was something else amiss. Benae moved her palm to the part of the chest exposed by the vest and concentrated again. Her spirit entered the mouth, coursing down the windpipe to the fine tubes that moved air through the chest. No matter where her spirit ventured, it was halted by glistening plaques of bodily humor. Benae grimaced, forcing a wave of nausea away. She withdrew her delving and knelt by the bed, a crushing agony in her own chest. This was just like her parents and she hadn't been able to help them.

"Lady, are you well?" Merel asked, her voice sharp in the quiet room.

"There is barely any air flowing into her," Benae whispered. "I don't know if I can help."

Mistress Orard returned and Benae pushed herself to her feet. She took the spoon and poured some tonic into it then placed it at the girl's lips. "Please drink, Elin." A trickle of the medicine slipped past Elin's lips and the girl swallowed. "That's right, dear, a little more."

Benae continued until the spoon was empty and then she poured two spoonsful into the bowl of water the mother had brought. She swirled the tonic through the water with her hand, battling despair. She must control this raging doubt. Healing couldn't be wrought amidst uncertainty, but how could she be confident when her last three attempts had resulted in death?

Benae continued to swirl her hand through the water, watching the liquid eddy around her fingers, mesmerizing herself. When her fears had subsided and her heart had halved its pace, she dropped herself into the deep, tranquil place in her mind, closed her eyes and began bathing the child with her tonic-drenched hand. As Benae moved her hand first to Elin's forehead and then her shoulders, chest and arms, she trickled a tiny weave of spirit into the child, soothing, coaxing and stripping the foul humors away. She didn't know if her labors had any effect on the chest, so clogged were the tiny tubes. Finally, she could do nothing more but send a final larger blast of spirit into the child and hope it would fortify her strength.

"She is strong," she said to the mother. Let her have hope at the last. Perhaps it would see her through the difficult days ahead. "I will leave the herbal tonic. You are to dribble a spoonful into her twice a day. Rub her throat so that she swallows. I want her to sleep on her side." She and Merel rolled Elin onto her side and pulled up the covers. "You must roll her onto her other side every two hours, even throughout the night. This will help the foul humors drain from her chest. Don't be alarmed if she coughs. If she is awake, encourage her to cough the matter up. It will make her stomach sick if she swallows it."

"Thank you, Lady. I will do all you say," the mistress said. "Now you must wash and join us for the midday meal." The woman allowed them to exit first. Benae's heart ached for her. She knew her instructions would only deepen the shadows beneath the woman's eyes and almost certainly for little gain.

Benae met Ramón's anxious gaze as she re-entered the living area. His concern was a balm for her raw nerves. It felt good to have such a solid friend, if she could call him that. He clutched her hand. A bolt of heat speared her core and rose to her cheeks. How could he do that with just one touch?

"How is the child?" he asked.

"She is gravely ill," Benae said, shame sending prickles over her scalp. How could she take his innocent touch and allow it to inflame her desires? Really! She must take hold of herself. "I've done what I can."

"Then it's time to eat," he said. "We must be on our way."

The five of them sat at the table, the fare simple and nutritious. While they ate, Benae told of her estate far to the northwest, in the neighboring kingdom of Tylevia. The seasons had been kind to the Orards. They had been able to pay their tithe to the prince and then some. But they missed their son's help on the farm. If he didn't return from the army, next harvest would be a different story.

"And the dark elves, Lady," Master Orard said. "They be troubling folk to the north. If we don't stop them there, sooner or later they'll be on our doorstep."

"My betrothed will see they penetrate no further, Master Orard. He has plans to travel north to secure my estate and seek help from neighboring kingdoms."

"I'm sure you're right, Lady. May the Goddess protect the prince on his travels."

The meal was soon over. Benae returned to Elin's bedroom for one last check of the child. Was her breathing easier? Her fever had certainly broken.

"You've saved her, My Lady." Mistress Orard kissed Benae's hand. "How can I ever thank you?"

Benae ignored the surge of hope that rose within. "Remember what I said, Mistress. You must turn her every two hours. She's not back with us yet."

Benae swept from the room, closing her heart against the poor mother's tightly pressed lips and slumped shoulders. Mistress Orard couldn't afford to think her daughter would be healed without further effort. She must continue to nurse the girl until she rose from her bed. If in fact she ever did.

Ramón helped Benae into the carriage. "Mistress Orard looks upset. What did you tell her?"

"The girl's fever is broken but her mother must not believe the battle is won. Elin needs all her efforts."

"Could you not have given her one shred of hope?" Ramón's face had gone red and a muscle twitched at his temple.

"Hope won't save her daughter, just as it didn't save my parents. I did my best, as I did with Mama and Papa. Only the Goddess can know if it will be enough."

Ramón's face had switched from beet to white. "I'm sorry, Benae, I didn't know."

"Didn't know what?" she snapped.

"That you had nursed your parents and …"

"Go ahead, say it. I nursed my parents and failed. I nursed my brother and failed. I used all my skills and I couldn't even save my own. Sometimes we have no power and Mistress Orard must accept that."

"It sounds as though she's not the only woman who must accept that." Ramón bowed and closed the door of the carriage.

Benae scowled at the closed door. She *had* accepted her lack of power. She had been forced to. Perhaps that was really it. Her powers had truly deserted her. Had she been reduced to the level of the peddler who sells tonics, knowing they can never cure anything? What did it matter? All the people she had ever loved were dead. She was building a new life for herself, making choices that would save those on her estate from starvation and the dark elves. If she could not heal, then so be it. *If only I could know if my talents have really deserted me.* The child's fever had broken but so had Benae's parents' fevers…just before they died.

"The child is gravely ill, Lady Benae," Merel said, her big brown eyes oozing sympathy. "You have done your best and must not blame yourself."

"I don't know what I would have done without your support these last months, Merel, and again here today. You anticipate my needs before I know them myself. It's a special gift you have."

Merel laughed. "You make it easy, Lady. It's an honor to serve."

Benae smiled at the maid and settled into the seat. As the carriage rolled away, she said a prayer to the Goddess to heal Elin and protect her parents and brother.

* * *

Ramón shook himself from the trance he had fallen into. The afternoon had been uneventful, but he was bone tired. Two nights without sleep had robbed him of his usual resilience. Tonight, he would retire early and not take part in the watch. Just thinking of his blankets made his eyelids droop. They arrived at a stream on dark. The watercourse marked the beginning of a forest and he gave the order to set up camp in a clearing. Dark shadows under the trees sent shivers of unease down his spine, but the merry gurgling of the water eased his fears.

Ramón set two soldiers to guard duty while he helped the others pitch the tents and tend the horses. As soon as the water over the fire had boiled, Merel took a pitcher and bowl into the carriage. Ramón felt a tightening in his breeches at the thought of Benae's legs, bared, as they were the night before they left. He relived the scene in her bedroom when she had tempted him, thrown her arms around him and he had nearly succumbed. It had been a close-run thing, but in the end, honor had won out. Nothing good could come of his laying hands on Benae.

When the camp was set, he sat by the fire awaiting the evening meal. The men brought out a skin of wine and shared it around, but Ramón declined.

"Those with watch duty are only to have two swallows," he said. That brought back-slaps and stories about how one or the other believed they fought better with a little wine or ale under their belt. Ramón smiled at their bluster, but his mood soured at his next thought. He should be on the road in his search for the princess, not escorting Lady Benae across the countryside to Wildecoast. Instead, the hunt had been wound down just when the prince should have been throwing everything into finding his daughter. The longer she stayed with Vard Anton… If Ramón thought about what the two of them were getting up to on the road he would never sleep again!

Despite the disconcerting thoughts of Vard and Alecia together, that mission would be a far less complicated one than this was proving to be. Not for the first time, he cursed Prince Zialni for choosing to travel north. All Ramón's efforts at avoiding Benae had gone to waste. Now, she was under his nose by day and haunting his dreams by night. As often as he pushed her image away, it slid back to torment him.

Benae brought out his best and worst characteristics. He wanted to protect her, but she was too capable. He wanted to be angry with her for not quelling Mistress Orard's fears, instead discovering she blamed herself for the deaths of her parents. Would she carry guilt with her for the rest of her life? He knew all too well how guilt ate at the soul, how secrets festered. He was ashamed of the secrets he held, and he regretted them, more than he could ever express. One was his part in allowing Alecia to escape with Vard Anton and the other…Suffice to say that if the prince discovered either of his secrets, his life would be forfeit.

His meal arrived and he ate it distractedly until the ladies appeared. He stood as they sat opposite him. "Lady Benae, Merel. I trust you've had a pleasant afternoon."

"Yes, thank you," Benae said. "Merel and I have been planning my wedding festivities. It proved a most agreeable pastime."

Ramón found himself discomforted at the thought of Benae's wedding. Why? Was it because she had flung herself at him, even while betrothed to his liege lord? He must focus on that. A complex lady was Benae; complex and intriguing. He couldn't help but wonder what it would be like between them: their love, their lives together. She had a zest for life, no matter how she suffered now, a knack for making the best of a situation. Her interest in him made him walk lighter, at least when he could forget whom she was destined for. Until Benae, he had never felt sought after by a woman. There had always been other men, who were more handsome, more riveting, more hypnotic than he.

He swallowed hard as the small but painful darts hit his heart. Alecia had always said he deserved a woman who would love him. He had not given up on the hope that it would be Alecia. In the meantime, there was duty, and it was his responsibility to protect Benae, even from herself.

Ramón realized Benae was staring at him, her eyes hungry, hunting, predatory. The expression was gone in an instant and she smiled coolly. It was such a contrast, with the steamy look it replaced, he convinced himself he had been mistaken. What on earth had they been discussing? He couldn't remember.

"We shall be on the road another two days and nights, My Lady, but we make good time, despite our long stop today."

Benae inclined her head. "I look forward to a proper bath and a soft bed." There was that fleeting expression again, as if she were on the prowl for a mate, instead of having already secured one.

Ramón's mouth had gone dry. He cleared his throat. "I —" *Get a grip, man!* "I'll endeavor to make the rest of the trip as comfortable as possible." There, that was better.

A nervous whinny floated from where Flaire was tethered and Benae frowned. "Flaire has been restless this afternoon." She paused as if listening. "I wonder what has upset him." She speared a piece of meat and delicately prized it off her knife, her rosy lips closing around the mouthful. Benae had wonderful lips, especially when they curved in that lazy smile she often had. It was as if she had some private jest at the world's expense. He imagined she would be full of mirth with those she trusted.

"It's likely just a bear or a wolf. I'll set an extra guard tonight. Nothing will get past to menace your mount." Ramón scraped the remaining stew from his plate and mopped up the gravy with a heel of fresh bread that the Orards had gifted them.

He turned to the man beside him.

"Play something lively for us, Henet."

Henet grinned and took up the flute that lay beside him. Sparkling notes filled the campsite, swirling through the brisk night air. One of the soldiers, Seve, drew Merel to her feet and twirled her around the fire. The shadows of his fellow travelers cavorted throughout the clearing, chasing the last of Ramón's uncertainties away.

* * *

Benae sat up in her bed, sweat droplets moistening her brow, heart pounding. Even awake, she couldn't dispel the images of the nightmare; dark shapes creeping through the night from tree to tree, man smell swirling up her nostrils. A nervous whinny sounded from outside. *Flaire!* The pictures in her mind weren't nightmares – they were from her stallion. They were real images that he was seeing. She pushed at Merel's shoulder and the maid groaned.

"Up Merel! The camp is invaded." Benae climbed over Merel and pulled on her cloak. "We must raise the alarm." She peered through the window of the carriage and saw a shadow slip past. "Awake!" she cried. "The camp is overrun! To arms!"

"What is it, My Lady?" Merel said, pushing her long hair from her face.

"For the love of the Goddess, get up, or you'll be killed in your bed."

Benae's words must have finally sunk in, for Merel screamed and threw herself out of bed. The maid reached into her knitting basket and withdrew a vicious, hunting knife from beneath the wool. The metal gleamed in the faint moonlight.

"I'll not let them rape us, Lady," she said.

Benae stared, half mortified, half wishing she had a weapon like it.

"You stay behind me," Merel said. "I'll defend us both."

Benae was struck speechless by her maid's bravery, but Flaire screamed at that moment and fear lanced through her chest. In her mind, she saw a dark figure grab the horse's head collar and start to untie him. The cries of men and the clash of weapons penetrated the relative sanctuary of their carriage. Benae pushed Merel out of her way and tore open the door.

What she saw made her pause. The camp was in chaos. One of her soldiers lay unmoving before the campfire, an arrow in his chest. The other members of her guard, including Ramón, were locked in combat with more of the dark figures she had seen creeping past the carriage. A hand appeared from nowhere and hauled her down the steps. She fell into the arms of a man whose bright white teeth gleamed in a dark face. As he spun her about and pulled her back against him, she glimpsed pointed ears. *A dark elf!* Benae felt the bite of metal against her throat and froze. The man behind her smelled of forest and sweat. She didn't dare move, but her eyes flickered to the right where Flaire was tethered. Another intruder was trying to untie the stallion as he leapt and plunged against his rope.

Benae was dragged across the clearing toward the trees. Still she dared not scream for fear that the man would slice her. She glanced to the left and her eyes caught Ramón's. Desperation bathed his face as he battled two of the invaders. They backed him toward the fire and then Benae did scream, for she was certain he would be speared on the short knives of the attackers or burned. One of the invaders hurled something onto the fire and it flared into the night sky. Ramón grunted as the heat shot past his body.

Benae's thoughts were torn from Ramón as Merel charged down the stairs of the carriage and flung herself at Benae's captor. She had a moment to marvel at Merel's flared nostrils and bared teeth, before the elf hurled her to the ground and met Merel's charge. Benae screamed as the man brought his short blade up to block Merel's knife thrust, then swung his weapon and sliced through her throat. Cold shock gripped Benae as her maid slumped to the ground, lifeblood pumping from a ruined gullet.

"Merel!" Benae hardly recognized the anguished scream that gurgled from her own throat. Her heart latched onto the hope that she could save the maid, but a cold, hard part of her mind told her Merel was beyond anyone's help. *Save yourself!* But Benae couldn't move. Her limbs seemed frozen to the cool ground beneath her. *Run!*

Even as the thought raced through her mind, Benae knew she couldn't leave Ramón and Flaire to the mercy of these invaders. Her attacker appeared as stunned as Benae was, staring down at the woman he had just murdered. His eyes met Benae's. He was young, not much more than a boy. She stood slowly, backing to where Flaire was tethered, knowing the stallion needed her protection. *I can't lose him.* Her foot came up against something and she glanced down to find the body of an elf at her feet. He must have been the man who was trying to free Flaire. She stepped backwards over his body but saw no movement of his chest. A gash marred his temple.

The approaching elf watched her, blood dripping from the metal blade in his hands. Benae came up against Flaire. He snorted and nuzzled her hair. He was fearful for himself and for her. He sent her images of them galloping through the forest, leaving the elves and the camp miles behind. She would never make it onto his back. Perhaps if she could slip the halter from his head he could flee. Her eyes fell on the discarded whip the driver used and she bent to retrieve it, bringing it up between her and the elf. Years of horsemanship had taught her how to use a whip. It could be an effective weapon. She flicked the long, sturdy handle and the leather cracker at the end popped, sending Flaire into a flurry of dancing hooves.

Benae swallowed down the fear that threatened to choke her. "Leave this camp now."

The man grinned. "I will take you and that horse."

He stepped forward and Benae brought the whip up and over her shoulder, ready to swing at him. His eyes flickered to the length of plaited leather that could trap an arm and the scrap of cracker that could blind.

"You'll get neither me, nor this horse." Her voice shook with emotion and the cold stole up her nightdress, making her knees shake. "Leave now." The tremor in her voice must have given him courage for he closed on her. She swung the whip with all the force she could muster. Before she could bring her weapon against him, he had closed with her and torn it from her fingers. His powerful arm curled around her for the second time, only now they were face to face. She barely reached his chest. He was too strong for her struggles to have any impact.

He laughed. "I like my women with fire." He grabbed her hair like he would a horse's mane and spun her around, the pain in her scalp bringing tears to her eyes. Flaire stood before her, his frightened brown eye rolling at the elf. Benae gazed up at her mount, sending soothing pictures to him of long days in the sun, of her calming presence on his back. He settled. The elf untied the rope tethering Flaire, hurled Benae face down over the horse's withers than vaulted onto his back. With a subtle squeeze of his knees, the elf had Flaire spinning and heading for the trees, one hand on Benae's bottom to steady her.

She sobbed as she realized he had won. She was truly being kidnapped. They gained the first trees, the ground flashing by and dirt flying up from Flaire's hooves. She closed her eyes to keep the grit from them and laid her hands down the horse's shoulder, the warm strong muscles moving beneath her fingers.

Several paces into the trees, Flaire's gallop suddenly faltered. The elf slumped against her then toppled to the ground. The stallion stopped the instant his rider fell, snorting and pawing at the earth. Benae pulled herself around on his withers and sat astride, her heart thumping, breath coming in gasps. As she soothed Flaire's neck she searched for the elf and found him with an arrow in his back. He didn't move. She scanned the path they had just taken, eyes desperately seeking the source of the arrow, but no movement could be discerned. It had to be one of her men who had loosed the dart, surely?

Benae didn't know what to do. Danger lay behind and before her. There could be more of the dark creatures in the forest and back at camp. She could hear nothing but the pounding of her heart.

Gently, she urged Flaire to return the way they had come, one step at a time. He didn't like the fear and scent of blood that hung over the camp. His whole body shivered in tune with hers, but he did what she asked, and she loved him for it. Benae ran soothing images through her mind to his, and calmed him with her hands; it helped to calm her too. They would face whatever they must together.

As they emerged from the trees, Ramón came to meet them. His face was haggard, and his once-fine clothes smeared with dirt and sweat. He held a short horse bow.

"Thank the Goddess, Benae," he said.

Benae sobbed, relief at the sight of him crashing over her. She slid from Flaire and threw herself into his arms, tears pouring down her face. His arms closed around her, the weapon flung to the dirt, and she breathed deeply, inhaling his warmth and strength. His closeness soothed her as she had tried to do to Flaire just moments before.

Ramón held her away from him, his eyes more fearful than she had ever expected. "Let me look at you. Where are you hurt?" His gaze fell upon her throat and he cried out. "He has cut you!" His fingers were gentle as they probed the wound. "Come and I'll tend it."

"What of you, Ramón? Are you hurt?"

"I've been sliced on my forearm and have some scrapes and bruises, nothing more. I'll see to them when I've helped you."

They walked together, past the bodies of soldiers and elves alike, Ramón stopping to check each one of his men as he passed. None had survived. Flaire shuffled along in their wake. When they came to Merel's body, Benae dropped to her knees and clutched the maid's lifeless hands.

"You should have seen her; she was fearless and see where it got her. Dead! Because of me. She was defending me. If only she had stayed in the carriage, she might have survived." Benae closed Merel's staring eyes and laid her hands upon her still chest. "I can't bear it, Ramón. She was goodness itself." Benae's heart ached, as though it would crack open. She couldn't stop the tears.

Ramón drew her to her feet, placed his arm around her shoulders and helped her into the carriage. He disappeared for a few moments and the image of Flaire, munching on a pail of oats, slipped into Benae's mind.

The squire was soon back, a lantern in his hands. He set the light on the hook over the bed and helped Benae to lie down. Her cloak fanned out around her and he pushed it off her shoulders, so she lay only in her nightgown. It was more modest attire than on their last bedroom encounter but still Benae was aware of his eyes upon her.

His hands brushed her throat. "It is but a scratch and some bruising. Can you heal it?"

Benae shook her head. "Alas, the help I can give others I can't provide myself. I'm afraid you must assist me." She handed him her favorite ointment.

Ramón bathed the dirt away from her throat and his gentle fingers rubbed salve into her skin. It stung a little. His hands moved down her throat to her shoulders and upper chest, wiping dust and grime away with the damp cloth she had used to bathe earlier in the night. He pushed the long sleeves of her nightgown up to examine her arms, gasping at a deep bruise on her elbow. It was where she had fallen when Merel attacked the elf. More ointment went there. He didn't open her nightdress but ran his fingers down over her lower chest and along all her ribs. Her blood stirred, warmed in her veins. He only examined her but…

"Ouch!" She said as his questing hands ran along her ribs below her right breast.

"It could be a broken rib and need binding. I must check."

"Please Ramón, it's nothing. Merely a bruise."

His hands ran down her nightgown to the hem and he began to haul it up, revealing her calves, knees. Thank the Goddess she had sensible pantaloons on this time!

"Stop, allow me." Benae pulled her nightgown higher until it was bunched around her hips. She lay down and pulled it up to reveal her chest, below her breasts. Ramón's gaze didn't stray, flying immediately to the large bruise on her ribs. "Can you bear ointment there?"

Oh Goddess, ointment there? Perhaps it would hurt enough that she wouldn't be reminded of his kisses, that his hands on her flesh wouldn't stir her desire. "Yes," she said, her voice merely a whisper.

His fingers were warm and gentle as he applied the salve to her skin, hands questing along the ribs to explore for breaks. It wasn't painful enough to keep her mind from imagining his hand in other, more intimate places. Her right breast moved in time with his massaging of the skin below it and her nipple hardened. *What sort of a woman am I to have these urges when our whole camp has been killed?*

"Ramón, there's time for this later. We can't be safe here. Surely, we need to hitch the horses and move on? We do still have the carriage horses, don't we?" Fear struck her anew as she contemplated being stranded in this place.

Ramón shook his head. "We have only Flaire."

Benae couldn't help the gasp that escaped her lips. "What will we do?"

"I must leave you and search the forest for a mount. At least that way we can ride the remaining miles to Wildecoast and send men for the coach and the bodies."

Benae imagined sitting in the carriage alone in the dark and her courage failed. She began to tremble. "Perhaps we could both ride Flaire?"

Ramón's concerned gaze was almost too much to bear. "It's too far for Flaire to convey us both in good time. He would have to be rested, leading to an untenable delay. We must gain Wildecoast in all haste, so I'll try to recover at least one of the horses if I can. I promise I won't be gone long." He completed his ministering to her ribs, pulled her gown to cover her hips, then ran his hands down her legs. Benae pushed unwelcome thoughts of pleasure from her mind. Damn her infatuation! She couldn't have him and yet she wanted every delicious piece of him.

He completed his examination and his hands left her body. Did she imagine reluctance as he drew her gown to cover her bare limbs? *Don't be foolish woman.*

"You're chilled. Wrap yourself in your blankets and I'll get us something warm to drink."

"Ramón, you can't go back out amongst all that death. They're your friends."

"It must be done," he said, anger in his tone. "Do you believe it will be easier to face at first light?" He stood, looking down at her, his expression unreadable. First so tender and now this …cold calmness. Perhaps he was in shock, just as she was?

"Stay here, do as I say. I'll move the bodies and cover them, so you don't have to confront their deaths." She knew he meant Merel. He cast her one long look, as if he sought to imprint everything about her into his memory, and stomped out.

Benae drew her cloak around her and crawled down the bed to peer out of the shutters. Ramón had thrown more wood upon the fire and placed the pot of water to boil. While he waited, he moved about the clearing, dragging the bodies of his men and Merel to the far side. The elven bodies he gathered several paces further on. Once the corpses were collected, he dismantled one of the tents and used the material to cover the Brightcastle dead. The elves he left in the open.

Ramón washed his hands and returned to her with steaming cups of herbal tea. Her heart ached at the exhaustion on his dusty face.

"I'll tend your wounds," she said, taking the tea from him. The first sip sent warmth radiating out, driving some of the chill from her body. "Mmm, this is good. You've added some whiskey."

"I thought we could both benefit from it. I'll wash and tend my wounds when we have drunk. Here, I found some gingerbread." He handed her two small pieces of the treat and Benae realized how hungry she was.

"Thank you. For everything."

"I'm just doing my job. And not very well, if I'm truthful. The prince will have my head for allowing this ambush."

"He will do no such thing. Jiseve will praise you for saving me. You couldn't have known."

"You raised the alarm. How did you know?"

"I had a nightmare of dark men creeping from tree to tree. It woke me and then I heard Flaire. I knew there was danger and gave the alarm. I just wish it could have been sooner."

"You gave us a fighting chance."

"It wasn't enough to save the others." She stared at Ramón, grief making her chest hurt. "Why are we here and the others killed? Merel gave her life for me."

"It's not for us to question the will of the Goddess," Ramón said. "All we can do is make their sacrifice mean something. We must make it to Wildecoast."

Benae rubbed her breastbone, trying to stem the ache in her heart. She nodded. "You're right. Somehow we must accomplish that."

Ramón stood and removed his tunic and shirt. Lantern light flickered over the smooth muscles of his chest and shoulders, the ridged planes of his stomach. *He is so beautiful.* A deep cut sliced the muscle of his upper left arm, but it had stopped bleeding. He had various small cuts across his shoulders and chest and one small nick beneath his right eye.

Benae tossed the used water from the bowl and poured fresh from the pitcher. She splashed a capful of her favored wound potion into the water and fetched a clean cloth. Gently, she washed the wounds and the rest of Ramón's exposed skin. He had been so fortunate that none of the gashes were serious. He gasped as she vigorously cleaned the cut on his arm to remove small particles of dirt.

"This one needs stitching." She fetched her needle and thread and began her task, ignoring the small noises Ramón made with each insertion of the needle. As she sewed, Benae dropped deep into her healing trance, imbuing the damaged tissues with vigor, willing them to knit and escape infection. This she could heal. If her skills were intact, this wound would heal within two days and the stitches could be removed.

* * *

Ramón gritted his teeth. It wasn't pain but desire he battled with. The lantern light outlined Benae's form through the nightgown, her perfect proportions imprinting themselves in his memory. No matter how often he tried to keep her at arm's length, the woman before him kept intruding. She was enticing; her head bent over her work, glorious dark hair gathered at her nape, ringlets escaping to curl at her forehead and ears. Cool air filtered in past the shutters, making him shiver, but Benae's attentions heated his blood. He groaned softly and tried to concentrate on the pain as the needle and the rough thread pierced his skin, but the discomfort was mild and the woman who toiled at the chore compelling. Benae seemed completely engrossed and he cursed himself for turning a clinical task into a seductive dream.

For he did dream of Benae. Almost every night since their first meeting, she had haunted his dreams, eyes full of mystery, her smile fueling his lust until all he wished was to kiss those perfect red lips. During the day he had more control. The weapons practice and running helped to focus his energies on matters that would benefit the kingdom and the prince. But at night he awoke in a sweat, heart racing and his manhood engorged beyond imagining. If he couldn't control his lecherous thoughts, he'd have to leave Brightcastle. Perhaps all would be well once they returned from this journey and he could resume his quest to recover Alecia.

"I'm sorry, Ramón," Benae said. "I'm being as gentle as I can."

"You're the epitome of tenderness, Lady." His gut clenched and a shiver of pleasure slid up his spine as her fingers traced the line of stitches. Benae had strong, artistic hands, made for healing – and pleasuring a man. He snapped his mind away from contemplating how good those fingers would feel on other parts of his body.

"Thank you," he said, his voice hoarse with emotion he couldn't dispel. He reached for his shirt and drew it on, wincing as the stitches pulled. "I should check on the guards that were stationed in the forest and see if I can find another horse…"

Benae gazed at him as if he were a particularly difficult blacksmith's puzzle. "Still running away?"

He froze in the act of opening the door and turned to face her. "We can't stay here a moment longer than needed, Lady."

She snorted. "Two steps forward and three steps back. Don't you feel it? This connection we have? You shut down every time I start to get close."

He shook his head. Did she truly not understand? "There can be no 'us' for so many reasons. Put it out of your mind and concentrate on gaining Wildecoast. That's what I am trying to do."

"I try but something keeps pushing me back to you. You're important to me."

"And you're important to me – as the lady of my lord."

Benae stamped her foot. "Tell me you don't want me."

"I don't."

"Liar!" Benae closed the gap between them and flung her arms around his neck, her lips against his, all the flesh he craved pressed to his hungry body. His response was instant, opening his mouth to receive her plundering tongue, his hands sliding down her body to cup her bottom. She parted her legs and leaned further into him.

"I have wanted you since I first saw you," she said, breaking away from his lips and pushing his shirt aside to plant soft kisses across his chest. Her hands fumbled at the fastenings of his breeches as she continued to rain kisses down the ridges of his stomach.

He closed his eyes to draw strength for what he must do; before he lost the last shred of control he possessed. "Benae," he said, grasping her questing hands. He swallowed hard at the passion and desire that blazed from her eyes. *Oh Goddess, what would it be like to have this woman?* The thought of her forever given to the prince was almost enough to push him back into her arms.

She straightened, tugging at the hands he still held. "You're going to say 'no'."

"I've already said it, Benae. I don't know what more I can say. Your path is with the prince and mine..."

"Don't say it again! Alecia has chosen another! Your quest to retrieve her and punish Vard Anton will be the end of you. Don't let her ruin you."

"I must save her. It's the only way I can atone for letting her go that night. Even if she and I have no future, this I must do."

"So, you finally admit your dream of a life with Alecia is only that. A dream. If my actions have helped you to see that, I'm glad."

"My dreams are my business." He wouldn't admit to the change in his feelings for Alecia. Benae couldn't know how hard it was for him to deny her or she would never give up on him. Somehow, he had to keep her focused on her marriage, unpalatable as the thought was. She had made her decision weeks ago and more depended on this than just his happiness.

Benae finally pulled her hands from his. "Go and do what you must."

To Ramón, it sounded like a final command. Perhaps that was truly what she meant. Benae had given up. Ramón buttoned his shirt and pulled on his tunic. "It's almost dawn. I'll return shortly after daylight, no matter what I have found. Stay in the carriage." He slammed the carriage door on his way out.

CHAPTER 9

BENAE dressed in a fresh traveling gown of russet satin, while mulling over her conversation with Ramón. Stubborn man! But she wouldn't give up on him. Her heart knew his on some deeper level and she couldn't ignore that. It meant something more than just lustful attraction. It went deeper than mere desire. Eventually he would see that.

The walls of the carriage seemed to close in on her as she paced the few steps back and forth. She had never enjoyed being cooped up. Still, she couldn't bring herself to leave the carriage until it was light outside.

By the time dawn touched the clearing, Benae could stand no more. An hour of straining her ears for sounds of Ramón's return, or that of the elves, had her nerves ready to snap. She left the carriage and set about making a breakfast of oatmeal and boiling a pot for tea. She topped up Flaire's oats for the hard day's riding ahead. Resting her forehead against his neck as he ate, her pounding heart slowed to match the heartbeat of the striking gray stallion. Time spent with Flaire never failed to calm her. His mind still raced with the events of last night, but they had become jumbled and Benae hoped in time he would forget his fear.

She left her mount munching his oats and returned to stir the oatmeal, her thoughts tumbling over themselves. If only life could be simple; she would marry for love, wouldn't be burdened with the care of her estate; might be free to come and go as she pleased, free to make a life of her choosing. Benae cut short her wistful musings. No one could do as they wanted in all things. Poverty constrained most lives and duty played its part as well. Even Merel hadn't been able to escape duty. It had cost her life. Benae glanced at the pile of covered bodies where Merel lay. There was none to mourn her, but Benae. Merel had been orphaned as a child and had grown up in Benae's household. She was the only living person who would miss the maid.

Benae's heart sank at the prospect of continuing without stoic Merel. She had been more of a sister than a servant, always there to give advice. Often that counsel had been gold. Merel must be given a court funeral befitting her importance in Benae's life.

Pushing sad thoughts of Merel aside, Benae scanned the trees surrounding the clearing, hoping to spy Ramón returning. The forest was silent, waiting. She began to see movement from the corner of her eye, but there was never anything when she turned.

"Silly woman," she said to herself. "Jumping at shadows like a child." She forced herself to concentrate on stirring the oatmeal, then dished up two plates and laid one by the fire. When the pot boiled, she brewed mugs of herbal tea and placed one beside Ramón's oatmeal.

Benae was halfway through breakfast when Ramón stepped from the trees, leading a brown horse, two bodies slung over its back. He avoided her eyes as he led the horse to the pile of kingdom dead and lifted the edge of the cover. Benae averted her face until the bodies were stored beneath the tent material.

Ramón led the brown horse to the carriage, tethered him beside Flaire and gave him a bowl of oats. He joined her by the fire and stood staring into the flames.

"Weren't there three men on duty last night?" Benae said.

"I couldn't find the third but there was a pool of blood where he had been stationed. The brown horse is one of the carriage horses. I found no others." He sat beside her and reached for the mug of tea. After a long swig he fell upon the oatmeal and finished it in short order. "Thank you for the meal, although I'm sure I told you to stay in the carriage. What if they had returned?"

Benae shrugged. "I don't think sitting in the carriage would have protected me for long."

Ramón sank into silence, a deep frown on his brow.

She couldn't abide the quiet. "How's your arm?"

"Fine." Brooding darkness sat on his shoulders like a cloak. It would do him no good to reflect on the night past. Or was it her he contemplated?

"What do you plan?" she asked.

"We must take the horses and ride for Wildecoast. I'll pack a tent and enough food and water to last us. Pack a satchel with what you need for the journey. If we ride hard, we'll reach the King's seat by midday tomorrow."

"Then I'll leave you to break camp." Benae stood and left to prepare for the journey.

They took to the road only minutes later. Benae rode Flaire, a satchel with medicines and personal items her only burden. A small bag of oats was tied behind her saddle. The feel of the horse beneath her had a calming effect on her nerves. She suspected the same couldn't be said for Ramón. He rode the carriage horse, which pranced and snorted for the first several miles. The beast wasn't used to bearing a man on his back and the added burden of the tent behind the saddle made him fidget more.

They made good time, alternately galloping, trotting and walking, to spare the horses. Luncheon was taken on the banks of a stream.

"This could be nice if the circumstances were different," Benae said as she chewed her way through a heel of stale bread and a chunk of hard cheese.

"You'd have to be a very optimistic person indeed to think this was nice," Ramón said, only half listening.

"There's no need to feel responsible, you know," she said.

He stared at her. "Who else is to blame for those deaths? A good leader anticipates trouble and prepares."

"You placed an extra guard that night."

"I thought the risk of attack was small. I was wrong. If only I had been on guard instead of Dawir or Alfrus…"

"Then you might be dead, and so might I." She moved closer to him and placed her hand on his shoulder. It tensed beneath her fingers. "You saved my life, Ramón. I'm so grateful for that. The prince will be as well. He'll not blame you."

He glanced down at her hand, then his piercing azure eyes met hers. Benae's heart melted at the doubt she saw there. It was clear he thought all was lost.

"We *will* make it to Wildecoast." She reached for his hand, his strong fingers closed on hers and butterflies fluttered in her stomach. No one had ever given her butterflies.

"This is not a situation I would have asked to be placed in," Ramón said. "Traveling with you unescorted places us both in a thorny spot. Even if we make it safely to the coast, another danger presents itself. Tongues will wag." His eyes strayed to her mouth and suddenly Benae didn't care what people thought.

"If they will speak, let's give them something to speak of," she said, planting her lips squarely on his. *Oh yes!* Ramón's mouth was soft and inviting and she took full advantage of it while he was too shocked to pull away. Both hands on his shoulders, Benae kissed him, willing all the passion she contained to flow into the glorious man below her. Ramón responded, his lips moving beneath hers, his tongue questing to push beyond her lips and explore the heat of her mouth. Benae not only allowed it, she welcomed his attention, pushing him back onto the soft grass of the riverbank, lying on top of him. His arms wrapped around her and slipped lower, his fingers on her waist, igniting warmth deep in her core.

She pushed herself up astride him, the bulge in his breeches sparking a tingle between her legs. There was no one to see and nothing to stop them. The long fearful night made her careless of the judgement of others, desperate to lose herself in Ramón's arms. She would take what he had and use it to sate the explosive need within her. Her lips ravished his mouth, his face, his neck. He groaned, thrusting his hips upward to meet her. She sat up and gazed down at him. His pupils were huge, dark, bottomless pools of need and she couldn't wait any longer.

She unbuttoned his tunic, while his hands slid beneath her skirts. His fingers slid up her legs to her inner thighs. A wave of longing nearly undid her, but she fought it down and continued stripping Ramón until his chest lay bare to the midday sun. She bent and kissed first one erect nipple and then the other. He groaned and rolled his head from side to side, his fingers searching for the ripe womanhood beneath her pantaloons. She was ready, desperate to accommodate the desire he so clearly felt. *But not yet.* This must be right.

Benae unlaced his breeches, leaving them on his hips but relieving his erection from its bindings. He was large! He would fill her as no one else ever had. She was wet just imagining his length buried inside her, thrusting until he poured his seed into her most intimate place. Her fingers closed around him and he reared up, gasping. She didn't allow him any respite. Filling her mouth with spittle, she released it onto her palm then closed her fingers on his manhood, running her hand up and down until he strained, panting, against her. He was a virgin all right and Benae reveled in the power it gave her. She could have him right now.

She abandoned his straining rod and stood, pulling up her skirt and discarding her pantaloons. Ramón levered himself onto his elbows and lay watching, panting as if he had run a race. Benae reached for the hem of her dress and started drawing it to her waist as she prepared to straddle him again. As she lowered herself toward his hips, Ramón clutched her forearms and pushed her a little down his legs so that she missed her target. She reached for his erection, but he stopped her.

"No."

"No one will find out, Ramón. There's no one to tell the tale. I know you want this. Tell me you want this."

"I want you with every particle of my being, but you're pledged to the prince."

"Can you truly deny me now?" Benae whispered. "I could give you release, pleasure, even love."

"You talk of the instant, but our lives, our loves are lived over a lifetime. What significance does this one moment have when compared to that?"

"Romantic rubbish! Listen to your body and give it that which it craves." She tried to pull her hands from his, but he wouldn't let her go. The passion in his gaze had cooled. Benae sighed as she realized the moment had passed. "Let me up."

Ramón released her hands. She stood and retrieved her pantaloons, being sure to allow him an eyeful of her legs as she drew the underwear on. *Stupid man!* Why couldn't he follow his instincts? Why couldn't he allow her some pleasure? The Goddess knew they had been through enough last night. They could be dead by tomorrow. Desire bubbled within her as she watched Ramón lace his breeches, stuffing himself into a space that had suddenly become too small. She smiled. Now she wanted him more than ever and she *would* have him, before she gave herself to Jiseve. One last fling wouldn't hurt.

* * *

Ramón had plenty of opportunities to contemplate Benae and her actions as they continued their journey to the coast. For that matter, he had time to consider his own actions as well.

Benae rode ahead of him, her delicious curves accentuated by the riding habit she wore and by the horsemanship she displayed. She and Flaire were as one. They had a special bond that Ramón had never known could exist. His thoughts turned to his black gelding, Arrow, which had been taken by the elves. He hoped the horse took a chunk out of whoever had stolen him. It would not be unusual for the beast to do so.

He was glad Benae hadn't lost her horse. She had lost enough of late. Perhaps that was the cause of her less than ladylike behavior. Loss and the threat of death could send a person crazy and what had Benae's actions been but insane? He went cold at the thought of what the prince would do if he knew the two had even kissed. Ramón didn't delude himself that the very least he could expect was to be banished from the kingdom. He'd lose all the respect he had gained from Jiseve Zialni.

Somehow, he must convey Benae safely to Wildecoast, and back to Brightcastle, without falling into her arms again. He was hard just thinking about her astride him, pantaloons discarded, his rod freed to the forest air. Only his honor had stopped him, but duty and honor wouldn't be his strength forever. He was only human, after all.

He pulled his horse back to a walk and called to Benae, but Flaire had already dropped his pace. He caught up to her. It was time to talk.

"We need to clear the air," he said.

She sent him a direct look, her vibrant emerald eyes amused. "I know what will clear the air, Ramón, but I don't think you have that in mind."

"You truly believe it would help if I bedded you?"

"It would make you see that what you feel for Alecia is infatuation. I know you have no experience of the sexual act. If you did, you'd realize there's more than fond thoughts in a relationship between a man and a woman."

"I can't see how coupling with you will make me feel differently for Alecia." No, Benae's very presence in Brightcastle had already accomplished that. "Unless you think I'll be so besotted with you that I'll forget she ever existed."

"That's exactly what I believe," Benae said, her flashing eyes stirring his blood no matter how he tried to douse the flames of his desire. "Alecia belongs to Vard Anton now."

"And you belong to the prince, or have you forgotten?"

Benae frowned and Flaire pranced as he sensed her disquiet. "I've not forgotten my promise to Jiseve. I came to Brightcastle in good faith. I thought I could turn my back on my past life and accept a marriage of convenience. I believed the salvation of my people would sustain me."

"What do you mean 'the salvation of your people'?" Ramón asked. Soon it would be time to move to the trot and he must resolve the situation with Benae. She had opened up to him now and he'd not miss the opportunity to understand her.

"My estates are poverty-stricken and my people starving." Her voice was strained, as though this was the last topic she wished to discuss. "I'm ashamed to say it's my fault. With Mama and Papa dead, the running of Branasar lands fell to me. I didn't take enough care with the money they put aside for hard times." She turned her beautiful face to him, tears pooling in her eyes. "It's all gone. You can't imagine the requests I had for fixing roofs and fences and replacing lost stock. The dark elves began attacking my remote farms and the menfolk defending them died. That left the women to carry on and they've done their best but…"

Ramón saw in his mind's eye, Benae's struggle to make her estate pay, even as she tried to deal with the grief of losing her parents. She blamed herself for everything and it wasn't right. In that moment, he saw her goodness and the tragedy that had befallen her.

He stared straight ahead as she continued.

"The last straw was when they carried my brother, Alvan, home from a skirmish with the elves. I felt something snap within me. With his last spark of life, he opened his eyes and begged me to save our estates." She slumped in the saddle, eyes closed, tears coursing down her face. "I couldn't save him either. He lived on for another hour and each of his breaths was like a stab to my heart."

"Perhaps he felt nothing that last hour." Ramón knew what it was like to lose a sibling; his twin sister, Elinor, had died in childbirth when they were only twenty summers old. Perhaps one day he'd be able to help Benae accept Alvan's death.

"You can't know that," she hissed, raking him with angry eyes.

"Be kind to yourself, Benae!"

She glared at him and looked forward again. "That day, I accepted defeat. The Goddess had challenged me, and I had to admit I had failed her test. I knew I wasn't equal to the task of saving my people, especially not with the dark elves on my doorstep. I heard Jiseve's call for a bride and knew I had to apply."

"You seek protection for your people? Why didn't you tell me?"

Benae's shoulders slumped. "I'm ashamed. How could I reveal my failures? I would rather have you think I'm a gold-digger than know I couldn't protect those who depend on me." Benae made to urge Flaire into a trot. "We should hurry along."

"Wait!" Ramón said, still determined to understand. "If you seek salvation for your people, how can you risk it all by seducing me?"

Benae pulled Flaire to a halt and swung to face him. "I thought I could sacrifice love for the sake of my people. Now I'm not certain I can. I have needs I can't deny, and you've shown me that perhaps there's a better life. I care deeply for you. I must be sure I can devote myself to Jiseve without giving up my chance of happiness."

"What about your people?"

"If I can't go through with my marriage, I'll find some other way to save them. Jiseve has ensured they are safe for the moment."

"So, you'll use me to test your commitment and use the prince to help your people in the meantime. He believes you're true to him!"

She had no answer to that, did she? Benae found herself in hot water and it was up to Ramón to extract her. He would see that she stayed true to her promises to Prince Zialni. It was the only course of action.

* * *

They pitched the tent well back from the road in a small stand of windswept pines. The water was almost gone so Benae moistened a cloth and wiped the dust from her face and hands. It had been a hard day, but they had made good time. Her discussion with Ramón had made her feel better, even if it was clear he disapproved of her actions. It was good to have someone to confide in. She had been on her own for so long. Merel had been her confidant, but there was much she couldn't discuss with the maid. A sob rose up in her throat. Merel had deserved so much more. Her death was just another of Benae's failures.

She wondered how things would be between her and Ramón now that he knew why she had come to Brightcastle. He had been there for her from the start, she realized, lending an ear even if he didn't want to. He was honest, steadfast *and* with a body and face that made her heart race; everything she needed. Benae realized with a jolt that he was much like her father. Jiseve, on the other hand, would keep her in diamonds but expect obedience. She doubted she would fit the bill for long. *Oh, what a mess!* Was it already too late to break her betrothal? Could she persuade Ramón to make love with her, to test the strength of her commitment to Jiseve?

Benae emerged from the tent to find Ramón seated by the fire, munching on the same old bread they'd eaten for two days. He smiled at her and desire stole her breath. How could a simple smile heat her blood so? Was this what love felt like? Did he feel the same? *No!* He had convinced himself that his feelings for Benae were simply lust. She favored him with a slow smile, allowing herself a leisurely study of his body. Oh, she would show her gorgeous squire what seduction was. Yes, she would!

She sat beside him and took the bread he offered. He poured her ale from a corked bottle. They ate in silence except for the cropping of their horses, tethered close by. When the meal was finished, Benae cleared her throat.

"One night left for us, Ramón. We've been given this. Let's not waste it."

He stared at her. "We're alone because of an ambush. People have died and you think only of lust?"

"Don't judge me, Ramón. It's the fact that we might have died last night that makes me bold. If I had been killed or taken, I would never have known your body. You would never have known what it is to be loved by a woman. Are you content to die thus?"

Ramón blushed. "I'm not content to die at all, but a betrothed woman shouldn't have those thoughts about another man."

Benae snorted and reached out to cup his cheek with her palm. It was deliciously rough. She shivered at the thought of his bristles against her skin, all over her body. Ramón had gone still; like a rabbit that hopes he won't be seen by the fox if he doesn't move. Yes, he was vulnerable to her. She leaned forward and brushed her lips across his. An almost overwhelming urge swept through her; to throw her arms around him and kiss him until he lost control. She kept herself in check.

"I wish to make love with you," she said. "I want to know you before I give myself to Jiseve. I want to understand what I'm sacrificing."

"Why should our coupling make any difference to your commitment? Should you so wish, you could still have any man after your marriage. You're giving up nothing."

She sat back on her heels. "I think I might be in love with you, but I need to be sure. You've shown me how it can be between a man and a woman. Tell me you feel the same."

Ramón shook his head. "The attack last night made me a little crazy, otherwise I wouldn't have acted with such little decorum at luncheon. I wasn't myself. Our talk has shown me how much you need the prince. You acted with honor when you sacrificed yourself for your people. You've gone too far to turn back now, Benae. I'll not let you throw the lives of your people to the devil. You'd never forgive yourself. Already you carry too much guilt."

"No! You can't decide for me." She flung herself at him and they toppled over. Benae ravished his mouth, her hands clawing at his tunic and ripping his shirt from his breeches. She felt him stir beneath her. She was winning!

She increased her assault and knew victory when Ramón rolled her onto her back and caught at her feverish hands. His mouth lowered to hers and slowly, reverently, he kissed her. Her lips parted beneath his and he explored the deepest reaches of her mouth. She groaned and pushed her hips against him, pinned by his body, her hands trapped above her head. Oh, how she loved the sensation of him atop her! Her body moved beneath his, without conscious thought, and she longed for the moment when he'd undress her, when she would free him, and they'd be one.

Ramón's lips left hers and she lay with her eyes closed, still lost in the moment, conscious of moisture pooling between her legs. She looked up to find him standing over her, his hair in wild disarray, chest heaving, eyes burning with desire. "Ramón?"

"I'd like nothing more than to make love to you, here. I can only imagine, dream of, such ecstasy. But I can't let you do this."

Benae rose and tried to fling herself into his arms. He couldn't deny her! Ramón held her at bay, arms outstretched.

"Make love to me damn it!" She panted, not able to let him walk away.

"I'm steadfast in this, Benae. I'll not let you betray your betrothed or your people. You wouldn't be able to live with yourself."

"Allow me to judge what I can live with."

He shook his head. "I respect you too much. We must remain only friends."

"I don't think I can stop at friendship," she said, driven by the intense desire that tore through her.

"You must be content. We'll find a way to deal with this. It can't always be storm and tempest between us."

She gazed up at him, allowing her fingertips to trail down his chest, and saw what it cost him not to respond to her nearness. His strength was remarkable. "Can you walk away from this?"

"I must," he said, his voice hoarse as though every muscle in his throat was in spasm.

Oh yes, this restraint was costing him dearly, but if he wanted only friendship, then he would have it. "Friends it is." She placed her hand in his. He bent and kissed her fingers. Benae closed her eyes, fighting the surge of desire the simple gesture triggered. She must have Ramón. If that meant as a friend, so be it.

Benae woke the next morning to find the place beside her empty. Spears of sunlight struck her through the tiny stitching holes in the tent fabric. She groaned. A night of tossing and turning hadn't prepared her for entry into Wildecoast, where there would be questions to answer.

"Breakfast is ready, Benae." Ramón's cheerful voice, from outside the tent, interrupted her thoughts.

Why was *he* so jolly? Apart from having had a decent night's sleep that was. She knew for a fact Ramón had slept soundly. His gentle snores had mocked her as she lay trying to come to terms with his rejection. He wanted her but had put her aside. He was right, of course. It was the only sensible and honorable path. She was promised to the prince and should behave as a betrothed woman, not as a woman in love. *In love…* Benae rolled the words around in her mind, testing their fit. Yes, this might be love but, oh, what a poor time to discover it, when she had already pledged herself to another man.

Could she accept Ramón's friendship and want nothing more? Perhaps once she was back with Jiseve and planning their wedding all this would seem silly. But when she thought of Jiseve, she found it difficult to remember the touch of his arms around her, of his lips upon hers. Instead, other arms and lips were all too easy to recall. She shivered, delighting in the memory of times spent with Ramón. At least she would have those recollections to console her and later, children would fill her life. She was doing the right thing marrying Jiseve. She must make it work.

Benae stood, shook her dress out and washed her face. She brushed her hair until it shone then twisted it into a simple knot. Merel's loss hit her anew and not because the maid usually attended to these tasks. Benae had enjoyed chatting to Merel first thing in the morning. Her soft voice and calm nature had soothed Benae after many a difficult night, especially since the loss of her family. She had come to depend upon her maid. Tears pooled but she would not shed them. She breathed deeply. Once her emotions were under control she stepped from the tent.

"Good morning," she said, uncertain of how to behave with her new 'friend'.

Ramón swept a bow, handed her a mug of tea and ushered her to a log beside the fire. "Only the stale bread and a hunk of cheese remain I'm afraid, but we should be at Wildecoast by midday and able to fill our bellies then."

"You're in a very cheery mood this morning," she said. For some reason, his happiness grated.

"Yes, of course. Our journey will soon be at an end." He smiled and Benae could find none of the torment of yesterday in his gaze. "I'll fold the tent while you have your breakfast. Then we must be on our way."

Benae watched as he worked. He was graceful for a man and showed the economy of movement typical of someone who was always busy. Her eyes fell upon his broad shoulders as he folded the tent. Her stomach clenched. Best not to watch that if she didn't want to be throwing herself at him again. She turned away and when she looked back, she was greeted with the squire's muscled buttocks as he bent to pick up the tent. Her heart skipped and raced away, and she took deep breaths to calm herself. Best not to watch at all.

CHAPTER 10

THE wind increased as they traveled closer to the coast and they were soon riding into a gale. Ramón cursed the weather for it slowed them and stung their eyes. Even the horses felt the discomfort. Approaching noon, clouds covered the sun and the temperature dropped. Their cloaks whipped about their bodies, supplying hardly any warmth. Ramón welcomed the discomfort for it kept his mind from worries about Benae and the reception awaiting them. With luck the pigeons sent to announce their visit had reached Wildecoast, but the king wouldn't expect Benae to arrive accompanied only by him.

Finally, they reached the cliffs of Wildecoast and were within sight of the King's seat, a lonely keep that sat atop a rocky hill overlooking the ocean. The city spread out around the castle and a high stone wall gave protection. They pushed their horses into a canter and soon reached the outer gates of the city. Kingdom soldiers were on guard in their red livery, the golden Zialni crest on their left breasts and on their shields.

Ramón and Benae stopped, pulling down the scarves they had used to protect their faces. Ramón dismounted and led his horse forward. The guards eyed Benae boldly and a bolt of anger surged through Ramón's gut. He fought it down and presented himself to the sergeant in charge.

"Squire Ramón Zorba of Brightcastle and the Lady Benae Branasar to see King Beniel Zialni and Queen Adriana."

The sergeant, a small man with a hawkish nose and a neatly trimmed moustache, smirked and said something to his fellows that caused them to snicker. Ramón felt his anger rise again.

"Where is your escort, Squire?" the sergeant said. "*Ladies* don't travel about the countryside with a lone male for company unless they're seeking trouble." His eyes ran over Benae and settled on her chest.

Ramón watched as Benae's neck and face flushed under the guard's impudent gaze. She was more than capable of putting the fellow in his place, but Ramón didn't want Benae to concern herself. She had enough to worry about and had been quiet all morning.

"We met with trouble on the road," he snapped. "Dark elves attacked our party and killed all but the two of us. We left the carriage behind. I need you to organize recovery of our conveyance and the bodies at the earliest opportunity."

The sergeant surveyed Ramón with his beady eyes as if trying to judge the truth of his words.

"There is no need to stand here, man," Ramón said, his patience at an end. It was cold and Benae needed to be out of the wind with a warm drink in her hand, not sitting here beneath the stares of common soldiers. "Get us an escort."

"First I must verify that you are who you say you are." He turned to the six men with him. "Can anyone tell me if this is Ramón Zorba, who was sent to Brightcastle to take up the position of squire to Prince Zialni?"

"It might be him," ventured a short squat man. "He has more the look of a highwayman than a noble as he stands here before us."

The guards laughed and Ramón gritted his teeth. "Bring an escort and we'll let the steward decide. He'll vouch for me."

The sergeant frowned at Ramón for long moments then seemed to reconsider making fun of him. He dispatched two of his men to bring an escort from the barracks. Ramón mounted his horse once more and sat beside Benae in silence, ignoring the stares of the remaining guards who continued to snicker.

A clattering of hooves announced the arrival of eight mounted soldiers, whose leader conducted a brief conversation with the gate sergeant. The hawk-nosed man turned to Ramón.

"Lieutenant Formosa and his men will conduct you to the steward who will verify your identity, or otherwise. Don't stray from their protection. I can't ensure your safety if that were to occur." The sergeant appeared as though he would love to see them wander away from protection.

"Thank you, sergeant," he said, "you've been most helpful."

The self-important guard smirked at Ramón, fully aware he had got under the squire's skin.

Ramón put the sergeant from his mind and ushered Benae before him toward the waiting escort. They formed up with three in front, one man each beside Ramón and Benae and three behind. To Ramón, it felt more like a guard than an escort. The bleak look in Benae's eyes said she felt it as well.

Ramón tried to converse with the lieutenant who rode beside him. "Formosa…I have a second cousin with that last name." The man looked only a little older than he. "What name do you go by?"

"Josef," he snapped, his bearing stiff and his eyes straight ahead.

"It *is* you," Ramón said. He could see the slight resemblance to his family although Josef's hair was a dark honey blond and his eyes were gray rather than blue. He supposed many would consider Josef handsome, and his uniform would certainly have the ladies' heads turning. A pity he seemed such a pompous ass.

Josef flicked a glance Ramón's way and his eyes narrowed. "So! It's no wonder I didn't recognize you. The last time we met, your face was covered in pimples and you were so thin, one would think you were perpetually starving."

"That was ten years ago, cousin. We've both changed much. If I remember, you joined the King's army soon after and were off to see the far reaches of Thorius."

"I did, while you chose the life of a servant, albeit nobility. I heard about your appointment to the prince. You've been gone less than four months. Has the king's brother found you wanting?"

Ramón smoothed the frown from his brow with difficulty. Now he remembered; Josef had always been abrasive. Ramón wouldn't rise to the bait by defending himself. "I've been charged with the task of escorting the prince's betrothed, Lady Branasar, to be fitted for her wedding gown."

Josef turned to Benae and inclined his head. "I'm pleased to make your acquaintance, Lady Branasar." His eyes ran over Benae's dusty raiment and frowned. He turned back to Ramón. "Is it true that you were beset by dark elves?"

"The night before last. We barely escaped with our lives. Those you see before you are all that is left of our party. You must dispatch men at once to retrieve the bodies of our soldiers and servants and the carriage with the lady's belongings."

Josef raised one eyebrow at Ramón and then pulled his horse from the procession, signaling for the man beside Benae to do likewise. As the rest of the party continued, the lieutenant and his man had a brief discussion and the soldier raced ahead while Josef re-joined the escort. "Pick up the pace," he said and urged his horse into a trot.

* * *

By the time Benae reached the inner keep and castle, a detail of mounted soldiers fifty men strong had amassed in the marshalling area. They all wore the red tunic and white breeches of the kingdom, except for one man who wore gray. This man met them on horseback as they drew to a halt inside the keep wall.

"Lieutenant Formosa," the man in the gray uniform greeted Josef. "What's this I hear of an ambush to the west?"

"General Jazara." Josef saluted stiffly, a scowl on his face. "This is my cousin Ramón Zorba, squire of Brightcastle, and his companion is Lady Branasar. Their party was attacked by the elves less than two days ride west of here. All were killed except these two. A squad will be needed to retrieve the bodies and the carriage."

The general raised one eyebrow. "We'll find the site of the ambush and draw our own conclusions as to the identity of the attackers. The victims will be buried where they died. A priest will go with us. How large is the carriage?"

"There were four carriage horses," Ramón said.

Jazara stared at Ramón's horse as though trying to decide if he rode one of the carriage horses or if the squire just lacked discretion when it came to horseflesh. Flaire snorted as though daring the general to find fault with him. The general ignored Benae and Flaire completely.

Benae grabbed Ramón's sleeve. "I can't allow Merel's body to be dumped in a mass grave," she hissed. "You must make them bring her here so she can have a proper burial."

Ramón cleared his throat. "There's one body that must be retrieved, General. The lady's maid was killed defending her mistress. Her body must be recovered so that she can have a fitting burial."

"That's why I'll take a priest. Surely you can have no problem with that?"

"On the contrary, General," Ramón insisted.

Benae bit her tongue to stop herself from interfering. This man obviously set no store by a woman's word. He had refused to even acknowledge her. Flaire fidgeted as Benae's hands shook on the reins. In the end, she just couldn't remain quiet. "I insist you bring the maid's body to Wildecoast for burial," Benae said. "Prince Zialni would expect the servant of his future wife to be buried with full kingdom honors."

Ah! Now the haughty leader notices me! His eyes flickered over Benae and Flaire, but his face remained impassive. She didn't like him one bit. To think that she must rely on this man to retrieve Merel's body, and the carriage, stirred the last shred of fire remaining in her. She lifted her head and stared down her nose at the military leader. He smirked at her. *Smirked!*

"Very well," Jazara said. He swung his coal-black stallion around and shouted at his men. "Fetch a priest. Hitch the supply wagon. We leave within the half hour." Without a backward look, Jazara trotted away.

Ramón's eyes met hers. "That man must be related to Vard Anton," he said, bitterly.

Benae smiled. "If he does what he has said he will, I don't care how he behaves." Jazara's arrogance *had* left a sour taste in her mouth.

"Come along," Josef said. "I'll find the steward and see that you're presented to His Majesty."

Benae eased into the steaming bath, flinching as the water contacted her various abrasions. The maid who had been assigned to her, a woman called Joletta, set about washing Benae's hair. The firm fingers massaging her scalp felt glorious and her shoulders relaxed for the first time in days. The woman might be quiet, but she certainly could work magic with her hands.

"You won't mind accompanying me to Brightcastle, Joletta?" Benae asked.

"No, My Lady."

Benae frowned at the maid's words. There was simply no way to ascertain whether Joletta was indeed happy to take the position as Benae's maid even if it was only temporary. Which it would be. She must find a maid more like Merel, one who understood her. This woman would not do, no matter how skilled her fingers were…and they were expert. She allowed herself to drift away, remembering happier times when those she had loved had still been with her. A tear escaped her closed eye.

"What is amiss, My Lady?"

"Nothing to trouble yourself with, Joletta." Benae felt suddenly cold. She had loved Merel like a sister and had never fully appreciated the fact. How stupid of her not to see what was right beneath her nose. Now she was gone. If Merel's actions weren't those of a sister, then… The pain in her chest grew until Benae couldn't suppress the sob that rose; couldn't hold back the torrent of grief that swept over her. Tears rolled unchecked down her cheeks and all Benae could do was cover her face with her hands.

"Lady?" Joletta sounded distressed but Benae had no thought for her.

"Out! Leave me alone!"

"But, My Lady —"

"I said leave. Now!" She heard the quiet bump as the chamber door was pulled closed.

Benae rested her face on the edge of the bath and sobbed until the water was cold. Slowly the tears subsided, and she stood and rinsed her hair free of soap. That water was icier than the bath water, leaving her chilled. So much for a lovely, warm bath. She wrapped herself in a linen towel and curled another around her head, slowly drying her long, thick hair. There was no one left. Ramón was delusional to believe they could be friends. Jiseve wouldn't allow him close enough for any meaningful friendship. She may as well get used to her new situation.

Benae called Joletta in and the maid helped her to dress in a beautiful gown that had once belonged to the Queen. The fabric was gold embossed and hugged her curves as though it had been made for her. It was a little long, but she could lift it above her slippers when she walked. As Benae sat before the roaring fire, Joletta brushed her hair, allowing the draught from the blaze to chase the remaining moisture from the luxuriant waves. The maid left Benae's hair down, restraining it only with the golden tiara, also supplied by the Queen. Last, Joletta fixed Benae's face with the powders and kohl liner she had brought with her, adding a touch of strawberry lip balm.

All would be well. From this disaster she would rise, like a sword forged in fire, and she would be tougher than before. She had to survive. There was no other possibility. She thanked Joletta, squared her shoulders and stepped from the chamber.

* * *

Ramón knew where Benae had been housed but he awaited her in the antechamber of the King's audience hall. It wouldn't do to appear overly familiar. He must be aloof, formal, detached – even though he longed to comfort her. She had looked lost, when led away to her chambers, and hadn't asked about Flaire's lodging. That wasn't like her at all.

The familiar palace sounds soothed the turmoil within him. It was good to be back inside the castle where he had trained. Nothing much ever changed around the old place. Many of the retainers were well into their forties and fifties, training men and women of his age to take their places. There was a stability here that was missing from Brightcastle, a constancy that settled him. A sudden autumn storm rattled the windows and he smiled. He even loved the weather here. The waves would be crashing on the nearby beach, hurling themselves against the cliffs upon which the castle was built.

Benae approached him accompanied by the steward. He stood. She was exquisite in her borrowed dress and tiara. No one would guess they were not her own. Benae smiled at him, but it didn't reach her eyes which were red as though she had been crying.

He bowed and reached for her hand before placing it upon his arm. Her fingers tightened and then quickly released. She sighed.

"What's wrong?" he asked.

She shook her head as if not trusting her voice.

"I've released Flaire into the care of the head groom," he said. "He seems content."

Benae smiled and Ramón was gladdened to have supplied a distraction.

"Thank you, Ramón," she said. "I'm not myself this evening."

"Small wonder after what you've been through."

Sadness cloaked her gaze once again.

"Let's greet His Majesty," Ramón said, stepping forward.

The steward threw open the doors to the hall and announced them. Fires burned on either side of the large chamber and several lords and ladies stood along the walls, chatting. They all turned to stare as Ramón and Benae were announced. He escorted Benae to the foot of the dais where King Beniel and Queen Adriana sat.

Ramón bowed low while Benae curtsied.

"Welcome back to our court, Squire Ramón. I well remember your courtesy when we visited our brother at Brightcastle." He turned to Benae. "Lady Branasar, soon to be Princess Benae, welcome to the family. My brother sent pigeons to inform me of your advent. His missives didn't do you justice. He has indeed found a beauty to share his life with."

Benae bowed her head, while Ramón's stomach turned sour at the thought of her life with the prince.

"I'm delighted to meet my future brother-in-law, King Beniel," Benae said, "and his Queen." She dropped a deep curtsy for Adriana.

Ramón thought the Queen had never looked lovelier, her dark hair swept up in an intricate knot and restrained by a silver circlet. She wore an emerald gown that exactly matched her eyes. Adriana could have been Benae's older sister, so much did she resemble the lady, but Benae was more beautiful.

"Lady Benae, welcome," Adriana said. "I hope we shall be friends as well as sisters." The Queen stood and came down the stairs to embrace her sister-in-law. A buzz swept through the assembled audience. Ramón supposed it was a ringing endorsement for Benae. Adriana turned to Ramón.

"Squire, welcome. You have our thanks for bringing our sister-in-law to us in safety."

Ramón bowed over her gloved hand and kissed her fingers. "I've merely done my duty, Your Majesty."

Adriana's eyes speared Ramón where he stood. "It could never be said that life was dull in Brightcastle and now it seems you bring trouble with you. I'm disturbed that dark elves should range so close to Wildecoast. I believed that blight confined to the north."

Ramón contemplated the events of the past months. First, unrest in the principality of Brightcastle as Jiseve Zialni made his rule felt, then the murder of former squire, Jorge. Then the assassin in the garden at the ball where Vard Anton was wounded. Ramón shied away from examining that event too closely, especially how the assassin came to be in the garden. Alecia's vendetta to kill the mercenaries responsible for the death of Squire Jorge had resulted in her near-death at the hands of one of the mercenaries. When the prince found out about Alecia's involvement, he imprisoned her to await the day of her betrothal, rather than reveal his daughter's outrageous activities to the populace.

All through these dramas, Vard Anton had been Alecia's protector. *Huh! Some protector he proved to be!* Just being around the man had given Ramón an itch he couldn't scratch. If only that assassin's aim had been true, the blight of Vard Anton would be just a memory. Instead, he had brought the kingdom to its knees.

Ramón came out of his reverie to find the King and Queen staring at him, frowns on their faces. "I confess I thought the elves were a northern phenomenon as well, Your Majesties. Prince Zialni is, at this moment, traveling north and west to assess the seriousness of the incursions. It seems, from our experience, they have penetrated further than first thought."

"That is an understatement!" King Beniel said. "We cannot have the cursed elves on our lands less than two days ride from our home. We must send soldiers to sweep the vermin from our kingdom."

"Some mobilization of forces seems appropriate, Your Majesty." Ramón hoped the audience would come to an end, *before* it turned to the topic of Benae's unescorted journey.

"Perhaps you can be of some assistance when it comes to deploying our forces, Squire," King Beniel said, "but for now there is another matter I must address." He leaned toward Ramón and Benae. "This lady has been unescorted, in the presence of a man not her betrothed, for more than a day. There will be gossip that my brother will not appreciate. How do you propose to stop the wagging tongues?"

Ramón frowned. "I don't see how we can stop them, Your Majesty, but I wish to assure you our conduct was of the highest standard at all times." He felt heat climb his neck and feared the blush was a dead giveaway, even if the monarchs assumed it meant he had inappropriate thoughts. Oh, he had been tempted all right, but now he and Benae could move on, as friends.

"You are sure there is naught I should report to the prince?" Beniel asked, his sharp gaze spearing them both.

"We were fighting for survival at first, Your Majesty," Benae said, "and then running for our lives, not ever sure we would reach

Wildecoast. Those are not ideal circumstances to conduct a romance, even should I wish to. I find Jiseve is enough for me to contemplate."

Oh bravo, Benae, Ramón thought. She would make a fine wife for the prince. She would hold her own at court, and with ambassadors and their wives, no matter how sharp their intelligence. And she hadn't lied.

"Indeed, Lady Benae," the Queen said. "We must discuss the matter at length when we have more privacy."

The king cleared his throat. "I will leave such matters to you, my dear. In the meantime, let us adjourn to the dining hall for our repast."

CHAPTER 11

THE dinner went long into the night with fifteen courses served, including Benae's favorite, pheasant. Despite the fine food, she cursed the need for the display of welcome. All she wished was to curl up on her ridiculously thick mattress and go to sleep. *For a lifetime. Long enough to awake and find that this life was all an absurd dream.*

The woman to her left was talking. She had a face longer than Flaire's and unfortunate piggy eyes that no amount of paint could improve. Benae supposed her golden hair was pretty enough. *Oh, Goddess, that wasn't very charitable.* It had been a long few days. She returned her attention to the blonde woman. Her name was Lady Feolinde or some such. Benae was not in the mood for remembering names; besides, she had always found it easier to recall men's names than women.

"Don't you worry about the court gossip, Lady Benae?" Feolinde said. "Ramón Zorba is a handsome man and to be alone in his company for more than a day…" She fanned herself with her napkin and nudged Benae's elbow. "I wouldn't let such an opportunity pass."

"Perhaps you forget I'm betrothed, Feolinde?"

"Yes! That's another interesting topic. The court here was abuzz when it heard of the contest. How many of you competed for his hand?"

Benae suppressed an angry retort. "That doesn't matter. *I* was successful and now I can't wait to become his wife. He's a most loving and considerate man, the prince."

"Not what I heard, Lady Benae," Feolinde said, bumping her elbow again.

Really! The woman had better stop her elbowing or she'd soon find a fork through her hand. Benae smiled sweetly. "Oh, I can't fault his manners. He has been the perfect fiancé since our betrothal."

The man on Benae's other side, Lord Korert, snorted. She turned to him, thankful for the interruption.

"He's not bedded you yet then?"

Benae nearly choked on the wine she had just taken a gulp of. In fact, she was a tad tipsy. If she didn't escape soon, she would either say something she regretted or fall asleep in her goblet. "That wouldn't be appropriate, Lord Korert." She smiled.

His paunch jiggled with his laughter. "Propriety didn't stop you traveling alone with the squire, did it?"

Suddenly Benae couldn't bear it anymore. She stood abruptly causing her chair to fall over. Lord Korert leapt to his feet, suppressing a snort of nervous laughter, then righted her chair.

"I'm afraid I'll have to take my leave." Benae nodded to Lady Feolinde and Lord Korert. She stopped by the king and queen, who were seated at the head of her table, gave her thanks for their hospitality and swept from the hall.

Back in her chambers, Benae endured Joletta's ministrations and dismissed her as soon as she was dressed for sleep. She shivered as a gust of wind shook the casement windows. She adored cold weather but couldn't abide wind that sliced through clothes and left a person shivering. This was her first experience of the coast. The brief glimpse of sand and waves she had as she arrived, was enough to tell her that she couldn't live here.

Benae preferred the quiet forests and rugged mountains of her northern home. Her people eked out their existence by reclaiming forestland for small farms, by woodcutting and hunting the forest creatures. It wasn't an easy life and the past two seasons had seen harsh winters that made life on the smallholdings more difficult. Dark elves were the last blight her estates needed and might easily amount to the end of her rule. Of course, now it would be Jiseve's problem, but she couldn't help worrying about her people.

She sighed. If only she could talk to Ramón, but they could not risk being seen together, especially not now. Anyway, he planned to visit his family and she would be busy with fittings for her dress. Benae paced the sitting room of her chamber, the floaty hem of her nightgown swirling about her ankles. There was a ball planned for tomorrow, which would be more of an endurance test than tonight's dinner. She felt like a caged beast, pacing up and down. *Ramón, where are you? Do you wish you could speak to me right now?*

* * *

Ramón paced the stone floor of his small sitting room, occasionally pausing to stare south, through the gentle light of dawn, toward his parents' estate. He longed to visit them, knowing they would be the balm his restless spirit needed, after the turmoil of the past months. First Alecia, now Benae consumed his thoughts, and the ambush on his convoy had left him floundering. What he needed was a long talk with his father and mother. They would each know just the right advice to give him. And he wished to see his sisters.

Nyon, older by a year, was wed to a senior apprentice of the city's shipbuilder and already had three sons. Alique was three years younger than he and one of Queen Adriana's ladies-in-waiting. He'd see her tonight at the ball. Then there was Elinor, his twin, who had left such a gaping hole in his life. He still felt a connection to her, even though she had been dead four years.

From his window, Ramón could just see the whitecaps as they rolled in toward the rocky shore. How he had adored skimming over them in his sailing boat, until his recent posting to Brightcastle. The weather was too rough today for sailing, but he hoped the seas would calm before his departure and he could enjoy the wind and spray in his face once again.

He was just as restless as those waves this morning, trapped within the palace for another day to attend the ball. He knew he would most likely dance with Benae that evening and was scared to do so. *Friends!* He feared she would read the lie in his face, in his very body. His determination to keep their relationship platonic had lasted less than twenty-four hours. After spending days in her company, cursing the way she made him feel, now he missed her smile and wondered how she fared. He suspected he could never be satisfied with friendship. She had seized a piece of his heart and made it her own.

Benae was not the only source of his unease. Until recently, his whole purpose had been focused on finding Alecia and destroying Vard Anton. Now that goal was out of reach. Even if he was able to resume his quest on returning to Brightcastle, Benae had made him see his future may not involve Alecia. He no longer believed the princess was the only woman for him, so when she returned—and he had to believe she would— the picture of he and Alecia together was no longer clear. The foundations of his life had crumbled, and he was uncertain of his future.

Ramón grabbed a linen towel from the washstand and headed for the bathing chamber. It would be quiet at this time of morning and would have been freshly prepared for the day's royal bathers. The buzz of activity as he stepped into the hall surprised him. Maids scurried about with trays and piles of linen; doors opened and closed on all levels. Perhaps the baths would not be as deserted as he thought.

The baths were something of a novelty in the kingdom. They lay deep beneath the castle in the rock and were fed by hot springs that bubbled up from below. There was a legend that told of a dragon that inhabited the springs, but only children believed the tale. As Ramón walked down the corridor hacked through the mountain itself, past flickering torches, he found himself remembering the fairy stories of his childhood. These dark passages were just the place a dragon might call home. He stepped into the bathing cavern and was at once greeted by warmth and steam. The rock walls glistened in the torchlight and he inhaled deeply of the humid air. The huge pool was indeed freshly filled so he shed his clothing and stepped straight in. A bath maid soaped his hair and shoulders. He dismissed the girl and sat for long moments submerged, reveling in the loss of sound and allowing the water to support him.

He couldn't lie beneath the water forever and, reluctantly, pushed himself out of the pool then turned to collect his bath sheet and clothes.

A small crowd of ladies stood in the shadows near the entrance. Among them were Queen Adriana, Benae and—*has the Goddess no pity?* — his sister Alique. Ramón nearly choked on his gasp of shock and the ladies appeared frozen where they stood. His skin tingled as ten sets of feminine eyes slid over his skin from hair to toenails. Not even the dim light could hide him from them. He grabbed the towel and wrapped it around his waist.

"I'm sorry, Your Majesty, Lady Benae. I didn't expect anyone here this early."

The queen's eyes gleamed appreciatively. "Do not be sorry, Squire. Stay and join us." Her gaze lingered on the part of his anatomy now concealed by the sheet.

He glanced at Benae. Her mouth was still open, eyes wide, as if she had never seen a naked man before. As he watched, her mouth snapped shut and she bit her lower lip. She walked past him to deposit her towel on a bench set aside for the purpose.

"Good morning, Squire," she said, her voice cool.

"Good morning, Lady Benae." Ramón swept his clothes up, bowed to the queen and her ladies and hurried from the cavern.

He got more than a few stares as he returned to his chamber. One didn't see a man clad only in a towel in the castle hallways every day. Once in his rooms, he dressed before the fire, slowly warming after the chill trip from the bathing cavern.

Far from dousing the rumors about himself and Benae, Ramón was certain this morning's debacle, where he had flashed his crown jewels for all to ogle, would bring fresh speculation about what might have occurred between squire and lady before they reached Wildecoast.

* * *

Benae gritted her teeth and slid into the deliciously warm water. Of all the places to catch her first tempting glimpse of Ramón's fully naked form, this was the last she would have expected; certainly not before the stares of the queen and her ladies-in-waiting, one of whom was Ramón's own sister.

If the sight of Ramón naked before her had not pushed all coherent thought from her mind, if his muscled form and glorious manhood had not set her heart thumping, the experience would have mortified her. As it was, mortification would have to take a back seat to… rampant desire. Even now, her nipples were tight with longing and the heat in her core…It seemed just when she had mastered her wayward emotions, something always happened to force him into her thoughts. She didn't think she would ever forget the vision of his golden body, burnished by the flames of the torches, glistening with hot water as it sluiced over his…

I must stop this. Benae closed her eyes and concentrated on steadying her breathing.

The queen had other ideas. "Over a day alone with a man who has the physical attributes of a god and you say you were not moved?" Adriana fixed her gaze on Benae and suddenly she felt like a mouse stalked by a cat. "*I* would not have been able to restrain myself, no matter how I love my Beniel."

Benae decided that didn't call for an answer.

"What say you on the matter, Lady Alique?" the queen said. "You're the squire's sister after all."

Benae swallowed and her eyes found the beautiful young girl the Queen addressed. She had Ramón's blond hair and sensuous mouth. She shared his startling blue eyes as well, if Benae wasn't mistaken.

"I'm sure I don't know what to think, Your Majesty. My brother was not so well-endowed last time I saw him, but it's a number of years since I saw *that* part of his anatomy."

The other ladies-in-waiting tittered along with the queen.

Adriana drew Benae away to a quiet corner of the bath, leaving the ladies to a game of splash.

"You are very quiet," Adriana said, her green gaze boring into Benae. "I am led to believe you are not so unmoved by the squire as you would have us believe."

"I've told you, Your Majesty, nothing occurred between us. We were fighting for our lives. Ramón is a dear friend, no more."

"I do not think my brother-in-law would be pleased for you to have a *dear friend* who looked thus." She slid closer. "Listen, Benae, I do not judge you. I would not say no to Ramón should he darken my chamber door, but you must be discrete. Jiseve will not tolerate rumors about his wife."

The queen left her and glided through the water to the other ladies. "Well, what a stimulating start to the morning, my dears. Let us hope this evening holds us in its thrall, as the squire's assets did just now. It will be an evening to remember."

Benae groaned inwardly. She agreed the ball would be one to remember, it just remained to be seen in what way.

* * *

Ramón was satisfied. The ball was now in full swing and he had managed to avoid Benae. The closest he came was when one dance finished, and she had been two men away from dancing with him. He had promptly spun and taken the hand of the lady with him, leading her to the opposite side of the room. Ramón had no shortage of lovely young women ready to dance with him. Even the queen had claimed him for three dances, one of which was a waltz. He remembered her reaction to Vard Anton when she and King Beniel had visited Brightcastle. It seemed Queen Adriana had a wandering eye. At the time he had thought it just Anton's ability to have every female under his thrall, but it seemed that mere mortals like Ramón attracted her as well.

He wouldn't be honest if he denied being flattered by her attention, but a ripple of unease set his teeth on edge. He didn't want trouble.

Alique appeared, her gorgeous eyes sparkling with mischief. "Won't you dance with me, brother?" She had always been the troublemaker of the family. "We have much to discuss."

"It's good to see you, Ali," Ramón said, standing and leading his sister onto the dance floor. Unfortunately, the dance was a waltz, suited to intimate conversations. Braced for more questions, he swept Alique into the dancers.

"It's lovely to see you too, though I hope I shan't be seeing so much of you in future."

Ramón knew a flush was winding its way up his neck and over his face. Damn his reactions! If only he could be cold like other men. "I'm so very sorry for that. Most embarrassing for you."

"Oh, I don't mind," she said airily. "I'm quite in demand now, because of you. All the ladies wish to talk with me about my gorgeous brother. Some of them have even asked me to organize a meeting between them and you. At the soonest possible opportunity, no less! And that coming from women who didn't see your display this morning. Rumors are certainly flying around this castle, brother."

"I don't suppose you discourage them, sister?"

"Why would I? It's one of the most exciting things that has happened this autumn. Coming on top of your arrival with the unescorted Lady Benae Branasar, it has people even more inclined to whisper. Were you really attacked by dark elves?"

Ramón squashed the blast of anger at her words. "Yes, we were, and people died. There is no cause to use tragedy to fuel gossip."

"People die every day, Ramón," she said, not a trace of distress on her face. "You always were inclined to the dramatic. What we all wish to know is what there is between you and Lady Benae. I notice you've been careful to avoid her this evening."

Now he was furious. Alique had always been able to get under his skin. "I. Am. Not. Avoiding. Her," he said through clenched teeth. "We are friends, no more. You should know better than to accuse me of disloyalty to the prince."

"From what I hear, Jiseve Zialni doesn't inspire much loyalty, so I thought perhaps this marriage of convenience wasn't exclusive. The old boy wants a son, after all. Who would care if it wasn't his?"

"In the name of the Goddess, Ali!" Ramón's brain struggled feverishly to process her words. Was this what the court at Wildecoast was saying? "Benae isn't even wed and you already have her unfaithful? She is loyal to the prince…and so am I."

Alique gazed up at him as if he had confirmed her suspicions, though nothing he had said would lead her to that conclusion. "Thank you for the dance, Ramón." She curtsied and swept back to the queen, leaving him staring after her, oblivious to those around him.

Finally, he turned to leave the dance floor and bumped into Benae. "I'm sorry, My Lady." He bowed and would have walked away but she clutched his sleeve.

"What's going on?"

"What do you mean?"

"Let's dance," she said, moving into his arms as if it were the most natural thing in the world.

She felt good; her petite frame, her curves. Suddenly his mouth was dry. He straightened his arms to keep her at a safe distance. "It's good to see you again."

A brief flash of despair transformed her features and was gone. "I've missed your company."

Her eyes were liquid pools of emerald, but they were so sad. What had happened to the joyful lady he had first met only weeks ago? He felt himself falling into her gaze and hauled himself back. "We can't enjoy each other's company. The eyes of all are upon us."

"That doesn't make this easier to bear," she whispered. "I need you." Tears glistened in her eyes.

Oh, Goddess, please don't let her cry. He ached to hold her tight. Instead, he swept her along, saying nothing, allowing her moment of weakness to pass. Benae was strong. She knew what must be done. The music swirled around them and he concentrated upon it, embracing the joyful chords, allowing the beat to surge through his body, willing her to do the same.

The song ended and he led Benae from the floor to the buffet table. She lifted a glass to her lips, and he was relieved to see her composure restored.

"Don't fear for me, Ramón. I will prevail. Tomorrow the dress fittings begin and soon we'll be back in Brightcastle." She seemed to steel herself before continuing. "I shall wed Jiseve and bear his children and there will be no scandal." She raised her gaze to his and he almost gasped at the raw longing she revealed to none but him.

There was nothing he could say to set her at ease. "I promised the queen another dance," he said. "It won't do to keep Her Majesty waiting." He bowed and walked away; downing the goblet of wine he carried in one long swallow.

CHAPTER 12

B Y the morning of her fourth full day in Wildecoast, Benae's grip on her composure was fragile. Two days of dress fittings, where she stood for hours to be measured, poked and pinned, had eroded her tolerance. Even worse, the queen or another female member of the nobility was always in attendance at her fittings. As much as Benae wanted to forget Ramón and his hold on her heart, she could not when his name was on the lips of every woman who visited with her.

The lady keeping her company that morning was Ramón's sister. Benae tried not to look at Alique, for she reminded her so much of the squire. The young woman kept moving into Benae's line of sight whenever the dressmaker altered her position. Alique had been chattering about Ramón's childhood.

"How well do you know my brother, Lady Benae?" she asked, her gaze altogether too penetrating.

"Hardly at all, really, although we talked a little after the ambush."

"I should say so. There was no one else to talk to." She fell silent for long moments and Benae wondered what was coming next.

"Do you find Ramón handsome?"

"I don't see the point of this topic, Lady Alique. Can't we talk of something else? Perhaps my upcoming wedding?" Benae hoped that would put Alique in her place but she had underestimated the woman.

"How can you give up your life for such an old man?" she asked. "There must be more to that story. I've heard your estate is impoverished. Is that the reason for your betrothal?"

"That's enough!" Benae simply couldn't believe she had to tolerate this, but if she asked Alique to leave it might appear she had something to hide. Or perhaps not. Her words were insulting. "The arrangement between the prince and myself is none of your business but there is real warmth in our relationship. I anticipate long years of fulfilment." Even to Benae's ears, it sounded less than ideal.

Alique laughed. "Keep telling yourself that and you might believe it one day. I've seen the way you look at Ramón and he at you. If I know him, it's he who holds you at arm's length. He did always have too much honor for his own good."

Benae didn't know what to say and so she stared at Alique, willing the girl to leave. The old dressmaker chose that moment to stick her with a pin.

"Ouch!" Benae was instantly distracted from Ramón's sister. When she turned back to the lady-in-waiting, Alique had left the room.

"One more adjustment and we'll be finished, My Lady." The dressmaker smiled at Benae. "You'll be a picture on your wedding day. Return to me an hour after luncheon and I'll make the final changes."

"Thank you, Mistress," Benae said. "You've created a beautiful gown for my special day." Benae stepped from the gown, dressed and hurried out before the woman could see the tears in her eyes.

She strode to her chambers, the need to flee building within. Perhaps after her final fitting this afternoon, she might saddle Flaire and give the stallion a run along the beach. She sent the thought to her mount and felt his excited response deep in her mind.

Ramón rode with his father along the narrow lane that wound between farms on the Zorba estate. The wind was strong and the crimson dress tunic he had worn to please his mother did little to stop the chill cutting through to his skin. He felt a driving need to be back at the castle. Benae would be anxious. Castle gossip hadn't been kind to them since their arrival four days ago. He had spent the last two nights with his parents and could almost forget the traumas of the past week. His older sister, Nyon, had visited yesterday with her husband and three sons, her belly round with their fourth child. She seemed content and was proud of Ramón's position at Brightcastle. She had said not a word about Benae, nor asked him about her. Instead, she had sat with her arms encircling her stomach and listened as he related the story of Princess Alecia and the events leading to her departure from Brightcastle.

Two evenings and a day in the company of his parents had eased his worries of the future, and now he was ready to return to Wildecoast keep. His mother had instantly known Ramón was changed from the man who had left her. Her eyes glowed with pride at the broadness of his shoulders and the way he now carried himself. She and his father had set about gently probing the root of these changes. He had confessed to them his original goal of finding Alecia and marrying her. His mother had helped him to accept that, though Alecia might one day return to her rightful position in Brightcastle, she would likely never marry him.

He must face the fact that his future was with some eligible girl, possibly one of the queen's current ladies-in-waiting. He wouldn't stay in Brightcastle forever. The return of Princess Alecia was still a priority and he would ensure she was recovered, but he should no longer dream of her as his wife.

His parents had drawn him out about the elven attack and the fears and guilt Ramón still harbored over that event. Just like that, a weight had lifted off his shoulders and he could breathe easier. None of the distressing events were his fault. He could move on to the next phase of his life with courage, dignity and integrity.

Now, as they rode, his father's voice washed over him, the honor and pride the man radiated so inspirational to Ramón. His parents believed he would make something of himself. He didn't discuss his feelings for Benae, but they fathomed his strong attraction to her, for they kept talking of honor and the importance of Benae's marriage to the kingdom of Thorius.

He came to understand he and Benae were only a small part of a greater plan. Their sacrifices and sufferings made the kingdom strong. He had made the right choice in holding Benae at a distance and she would thank him one day. It was difficult for her to see that now; when she was in the grip of whatever feelings she had for him.

A happy glow warmed Ramón despite the chill of the day. That a woman like Benae found him attractive boosted his ego. More than that, he had been able to save her from the dark elves. Next, he would retrieve Alecia and the prince would never again doubt his worth. Steely resolve straightened Ramón's shoulders. If he could save the lives of the prince's two most treasured women, his worth in the kingdom would be beyond measure.

Benae stood again in the dressmaker's fitting room, turning this way and that, as the final adjustments were made. Her wedding gown was breathtaking. It hugged her curves from her breasts to her hips, scooping low across her shoulders to reveal a decent amount of cleavage. The sleeves were long, finishing in points over her hands and the skirt flared out from thighs to feet. The entire gown was delicate lace over satin and the train extended five paces behind her. A gorgeous lace veil completed the ensemble.

The fitting was almost complete when there was a knock at the door. The queen entered. She was dressed in a body-hugging gown of crimson velvet that also left a good deal of her breasts on display. Her flashing green eyes lit up when they saw Benae.

"My dear, you make the most stunning bride!" She advanced and kissed Benae on both cheeks.

Taken aback by Adriana's display of enthusiasm, Benae curtsied, wondering what the queen would say next. This day had been difficult and the only thing that held Benae's nerve at that moment was the thought of a ride in the wild wind with Flaire. Already excitement bubbled in her stallion's veins.

"No need to curtsy when we are alone, Benae. You and I will soon be relatives. In fact, that is why I am here. I wish to give you some sisterly advice. I fear there may not be another opportunity." She turned to the old dressmaker. "Leave us."

The woman curtsied and left without another word. What did Adriana have to say that required dismissal of the servants? Benae rubbed at the sudden tightness in the muscles of her neck.

"I know you have a hankering for the squire – who could blame you? But Jiseve must not know. He is insanely jealous. There is no telling what he might do if he discovers your feelings for Ramón."

"Your Majesty, I've already explained we are merely friends."

"Nonsense, Benae," Adriana said, a frown marring her beauty. "I have seen the way you look at him. You must not give Jiseve reason to believe you have been unfaithful."

"I have not!"

"Perhaps that is so, but that won't be the case for much longer, if I am any judge."

Benae turned and walked to the window. She couldn't bear this. It wasn't any business of Adriana's. Or was it? Was she simply trying to safeguard Jiseve and the kingdom's heir?

"You are very much like me, Benae. You could easily be my younger sister. I understand your passion. Jiseve is an older man. You will stray. You want to already."

Benae spun to face her. "We would never betray Jiseve as you describe. Please, I don't wish to speak of these matters."

"Take Ramón as your lover, Benae."

Benae gasped. *Why would the Queen say these things?*

"I know that is what you wish. Your passions drive you and Ramón is an easy man to love. It is my belief that, until you and he are one, your hunger for him will be there, upon your face, for all to see, including Jiseve. Find a way to sate that passion, that longing, and you will disguise it more easily."

"That's outrageous, Adriana. I won't speak of this any longer with you." A flash of intuition came to her. "You've taken lovers!"

"Of course, I have. Beniel, the Goddess bless him, is not always able to perform and our childlessness is no secret. I blame him for the lack of an heir even though officially *I* am barren. When the urge takes me,

I have several *friends* I call upon." A wistful smile curved the queen's lips. "Anyway, I see a deep sadness within you, Benae, and I wanted to assure you that, despite your marriage of convenience, there is no need for you to be unhappy or to settle only for Jiseve."

Benae stared, unable to believe what she was hearing. She had heard of the fairy tale marriage of the King and Queen of Thorius and now she knew it was pretense. Oh, Adriana was very fond of Beniel, perhaps even loved him in her own way, but the superficial nature of the queen's life depressed her. Could she enter into the same sort of marriage with Jiseve? Was he impotent and that was the reason he had not yet bedded her? When she thought back, she couldn't remember his rod swelling during their romantic interludes. Fear gripped her heart. Had she promised herself to a man incapable of satisfying her sexual cravings?

She couldn't help the tremor that shook her. She must think this through, now.

"Please help me from this dress, Your Majesty." Benae reached behind to the dozens of buttons that ran up her spine and began to undo the uppermost fastenings. Adriana stepped forward to help her. They soon had the garment off and laid across a chair. Benae slipped into the sea-green riding habit that Adriana had loaned her.

"You look exquisite in that, my dear. You may keep it. I hardly ever wear it anyway. I take it you plan to ride this afternoon?"

Benae nodded, unable to trust her voice. She must hold herself together until she and Flaire were away from the castle and from the city; until they were flying along the sand and a few tears wouldn't be noticed.

"Take an escort and don't be away for long," the queen said. "There is a storm brewing."

Benae swept a curtsy and hurried from the dressmaker's chambers. In her room, she paused only long enough to throw her cloak around her shoulders before taking the servants' stairs to the stables. She *had* to be alone; needed time to think.

The stables were deserted, though she heard a murmur of voices from the rear of the building. She must be quick to saddle Flaire before one of the attendants insisted she be accompanied. Benae found her stallion and sent him a mind message for quiet. He scarcely breathed as she saddled him and drew on his bridle. Her insides quivered as they left the stable and walked agonizingly slowly past the other horses. Flaire's hooves made barely a sound on the flagstones but there were quiet nickers from some of the other horses. She could tell from Flaire's response that most of the other inhabitants were envious of the stallion's chance to escape.

Once out of the stables, Benae mounted and walked in a leisurely fashion through the castle forecourt and out through the gates, nodding to the guards on duty as if she rode out on her own every day. Out of the corner of her eye, she saw the sergeant send one of the guards running. It wouldn't be long before an escort was dispatched to retrieve her, but she would make the most of the time she had. Ramón had shown her a trail down to the beach when they arrived at Wildecoast, so she retraced her steps and found the steep descent to the seashore.

Her spirits soared along with Flaire's as they reached the sand and stared out at the wind-tossed waves. The darkening clouds seemed to touch the ocean and Benae spied a flash of lightning on the horizon. Flaire snorted, excited by the strange salty tang on the air. Neither of them had seen the sea before, but Benae had learned to swim in the fast-flowing rivers of her native northern lands. Peering down the beach to the south, she spied a rocky causeway that jutted out into the ocean.

"Let's race to those rocks, Flaire," she whispered into the stallion's ear. He went from a stop to a flat-out gallop in seconds. Excitement gripped Benae as the wind ripped at her hair and sent her cloak flying behind her like a flag, tugging on her shoulders as though it wanted to rip her from the saddle. They raced along the beach above the waves, past driftwood and exposed rocks and Benae felt freer than she had in months. This was living, not the stuffy existence most people knew. She hoped Jiseve didn't expect her to live the life of a princess, stuck inside castle walls, embroidering and waiting to die. He would never expect that, would he?

The waves swept in from the ocean and surged up the beach to ripple against Flaire's hooves. The stallion shied to avoid the water and stumbled over a rock. Suddenly Benae was flying through the air. She landed on her back, the reins still in her hands, and lay there, unable to breathe. Shooting pain slammed through her skull, along with panic, and she was momentarily confused—she wasn't hurt, was she? A scream rent the air along with another burst of pain through her skull. She turned to see Flaire hobbling toward her, his left foreleg hanging limply.

"No, Flaire, no!" she cried, careening toward her horse as he again tried to place weight on the damaged limb. She threw her arms around his neck to ensure he stayed still. Great tremors wracked his body. He stood with his head down, blowing, sweat dripping from his neck and flanks.

Gently, Benae touched his injured foreleg, hardly daring to breathe as she probed the bones and sent a flow of spirit into the limb. Agony seared through her mind and she gasped. He had broken it! Benae fell to her knees, cradling the injured leg in her hands and placing her forehead against his leg above the knee.

"Oh Flaire," she said. "I'm so sorry."

He nickered softly and nuzzled her head. He was always more concerned about her than himself. Tears sprang to her eyes at the surge of love and confidence that flowed to her from the horse. He believed she would fix his leg! Her heart skipped a beat as she contemplated the extent of the injury. Could she heal such a catastrophic break? She had never attempted a bone repair of this nature before. A sob tore through her. She had to try even though her recent record was abysmal; even though the largest break she had fixed on anyone before had been a finger bone.

"What was I thinking?" she grumbled. "We should never have been galloping where we weren't sure of the footing." She let his leg down gently and rose to kiss his forehead. He pressed it against hers.

If the horse died because of this…she simply wouldn't allow herself to imagine that.

Drawing together the shreds of her courage, Benae dropped once more to the sand and clasped both hands around Flaire's injured cannon bone. She constructed a weave that would numb some of the pain from the damaged limb and Flaire relaxed. Benae closed her eyes and formed the delicate weave of spirit that would knit bones, moving the displaced bone fragments into place with the help of pressure from her hands. One fragment was stubborn, refusing to move. Flaire pulled his leg away but Benae soothed him with words and thought.

"Be strong, my brave stallion." She took a deep breath, swallowing the fear that rose. She would succeed, she must. She couldn't lose Flaire too!

The fragment clicked into place and she let out her breath, forcing the tremor from her fingers, willing her heart to beat slowly, concentrating on knitting the bones. Sweat poured from her, wetting her gown and making her shiver in the blustery conditions. Flaire nudged at her shoulder, his love and faith bringing fresh tears to her eyes. What if she couldn't make the healing firm enough to walk on? Injuries like these were disastrous, unhealable, weren't they? She closed her eyes, delving the wound, checking the bones she had knitted. They weren't full strength, but perhaps it would be enough to get him to the castle. Benae wove one last healing and placed the hoof gently on the ground.

Flaire gingerly tested the leg. Benae registered a dim ache from the injury, not the shooting stabs of agony that the stallion had experienced before. She breathed a ragged sigh as relief crashed over her. His suffering had nearly been her undoing.

"All will be well, valiant friend," she said, soothing him with her hands, "but I won't ride you until strength has returned." Perhaps her skills remained intact? Maybe Ramón was right? There were some things she couldn't heal. She had done her best with her parents and her brother, but she wasn't a worker of miracles.

The thought of Ramón shot a spear of anxiety into her heart. She couldn't bed him and stay true to Jiseve. Ramón wouldn't agree anyway. He had too much respect, for both herself and Jiseve, to allow it. He was strong where she was weak. She listened to her desires while Ramón carefully thought through his decisions and sought the best course for all. The queen was wrong. Benae couldn't have both Jiseve and Ramón. It was just not right. Benae must choose one or the other, but could she live without Ramón? Could her people survive without her alliance with Jiseve?

She howled in frustration. Casting her eyes to the heavens, Benae began a prayer to the Goddess.

"Holy Mother, look down upon your daughter and give her solace. Bless her with your wisdom so that she might make the right decision for all. Guide —"

A strange keening interrupted Benae's prayer. It seemed to be coming from the sea. She looked out to the waves, realizing Flaire's accident had occurred close to the rocky causeway that jutted into the ocean. Fascinated, Benae led Flaire onto the rocks, ignoring the part of her mind that urged caution. She turned her head this way and that, trying to judge the direction of the keening.

The strange song seemed to come from the very waves themselves. A larger wave rolled over the causeway, startling Benae and wetting her slippers. The sea had become angry cliffs of foaming whitecaps. The advancing storm rolled out of the south and dark gray clouds hung over her. The song continued. Benae couldn't be concerned for the storm or her safety when such notes trembled in the air, formed of her very emotions: grief, anxiety, frustration, fear. They were all in the song.

As she stood transfixed, concentrating on the music and oblivious to the choppy seas that snapped at the rocks like angry dogs, a freak wave crashed over the causeway. Benae was knocked off her feet and swept over the side.

The shock of the cold water made her gasp and she inhaled a mouthful of the sea even as her hand clamped on the reins. The wet leather halted her headlong rush into the water, but her body slammed against the rocks of the causeway wall. Through the fog of cold and fear, she realized she had to keep a grip on her lifeline. Flaire would drag her from the sea. She concentrated on trying to breathe but her throat had closed, her body shocked by the salty invasion. When she did draw breath, a stab of pain shot through her chest.

A swirling wall of water hit her, and she lost her grip on the reins, grasping hold of a rock in the wall of the causeway to stop herself from being washed away. Now most of her body was submerged in the freezing sea. Dimly she watched Flaire dance to the very edge of the causeway, his muscles bunched as if he would leap in after her. She prayed for both their sakes that his training would keep him on solid ground.

CHAPTER 13

TERROR gripped Ramón. He whipped his horse through the forecourt of Wildecoast Castle and tore into the crowds that milled before its gates. Benae was out there, somewhere, perhaps lost or injured. Pressure mounted in his chest and his heart beat faster than a tiny bird's. Having returned from his parent's estate mid-afternoon, he was told that Benae had gone riding after her final dress fitting. She had been absent for over an hour. How could she think it proper for her to leave the castle unaccompanied? What had made her take such a terrible risk?

He couldn't wait for the search party that mustered in the yard. Benae was *his* responsibility and he couldn't lose her too. *Thank the Goddess she's with Flaire!* Where would she go? He had no idea where to start, except to make his way out of the city. The crowds in the streets frustrated him, townsfolk scurrying to and fro as they retreated to their homes amidst the squally conditions. They continually leapt into his path as he hurled headlong through the streets. When he almost flattened a small boy, Ramón pulled his horse over to the shelter of a wall. It was no good. He'd kill someone this way. He forced himself into the center of the street, restraining his horse to a brisk walk, avoiding further close shaves as he wove his way, through the dwindling pedestrians, to the city's gate. The guards were clustered in the watch house, likely around a fire, and a lone soldier waved him through.

At last he was free, and he touched his heels to his mount, wishing for the first time that he wore spurs. Where should he search? If he were Benae, where would he go? The beach? Perhaps. There was nothing like a gallop along the beach to clear the cobwebs from long days of being cooped up indoors.

Ramón changed course and headed for the cliffs, pulling his horse up in a flurry of rocks at the edge of the precipice. He peered up and down the beach, but visibility was poor and the rain in his eyes wouldn't allow him to focus for long. He dismounted and used his horse as a windbreak, shielding his eyes as he peered first to the north and then to the south. Finally, a gust of wind cleared the sea spray for a moment, and he spied movement on the causeway. Was it a horse? A gray horse? If it was, he had seen no rider. A cold hand clutched his heart and squeezed. Physical pain seared his sternum. He threw himself onto his mount and galloped to the nearest path down to the beach. Benae must be alive, she must be safe.

Ramón's reckless plunge down the steep and treacherous path nearly unseated him a half-dozen times but with each slip he managed to claw his way back into the saddle. His mount's familiarity with the trail was the difference between life and death. Reckless didn't begin to describe his descent, but he reached the cliff base in one piece and sent his horse galloping toward the causeway. Every so often, another swirling gust would clear the sea spray and he was able to confirm a horse did stand on the rocky breakwater. It was Flaire but where was Benae? He prayed his mount wouldn't stumble in the wet sand. Rocks jutted up at regular intervals and a fall could easily spell disaster.

Finally, he arrived at the base of the causeway and shouted to Flaire. The stallion whipped around, whinnying, his reins dangling below his head, but didn't move toward him. Benae was nowhere to be seen. Flaire turned to the swirling waves below his feet and threw his head down, his nostrils flaring, and eyes wild. His low nicker tore through Ramón. She must have fallen into the sea!

At first he didn't see her, but a flash of dark hair caught his eye. There she was, almost submerged, only her head poking from the water, the weight of her cloak and gown tugging her down. Waves broke over her head. She couldn't fight much longer. He approached cautiously, not willing to spook Flaire or be knocked aside. He reached out and laid his hand on the stallion's shoulder, felt the muscles shudder under his fingers. With soothing words, Ramón moved his hand up to the horse's neck and secured the reins. *Can I count on him to remain where he is and supply an anchor as I pull Benae free?* The stallion was out of his mind with fear – a precarious moment for Ramón to depend upon him.

He wrapped the reins around his left hand and stepped off the causeway, slipping down two layers of rocks before his grip on the reins pulled him up. He continued toward Benae, controlling his descent until his leather lifeline ran out. He shouted to her and she turned her head, green eyes blazing up at him through the tendrils of hair plastered on her face.

"Hold on, Benae. I think I can reach you."

A wave crashed over the causeway, nearly carrying Ramón with it. The only thing that kept him from being swept away was his grip on the reins and the solid mountain of horseflesh above him. As the water ebbed, he looked frantically for Benae. She still clung to the jagged rocks, just out of reach. Her eyes fluttered closed, chest heaving with the exertion of fighting the water.

He eased himself into a sitting position and tugged on the reins. Flaire moved a step closer to the edge. Stretching out his fingertips, he reached down. "Take one hand off the rock and reach for my fingers. I'll pull you up."

She looked at him, the muscles of her throat convulsing as she swallowed, her eyes red from the wash of salt water. She was nearing her limit. Soon she would slip from his reach and the sea would take her.

"Undo your cloak!"

With agonizing slowness, Benae took one hand from the rock and fumbled at her throat for the clasp. Ramón drew a ragged breath as the heavy material slipped from Benae's shoulders. He stretched his fingers as far as he could toward her.

"Grab my hand!" He wiggled his fingers and she stretched out, their fingertips brushing, but a wave swirled up and away at that moment. Benae clutched the rock to prevent being washed off.

When the water subsided, she again let go of the rock with her left hand and reached for him. As before, only their fingers touched, and Ramón couldn't get a proper grip. He tugged on the reins, but the stallion had planted his feet and couldn't be coaxed any closer to the edge. Ramón ground his teeth. *Stupid horse.*

"Hold tight, I'm coming down."

He waited until Benae had a firm grip on the rock, then released the reins and descended the slippery surface, falling rather than climbing, until he rested beside her. She gripped his hand as though she would never release it. Her lips were blue, and her chest heaved with the exertion of holding on.

Ramón slipped the fingers of his left hand into a crevice and gripped Benae's upper arm. "Climb up. I'll help you." He hauled with all his strength and Benae climbed rock by rock until she could reach the reins. Once she had them in her grasp, Flaire backed across the causeway, hauling her the rest of the way to the top. *Now the horse chooses to cooperate!*

Benae collapsed gasping at the hooves of her mount, Flaire nuzzling her head.

Now for me. Ramón removed his right foot from the crevice it had slid into and began searching blindly for a foothold further up the rocks. As he searched, his left foot slipped. Before he could steady himself, he slid a pace lower until most of his body was submerged. The rocks were slimy here and he couldn't get a decent foot or handhold. As he scrambled for purchase, he glanced up at Benae. Her eyes were wide and she was on hands and knees, shouting for him to hold on. She glanced at something behind him and shouted but it was lost as a wall of water engulfed him, tearing at his body and plucking him from the rocks. He had the presence of mind to take a gulp of air before the water closed over his head. A blinding pain seared through the left side of his skull and everything went black.

* * *

Benae knelt, frozen, on the causeway, her fingers gripping the rocks at its edge, as she searched for some sign of Ramón. What good to rescue her if she lost him? The reins were too short, but perhaps with a rope she could tie it around her and leap in after him. Flaire could pull them out. She pushed herself to her feet, not wanting to take her eyes off the churning water. *Hold on, my love.*

She fumbled through Flaire's saddlebags and came up with nothing. A sob escaped her throat and she pounded the saddle with her fist, not even noticing the pain. Her eyes fell upon Ramón's mount, twenty paces away. She sent Flaire a mental picture to stay put before running to the other horse. Her gown hung heavy around her and she was colder than she could ever remember being; her teeth chattered, her limbs moved like she was mired in mud. *Too slow! Keep moving!*

Movement would warm her up and it was the only thing that would save Ramón. She slowed as she reached the horse so as not to startle him and fumbled through the saddlebags. Two coils of thin rope lay inside. *Thank the Goddess!*

She jogged back with the coils and stripped out of her gown and petticoats until she stood only in her chemise and pantaloons. She joined the two ropes together in a knot that wouldn't slip, tied an end to herself and the other to Flaire's saddle, all the while sending him soothing messages and showing him what she, and later he, must do. He whinnied, on the edge of panic. He wasn't happy that she intended to leap back into the churning water.

Benae peered toward the spot where she had last seen Ramón, the deepening twilight hampering her sight. *There!* A flash of red tunic bloomed out of the dimness and her heart quailed. He was almost too far to reach with the rope, if she was any judge. She climbed over the edge of the causeway and began her descent, slipping and sliding to where the waves lapped. She took a breath and jumped in. It was bone-jarringly cold; the air whooshed from her lungs. She tread water and flung the rope behind her, then struck off into the churning ocean. It was almost impossible to see anything down at water level, so she kept swimming, trusting her sense of direction to lead her to him.

The rope pulled her up and she tread water again as she searched. He was still a pace out of reach but at least he floated face up. She couldn't tell if his chest was moving. Benae hauled on the rope but no more length was forthcoming. She cast a plea to her horse. Nothing but fear came back to her. Poor Flaire had reached the limit of his bravery. She smacked the water before her in frustration and a sob, like the cry of a wounded animal, broke from her. Ramón floated before her, just out of reach, blood oozing from a wound on his left temple. She started paddling the water away from in front of her and he floated a hand closer. Frantically she bailed the water before her but each time she brought him closer, the waves would take him from her.

Benae paused, exhausted by her paddling and from her efforts to stay afloat in the rough sea. The strange keening song that had drawn her onto the causeway in the first place, echoed across the water. Ramón slowly floated toward her. Benae stared, unable to understand what was happening. A large tail flicked out of the water then disappeared. *I must be more exhausted than I thought.*

Benae didn't have time to ponder further as she grasped Ramón and placed her hand against his neck. A pulse beat there, fast but faint. *I might still lose him!* She flipped over onto her back and drew Ramón against her then began to kick toward the shore, moving parallel to the causeway. It was difficult to find the energy to communicate with Flaire, but she sent him mind messages, asking him to walk along the causeway toward the beach. After a handful of kicks, the rope drew taught, stopping her motion toward the shore. Flaire hadn't moved. She snapped out a command through the mind link and got nothing back, so barked out another. A sluggish response trickled back.

Haul us in you great lump of lard! she cursed at him.

Harsh, came back his thought. At least that was how she interpreted it.

A gentle pressure gripped her chest as Flaire plodded along the causeway, hauling them toward the shore. Benae kept kicking to keep her distance from the rocks, so cold she couldn't feel her legs or arms. It seemed an eternity until she felt the coarse sand beneath her buttocks.

Without the buoyancy the water provided, resistance was greater. The rope cut into her unmercifully as Flaire continued to haul them up the beach. She flashed a quick request to stop her horse and the pressure on her ribs ceased. She rolled Ramón onto his side and shrieked when pain flashed from her cold, cramped muscles.

Ramón was so still she feared she had lost him. She braced herself to deal with another wave of pain and kneeled, placing her hand at his throat. *His heart still beats.* Benae collapsed across his chest, tears warming her cheeks. She levered herself up and lay a hand over Ramón's chest and forehead. At first her delving failed, and cold panic flooded her mind. *Breathe deeply. You can do this. You* must *do this!* She steadied her breathing and looked deep inside for the spark of spirit she had left, sending it spiraling into Ramón's still form. It curled around his heart and infiltrated his lungs, pushing a wave of water from his mouth.

He coughed and heaved a great breath, but his heart still barely beat out its faint rhythm; even though her delving hadn't detected any fault in the vital organ. *His head then.* Exhaustion swept over her. It was too much, all too much. Flaire nuzzled her hair and snorted his glorious warm breath against her cheek. His thoughts were of sunlight and galloping and love. She was momentarily distracted from the cold and fear. The spirit within sparked anew and she sent it sweeping through Ramón's skull. *There!* It was fractured at the site of his injury. A large swelling pushed his brain aside and the pressure was growing.

The doubts she experienced when trying to mend Flaire's leg were less now. She had healed her horse, certainly she could fix Ramón. First the bleeding must be stopped. It was a simple matter to apply pressure and knit the vessel that trickled blood into the space. Next, she wove a net around the swelling, compressing it. Ramón's chest filled with air and he coughed. His heart beat more steadily. She delved the vessel again to ensure the healing would be able to withstand the increased pressure the heart would place upon it. All was well. Last were the bones. She wove a web of spirit that settled over the injury and the bone fragments knitted together.

It was dark now and the storm howled from the southeast. Soon there would be heavy rain. Ramón stirred, muttering.

"Ramón, I need your help," she said, struggling to untie the wet rope from her waist. He turned his head. "Benae?"

"Yes, I'm here. You hit your head, but all is well now."

"I remember."

Benae sagged with relief. He had passed the last test; his memory appeared intact. Perhaps his brain had been spared permanent injury. "Where can we seek shelter? We're at the base of the causeway."

"Hut, a little further south along the beach. On a small rise above the high tide mark."

"Can you walk?"

He didn't respond and Benae seized his shoulders and shook gently. "Ramón!"

"Mm?"

"We must seek shelter." She gripped his arm and hauled him to a sitting position. "You must help. I can't lift you."

Ramón rolled onto his hands and knees and pushed himself to his feet. Benae guided him to Flaire's side.

"Mount. Flaire will keep you safe." She helped him place his left foot in the stirrup and gave his buttocks a shove as he hauled himself up. He landed in the saddle and Benae gripped his leg to steady him. She gave her stallion a pat on the nose and mounted the other horse, which had followed Flaire off the causeway.

"Gently now, Ramón, Flaire was injured and isn't capable of speed. You must take care."

"He's not the only one incapable of speed. Truly, I can walk if needed."

Benae's heart sang at his lucidity. Perhaps all was well. "He pulled us from the ocean, so he is able, just take care."

She kicked off and sent Flaire a request to find the hut in the dunes, directing him south of their location. He was calm now and she was confident he would find the sanctuary, his vision superior to that of humans. Not for the first time, she was glad of her link with the horse.

A mere four hundred paces along the beach, Flaire suddenly turned inland and soon stopped before a dark structure. Benae dismounted and came to Ramón's side, tugging on his left foot. "We're here, Ramón."

He slid to the ground, landing awkwardly. His arms curled around her and butterflies danced in her stomach. His hands slid lower until they rested on her hips, fingers curling around her buttocks. She swallowed the lump of emotion that leapt into her throat.

"This is some giddy dream, just like my dreams of Alecia."

Benae's butterflies turned to bubbles that vanished, leaving her cold. It always came back to that woman. One day she hoped she had the opportunity to meet the princess and claw her eyes out. Ramón's next words explained everything.

"You, Alecia, the mermaid who saved me: all are dreams to torment me."

It was his head injury talking. He didn't know what he was saying, what he was doing. Mermaid indeed! A fleeting memory of a tail amongst the waves came to her but she tossed it aside. This was no time for foolish fancies. Ramón needed rest and warmth.

She pushed him away, momentarily bereft as his hands left her body. Clutching his fingers, she led him to the hut and felt along the wall until she came to the door latch. The door swung open and the musty, pungent odor of fishing nets, mouse droppings and rotting seaweed assailed her. No matter, it was warm inside, or rather, less cold than the stormy beach. Benae settled Ramón on a pile of old netting then headed back outside.

She led the two horses to the rear of the shed where she found a solid post to tie them to. It would have to do. She grabbed the flint box from her saddle and after a brief mind link to Flaire, returned to Ramón.

The inside of the shed was almost pitch black, but she had noted a stone chimney from the outside, so moved toward the spot where she thought the fireplace must be. Miraculously, the tinderbox and flint were dry. The fireplace had been laid and Benae soon had a cheerful blaze going.

"I came to save you," Ramón said, "and instead you saved me."

She turned to him and was startled by the frank admiration in his gaze. *Oh Goddess, I'm in my underwear!* She stayed where she was, the fire at her back beginning to melt the block of ice that had formed inside her. "That makes a life for a life," she said, suddenly awkward. "You really remember what happened?"

"Most of it," he said. "It wasn't only you who saved me. Something, someone, rolled me onto my back and held me there, even pushed me a little. I think it was a mermaid."

She frowned at him, remembering the tail she had glimpsed, and nodded. "I heard a strange song. It lured me onto the causeway. I hadn't heard that mermaids saved lives, rather the opposite."

"We will solve the mystery of the mermaid later. For now, let's see what provisions are here." He rose, crossed to a sack suspended from the rafters and untied it from its support. Inside they found dried mutton, hard cheese and pickled onions. Ramón took a knife and cut the edges from the cheese then gave Benae a slice to nibble on.

While Benae mused on the events that had brought them to this refuge, Ramón stripped the wet clothes from his body and laid them before the fire. She grew hot at the sight of the squire in his smalls. The firelight made his body glow golden. As his hair dried, it took on the halo that was unique to Ramón. He was so beautiful.

They ate in companionable silence, she on an old rickety chair and he on an empty barrel. The warmth of the fire and the cheery light it cast, along with a full stomach, helped to restore Benae's hope.

"What were you doing, leaving the castle unescorted?" he asked, cocking his head to one side so his hair flopped across one eye.

"It seemed the answer at the time. I had no one to talk to and I panicked about the wedding."

"What's there to panic about?"

"I love you." It had to be said, had to be faced. "The queen has urged me to take you as a lover. In fact, many believe us already to be lovers. It's only by your choice that we are not."

"We agreed to be friends."

"Yes, agreeing to that was the only way I could have a relationship with you. Better to have you in my life as a friend than not at all." She paused. "Now I find that not to be the case."

"What do you mean by that?" He asked, warily.

Benae stared at him, uncertain how to respond. He had said "no" to her more than once. The odds weren't in her favor that he'd succumb to her tonight. He was so much stronger than she. Benae reached for the top button of her chemise and slowly undid each fastening to her waist, until she could pull the garment from her shoulders. It slid to the stone floor. *Goddess grant he can't deny me this time.*

Ramón swallowed hard, his eyes wide as they devoured her bare chest. His breathing picked up pace.

"Benae —"

"Hush, beloved," she said, reaching to place her finger against his lips.

She didn't shift her gaze from him. He seemed mesmerized, his eyes following as her fingers caressed her bared breasts and rolled back and forth over her nipples. He swallowed, his tongue moistening his lips. Benae imagined that tongue against her nipples and they became hard points of need.

Once she had allowed Ramón to feast upon her naked torso for long moments, with only the rolling waves and the crackling fire to serenade them, she stood and stepped from her pantaloons. "This night is ours, Ramón. Whatever happens tomorrow, we'll have this night." She stepped closer to him so that she could run her hands across his shoulders and through the fine golden hairs of his chest. He shivered beneath her fingers. "I want to know you, Ramón. I need that, and I believe you do as well."

Benae gripped his hands and brought them to rest on her hips. Just the touch of his hands on her bare skin was almost enough to make her lose control but she must be strong. With him seated on the barrel, they were the same height. His gaze dropped to explore her body. She moved her hands up either side of his face and kissed him briefly, tenderly. She sensed the longing in his full lips, knew he held himself aloof by the merest shred of control. Still she couldn't force this. He must be fully willing to cast his feelings for Alecia, and his loyalty to the prince, aside.

She kissed him again, this time deepening the contact, her tongue questing past his lips so she could explore the depths of his mouth. His hands gripped her hips tighter and his tongue forced its way into her mouth, tangling with hers, igniting a fierce need in Benae. She arched her hips against him, and he groaned. *Slowly, slowly.* Ramón wrenched his lips from hers and Benae nearly sobbed. Her dismay was short-lived as his mouth found first one nipple and then the other, sucking them just short of pain until she strained against him, desperate for release. She stepped back, breaking the contact, then took his right hand and brought it to her mouth, moistening his fingers and then guiding them to her core. Benae showed him how to stimulate her, her body moving with the rhythm of his hand, tightening and building. As his fingers pleasured her, his lips worked their magic on her nipples until she climaxed, shudders ripping through her body over and over, until she sagged against him.

Her skin against his felt so right, their chests resting together, their breathing ragged. They stayed like that, Benae lost in the ferocity of her orgasm, wondering if they would now consummate their love. Surely, he couldn't deny what lay between them. He wouldn't let honor deprive them of this moment, whatever happened in the future.

He stood and gazed down at her, both his hands now encircling her waist. His pupils were huge, dark, almost obscuring the blue of his irises. There was a haunted look to his gaze; reluctant, fearful, yearning. Passion drove him and he was unaccustomed to the war within. Would he allow passion to rule or would he succumb to honor yet again?

Benae gently stripped off his smalls until the extent of his arousal was exposed. The underwear dropped to the floor and she pulled him toward her. She gripped his erection in her right hand and squeezed. His eyes closed and he shuddered. She gripped again and he thrust a little toward her.

"We shouldn't," he said.

"Who's to say we shouldn't?" She knelt before him. "Doesn't this feel right to you?" Benae took his rod into her mouth and sucked, pulling him in and out of her mouth with her hand, forcing his erection to the back of her throat, then withdrawing him. She repeated the movement until she thought he was at the point of climax, his head thrown back, his eyes closed, body tight with need.

Benae pulled him from her mouth and lay down on the clothes he had placed before the fire, knees bent, legs parted so he could see she was ready for him.

* * *

It took Ramón a few moments to realize Benae no longer pleasured him. Goddess, what sensations she evoked! Of course, he had felt the need to relieve his tension from time to time but more often he found relief in a weapons session or a run. This was altogether different. He opened his eyes and found her spread on his clothes, her left hand dangling between her legs, playing with herself. Moisture glistened on her soft folds and Ramón lost all thought of resistance.

He flung himself down and crawled between her legs, his erection brushing her. His mouth found hers and there was no restraint, his tongue exploring her mouth, her hips straining against him, reaching to accommodate him. His rod seemed to move of its own volition, seeking Benae's center. It wasn't as simple as it seemed. Need drove him but his shaft couldn't find its target. He groaned with frustration.

"Don't fret, lover," she said, her hands guiding him, her fingers parting her folds so that he slid within. Her slippery warmth enveloped him. He began to thrust, Benae meeting him each time, her hands on his buttocks, letting out small gasps at each thrust. The tempo increased and Ramón's climax built, zeroing in upon his groin. Benae gave one last thrust and shuddered, her whole body tightening around him, his name shrieking from her lips. His seed burst within her and he thrust again and again, until he had emptied the whole of himself into her. He relaxed and rolled to the side, pulling Benae with him, so they stayed joined.

"That was wondrous." He smiled at her, gently pushing a strand of dark hair from her glorious emerald eyes. "Thank you."

She stiffened in his arms. "Don't thank me. It was a giving and receiving between two people who care for each other."

Why was she angry? "You made my first time special. I had always wondered how it would be. I thought —" He felt her stiffen further as if she expected Alecia's name on his lips. No, that wouldn't do. "Never mind what I thought. I'll always treasure this night and hold it in my heart. It will be something to remember when I can't hold you."

Her serious eyes studied him. "I won't allow you to walk away from me, Ramón. You and I are joined forever. Your seed lies within me. It might result in a child. I'd welcome such an eventuality. To bear your son or daughter would make sense of this cruel world."

A chill crept through his chest. He withdrew from her and stood, looking down upon her. "I can't be with you, Benae. You're betrothed. We must take our pleasure this night and never again. If you thought taking my virginity would bind me to you, you were mistaken."

Benae leapt up to confront him. "I didn't set out to trap you. Yes, it was selfish of me to seduce you, but I was desperate. I told myself all along that what I felt was desire only, that when I was married to Jiseve he would sate me. I reached the point where I could no longer lie to myself. I love you, Ramón! I think you love me, too."

Ramón's chest constricted, panic closing his throat. *She loves me!* He shook his head. She couldn't love him, must not. He fell to his knees, imagining the scene should the prince discover their adultery. Already he felt the heavy weight of guilt deep in his gut, knew he must hide another indiscretion. He had promised himself never again to act on impulse; never again to let passion dictate his actions. And here he was: Benae's lover. How had it come to this? How had he tossed his principles aside, nay his convictions, so quickly?

"It's love, dearest," Benae said, seeming to read his thoughts. "You and I; it is love. You torture yourself because you couldn't deny me." Love shone in her eyes. Love for him. He realized, in that moment, he'd do anything for her. He would risk his life, would stand by and protect her as she married the prince. He'd kill for her.

She sat in front of him, naked, and a hot blast of desire tore through him. He pushed her down into the clothes and kissed her until they were both breathless. If they couldn't be together forever, he'd at least have her one last time. He parted her legs and this time his rod found its home without help, thrusting into her slick, hot center. Benae cried his name and it sent him over the edge. He plunged into her again and again, no thought but pure, sweet pleasure on his mind.

CHAPTER 14

BENAE retrieved her pantaloons and chemise from where she had flung them last night. She hummed as she dressed, reliving the moment when she had awoken, Ramón's hands on her body, doing things she could never have imagined he would know. The firelight had danced along the muscular planes of his shoulders as he moved over her, kissing and fondling her breasts, licking her navel and then continuing to lick her all the way to her most intimate place. His loving had resulted in a climax she'd long remember. He was an instinctive lover and would be extraordinary with experience. The love-making had been as much a revelation for her as it had been for him; her first sexual experience with a man she loved. She had never expected to feel so connected, so complete.

The thought of their coupling brought a fresh surge of heat. She paused in her dressing and strode across the room to him, clad only in her pantaloons. Ramón drew her into his arms.

"I long to be one with you again, beloved," she purred, nipping the sensitive skin below his ear. "Can't we stay here today?"

His body shivered under her ministrations. She kissed the broad muscles across his chest, slowly working her way lower, until she grazed her lips across his nipple. He grew hard against her. She could never have enough of this glorious, sensual man. Somehow, all the sorrow she had endured was worth it to end up loved by Ramón.

"Search parties will be abroad," he said, his voice husky, his eyes dark with desire. "We can't risk being discovered here, like this." His hand stroked the side of her breast. "Already we've lingered too long."

"Let them find us," Benae said. "I can't be sorry for last night."

"We must continue the charade, love. You're a betrothed woman."

"I'll no longer lie about my feelings for you." She pulled his head to hers and kissed his full lips. *I could kiss him all day and never tire.* Her desire mounted.

Ramón placed her at arm's length. "We must talk."

"Talk?"

He frowned. "When we leave this place, we resume our past lives. You're to become a princess and I'll resume my life as a squire, servant to Prince Zialni. As such, you'll be my mistress —"

"Oh yes, I will indeed." She blessed him with a look designed to boil his blood.

His lips pressed into a straight line. "You deliberately misunderstand my words, Benae," he said, folding his arms across his chest.

She tried to push past, to ensnare his waist but he resisted.

"We both know there can be no more of this." His arm swept the hut and icy fingers clutched her heart.

"I love you," she said. "I can't stop loving you just because I'm betrothed to another. Don't expect me to walk away from this, because I can't. Can you?"

"I can do anything I'm required to. We've had our moment and to entertain 'us' as a possibility...well, it just can't be."

"I love you," she repeated. "I'm going to marry you and we'll be gloriously happy." Benae could see their children, girls on horseback galloping through her estate and the boys learning weapons from Ramón.

"You're betrothed to the prince. He'll never give you up. He would see you and me dead first."

A shiver sliced up her spine, but she ignored it. Ramón didn't know Jiseve as she did. Even after such a short relationship with her fiancé, she was sure he would accede to her will. He wouldn't want her if she couldn't give him all of herself. Jiseve was too proud for that. Ramón was wrong. Her betrothed was a good man.

"I'll tell him we have coupled, and he'll sever our agreement," she said. "Yes, he'll be hurt, but he won't want a wife who is in love with another man. He'll send word to one of the other ladies and they'll be only too happy to marry him, to bear his children, to supply the heir he needs. No one will be hurt."

"How can you be sure?" Ramón asked, his eyes troubled. "Had you considered the prince might be in love with you?"

She did so adore him when he was serious. He'd make a fine partner, father.

"I know men, Ramón. Jiseve isn't so attached to me that he'll refuse to let me go. If he were, he'd have consummated our relationship before I left Brightcastle. He brought me to the peak of longing many a time and left me there, unfulfilled. It drove me wild. That's one of the reasons I was so indiscreet with you the night before we left."

Ramón colored, a slow blush rising from his throat to cover his face. That was another thing she loved about him; his boyish blushes. She had never seen a man blush so delightfully. Joy sang in her heart. She would have the rest of her life to take pleasure in his company, to enjoy his eyes upon her, his hands working their magic.

"Are you sure we can't stay longer?" she asked.

Ramón pulled her into his arms and kissed her, one arm around her waist, the other hand at the nape of her neck. All rational thought fled as Benae responded to his touch, strained against his hard length, wove her fingers through his hair.

"We must go, beloved," he said, "but we'll discuss this further. For now, let's tell the court of our extraordinary escape from death, taking refuge in the hut and of our need to return to Brightcastle to prepare for your wedding."

Benae studied his face, uncertain how he felt about her. He had not admitted his love. Would he deny it still? Ramón had embedded himself in her heart and she believed she was as deeply set in his. Jiseve would understand. He'd release her from her promise and she and Ramón would find a way to save her estates that didn't involve sacrificing her happiness. It was possible; it had to be.

* * *

As Ramón saddled Flaire and his own mount, he mulled over the revelations of the night. He might be inexperienced, but he understood enough to know his desire for Benae was dangerous; for himself and for her. He could still feel her skin against his; he imagined he always would. No matter how far he traveled, it wouldn't be far enough to escape the memories.

A lump formed in his throat. Their relationship could never be. Somehow, he must persuade her not to reveal their betrayal to the prince and then she might be safe. He would leave Brightcastle and that would be the end to it all. He swallowed again at the thought of turning his back on Benae, but he must do whatever he had to, including denying her.

* * *

They shared Ramón's clothes, because Benae's cloak and dress had been lost in the ocean. Benae wore his shirt and cloak over her pantaloons and chemise; the squire dressed in his breeches and tunic. She couldn't help noticing Ramón's reticence as they rode north along the beach. Had she done the right thing seducing him last eve? Had it made her marriage to Jiseve easier to bear? How could it when every fiber of her being now hummed when Ramón was near? She wanted to speak to him of what was in her heart, but where should she start? If Ramón didn't love her, she must accept that. *No!* The emotions inside her were too powerful to deny. She had never envisaged caring this way about another human being. Last night had forged a connection between them that would endure.

An unfamiliar tension began to build within her as she rode toward the trail that led to the top of the cliffs. Eventually, Benae was able to name the emotion. *Fear.*

It was so new, this love she felt for Ramón. Its intensity scared her. The thought that he might not love her back frightened her. The niggling suspicion that Jiseve wouldn't release her terrified her. She couldn't be trapped in a loveless marriage. Once upon a time, Benae had reconciled herself to that fate but, since Ramón, it wasn't possible.

As she turned to speak to him, a shout sounded from ahead. Men and horses spilt from the cliff trail onto the beach. Ramón's cousin Josef led the party.

Benae moved forward but Ramón grabbed Flaire's reins. "Wait for them. Keep the story simple. The truth. I came looking for you, and you ended up dragging me from the ocean. We sought shelter in the hut. They have no proof that anything else happened."

Lieutenant Formosa pulled up in front of them, sand flicking from his horse's hooves. "I'm glad to see you, Lady, cousin. I was beginning to believe we would find only bodies." His eyes flicked from one to the other and Benae suspected he hadn't missed a detail. She pulled the cloak to cover her bare legs, but it was no use. At least Ramón's shirt was long enough to cover her thighs.

Ramón spoke up before she could explain. "I found Lady Branasar in difficulties and then needed rescuing myself. We were both nearly drowned and had to take refuge in the fishing hut overnight."

"That explains the state of your clothes." He examined Ramón's face. "You're bruised there." He pointed to the side of Ramón's head where Benae had set the bones.

"I told you I nearly drowned. I fell off the causeway and hit my head on rocks. After Lady Branasar dragged me from the water, I was in no fit state to return to Wildecoast. We took shelter from the storm."

Formosa's eyebrows rose, his expression speaking louder than words. "We'll escort you to the castle where you can have your wounds tended." He turned and trotted back to his men. Four horses peeled off to the side to form a rear-guard as Benae and Ramón fell in behind Josef and three of his men.

There was no talk on the return trip. The squeak of leather and jingle of spurs wore at Benae's nerves. Those sounds were usually music to her ears. All she wished was to be back in familiar surrounds with Ramón. She couldn't wait to leave Wildecoast and resolve her future, or lack of it, with Jiseve.

The king and queen awaited them in the castle forecourt, along with Kain Jazara. Weariness cloaked the general, his brow drawn in a deep scowl, his manner stiff and unfriendly. The queen stepped forward to embrace Benae, kissing both cheeks.

"I see you took my advice," Adriana said, a cheeky smile lighting her eyes. "I trust you are well?"

A spike of alarm shot through Benae at her words. No, she couldn't know, could she? "I'm well, Your Majesty. Ramón saved me from drowning last eve. It was rather foolish setting out on my own. I was washed from the causeway."

"And you, Squire?" King Beniel said. "That's a nasty bruise on the side of your head. What befell you?"

"He hurt himself in rescuing me, Sire," Benae said. Under the scrutiny of the monarchs, she was suddenly very conscious that she wore only Ramón's shirt over her underclothes.

"Let's not stand here talking," the queen said. "You must both go to your chambers and bathe. Only then will we talk of yesterday's events. Lady Benae, the body of your maid has been recovered. We must hasten to lay her to rest. On the morrow, if you please."

Benae curtsied. The sooner Merel was laid to rest, the sooner they could leave this cold, dreary castle and the scrutiny of its inhabitants.

CHAPTER 15

THEY were well into their first day on the road to Brightcastle. Ramón scanned the forest they passed, his eyes detecting movement where there was none. The one hundred soldiers with him didn't set his mind at rest. Who knew how many of the dark elves had amassed in the forests of Thorius?

Merel had been buried with full honors yesterday afternoon. The funeral had brought back all the grief pushed aside by more recent events. Benae had collapsed on Alique's shoulder and been led away by the ladies. Ramón ached to console her. Keeping his distance made him feel more powerless than ever. Benae had recovered somewhat since the funeral but her composure was like ice on a pond in spring.

Now they must confront the prince, or not. He still hadn't discussed the matter with Benae. As far as Ramón knew, she still intended to reveal their relationship. It would be disastrous. He stretched his neck, the bones clicking into place. The king and queen had questioned them after their return. Beniel was satisfied with their story, Adriana anything but. She seemed convinced they had coupled if her sly glances were anything to go by. Ramón didn't know what, if anything, the queen would do about her suspicion. Perhaps it didn't matter, especially if Benae ended up revealing their affair to Prince Zialni. He shook his head. *What a mess.*

And how *did* he feel about Benae? *That* he didn't care to explore. He had never imagined the act of joining could be so wonderful, but did that mean he loved her?

She seemed convinced of her love for him. A pang of guilt cut through him. His act, nay acts, of the night before last had been brutally disloyal to Benae's betrothed, and no matter the outcome, that could not be erased.

Benae's wedding gown was safely stowed in a large trunk but would it ever see the light of day? A cord of jealousy curled around his heart at the thought of her walking down the aisle toward Zialni. If it came to that he wouldn't stand by and watch his lover marry. He'd be long gone, on the road to finding Alecia, and after that, somewhere far from Brightcastle. But did all that mean he loved Benae, that they could form a life together if a miracle happened? *Too many questions!*

He had to tackle his problems one step at a time. First get Benae back to Brightcastle safely, then decide what to do about the prince.

* * *

Benae sighed and laid her head against the stuffed headrest of the carriage. They would reach Brightcastle later that day. She wished she could rid her mind of the swirling thoughts that possessed it. Sleep was the only respite she enjoyed from the crippling anxiety and guilt. She closed her eyes and used the relaxation exercises her father had taught her. Dear Papa had known her better than she knew herself. He realized she would suffer when he passed and had made her practice relaxation, even when she thought she didn't need it. Oh, how she wished he were still here. She wouldn't be in this position now, and more than that, she missed his sure presence at her side, his calm advice, his patient explanations, his love.

Tears threatened and Benae pushed the thoughts from her mind. Slowly, she contracted and relaxed her muscles, one area at a time. It did help; the tight bands that ran up her neck and down into her shoulders softened a little. Joletta was hardly helping, but she was a necessity. She couldn't travel to Brightcastle with Ramón and one hundred soldiers without a chaperone, so Queen Adriana had sent Joletta. However, over the course of the trip, Benae had grown weary with the need to converse when all she wished was to shut herself away in her box of pain. Joletta was a constant reminder that Merel was dead and Benae wasn't ready to replace the woman who had been as close as a sister. It wasn't Joletta's fault, but Benae had been driven to ask the maid only to speak when spoken to. Now the woman sat, lips pursed, working at her embroidery loop. She was never rude, but it was clear that Benae had deeply offended her. The way Benae felt now, she couldn't deal with Joletta's hurt feelings. They would have to be repaired later.

Ramón had been aloof in her presence. Was he trying to avoid suspicion, or did he truly want to distance himself from her? She loved him! She knew he had feelings for her, but were they strong enough for him to take a risk? Their night together had been magical, and she yearned to wrap herself around his body again. Adriana was wrong in one thing; coupling with Ramón hadn't quenched her desire, it had only fired it, confirmed her deep love for him. They had connected on a spiritual level and he was an ass if he didn't realize it. *Damn relaxation exercises!* Days of sitting in the carriage, worrying over the future, had her stomach churning, made her unfit for company. Flaire felt the same, probably because of her agitation. More than one soldier had commented on his prancing and snorting. Several had advised her not to ride such a flighty beast. *Oh, the arrogance of men!*

A wave of love passed through her as she thought of her stallion. His leg had healed brilliantly so far. By the time they reached Brightcastle it would be close to full strength. The first thing she intended to do was to take him for a gallop in the meadow. She sent him a mind message of them galloping through long grass and received joyful excitement back. Benae smiled. It was a treasure beyond worth to have this connection with Flaire and it had saved Ramón's life. *Ramón! Back to him again.* She sighed. Somehow, she would make their relationship work.

The carriage rolled to a halt in the castle forecourt but Benae didn't move. She couldn't bring herself to rise from her seat and alight, although Joletta stood waiting.

"You may leave the carriage, Joletta," she said.

The woman gave a low snort and descended from the conveyance. Ramón appeared in the doorway.

"Come, My Lady, let me help you down."

His smile was so formal Benae had to stifle a cry of frustration. "My Lady, indeed!" she hissed, turning to face him. "I won't allow you to do this, Ramón."

"Do what? Assist you from this carriage? Surely you've spent enough time in it of late?" His big blue eyes were the epitome of innocence. He didn't fool her for one second. She knew what he was trying to do, and it wouldn't work.

"We can't turn back the clock," she said, leaning toward him so her low words would carry. "What we did that night can't be forgotten, by myself or you. I won't marry Jiseve knowing I love you. I think you feel the same."

His gaze fell from hers. "My feelings are immaterial. Even if I understood them, they'd still be unimportant." His troubled eyes made her queasy. Perhaps she couldn't be so certain of his love. "The prince has first claim upon you and he won't step aside."

"How little you understand. Jiseve won't want me and I have time to decide how to tell him the truth. He won't return for days yet. I'll ensure we get what we want."

He reached for her hand. "Please, Benae, don't tell him. You risk everything if you do. You've made a commitment, now you must honor it."

"You and your honor," she said, frustration and fear sharpening her tone. She had been so sure of his love. Would he cast away his virginity if he didn't care deeply for her? Perhaps. She had given her maidenhead for a quick roll in the hayshed with a visiting lord's son. *What was his name? ... No matter.* At least Ramón had not given his away lightly. He wouldn't soon forget the night they had spent together.

"Please step down. The servants will gossip." He tugged on her hand.

"Is that all you care about? Appearances —" She froze as a familiar voice sounded outside the carriage.

"Where is she? The pigeons brought news of an attack —"

Ramón was shoved to the side and the bright light of two flaming torches held by soldiers fell upon her. Benae shielded her eyes but couldn't miss the sight of her betrothed, face set and sharp gaze raking her. He drew her from the carriage and pulled her to his chest, clutching her so tightly she could barely breathe. She accepted his embrace but couldn't bring herself to return it. He let her go and she dropped into a curtsy.

"Your Highness," she said.

The prince drew her to her feet. "So formal, Benae. There can be no ceremony between us this night. You are returned to me when I feared all was lost. Word came to me in the north and I cast aside my plans and returned home by the most direct path. I was preparing to ride east to find you." His eyes flicked to a point over her shoulder.

"Thank you for returning my lady to me, Squire," Prince Zialni said, his eyes burning. "I am in your debt."

Benae shivered at the chill in Jiseve's voice. Had he heard the rumors? Perhaps distraction was best.

"I lost Merel," Benae said, grief hitting her anew. "She died defending me against the dark elves. King Beniel granted her a heroine's funeral." Benae closed her eyes, her hands gripped tight before her and took a deep breath. "The queen gave me Joletta." She pointed to the maid, who curtsied.

Prince Zialni's eyes softened a touch. "You have endured much, my love. Come inside and tell me what you are able." Benae again curtsied to the prince and turned to Ramón. "Thank you, Squire, for bearing me safely home and for saving my life." She couldn't miss the concern in his eyes.

"Perhaps we'll talk of it later, My Lady." Ramón cast her a look that spoke volumes, then bowed and turned away, leading Flaire to the stables.

Benae knew he didn't wish for her to reveal their love affair, if love it was for him. He planned to resume his life, find the princess and earn the prince's undying gratitude. Benae wasn't part of his future at all. Yes, they must talk, and she must discover if there was hope for their relationship or if it was all one-sided. He would tell her once and for all. If the answer was no, she would marry Jiseve and make the best of it. A bleak shadow engulfed her heart.

Benae stood in front of the roaring fire in her chamber, fingers against her lips, her mind on the kiss she had just shared with Jiseve. So much had changed in the time she had been away. She had been irrevocably altered by Ramón, but was certain Jiseve had expressed more passion, more love in the early days of their relationship than he had just now. It couldn't just be her perception could it? How could he have discovered her infidelity or even suspect it?

The answer was he could not. Only she and Ramón knew the truth. The change she felt must be all on her side and due to her altered feelings. Could Jiseve sense her withdrawal? Perhaps that was it.

She hadn't seen Ramón since their arrival three hours ago and already she missed his steady presence. She must speak with him; must know if they had a chance. Her decision had appeared so certain on the trip home, but now she doubted her squire; doubted he really wanted her and her alone. There was a sound behind her, and she turned to find the tapestry, of a beautiful, golden-haired queen at her coronation, bulging inwards. Before she could move, Ramón stepped into her chambers.

"Oh, my love," she said, and flung herself into his arms. He trembled as he gathered her close, as if his desire warred with some other emotion. He lowered his head and his mouth captured hers. Days of holding in their emotions exploded in one heated, passionate kiss. He pulled away, his breath ragged. Benae clung to his arm. She didn't care if she seemed desperate, eager; she was all those things.

"Stay with me. Love me," she said.

"We can't risk it, Lady." The distance in his voice belied the agitation that was plain to see.

"How can you be so controlled?" she asked. "I *love* you. I can't stand to be parted from you. I want to know you feel the same!" Benae stared at him but, as the seconds ticked by and he made no response, fear replaced desire. "Ramón?"

"I desire you, but is that love? It doesn't feel pure and innocent; it's a raging fire and I dare not let myself succumb. If I did, I couldn't walk away. I'm holding myself by the barest thread. The days on the road have been agony. I couldn't keep my eyes from you and yet I knew if I gazed as I wished to, it would only bring disaster."

Benae drank in every word he said, like a thirsty woman in the desert. He did love her. The blazing fire of her love matched his. All would be well. "Lie with me. I need your body against mine, within mine." She watched the battle inside him and held her breath.

"I can't," he whispered, clutching her upper arms. He pulled her close and kissed her. Benae's knees went weak and she would have fallen if he hadn't held her. The kiss deepened, stirring her innermost needs, driving her mad.

"I won't lie with you again until we're free to love each other," he said. "We must do this the correct way now. No more sneaking around."

"Then let's tell him this night and be done with it. Once my engagement is over, we can be wed in all haste. Jiseve will step aside, I know he will."

Ramón frowned. "I hope that's the case."

Benae could see he didn't share her optimism, but no matter. If Jiseve didn't give his blessing, they would find some other way to be together. She'd never give up on him. "Let us wake him and tell him now."

Ramón shook his head. "We are both tired. Let's sleep on the decision and act in the morn. Meet me in the breakfast room an hour before the meal and we'll talk. We can tell the prince then if we so decide."

Benae nodded. "It shall be as you say."

Ramón walked to the tapestry and she followed. He turned back to her and she pressed a kiss to his mouth. She longed to make him stay but didn't know if she could. He was a stubborn man. Best to follow his wishes and he had said he wished to wait. She stepped away. He opened the wall and disappeared into the passage, the stone closing with a low grinding. *A secret passage!* Her mind buzzed with the possibilities, but she wouldn't need to sneak around to see Ramón after tomorrow. Somehow, they would be together.

One way or another, she'd have him *and* save her people.

CHAPTER 16

RAMÓN paced across the breakfast room, stomach in knots that no amount of tea would settle. Benae stood near the window, outwardly calm, but he suspected she marked the passage of every second that brought the confrontation with the prince closer.

He kept repeating the same mantra his father had always told him. *All will be well, have faith.* Last night, with Benae, he had finally admitted to himself he loved her. Perhaps he had loved Alecia as well, but what he felt for Benae was fire and tempest and he was unable to ignore it.

He had never thought of himself as a passionate man; more careful, deliberate. Benae unleashed a side of himself that surprised him, gave him courage, made him want to risk everything to secure her love, her happiness. She wanted *him*, not some aging prince who could give her prestige and possessions.

They both jumped as Prince Zialni strode into the room. He came to an abrupt halt as he saw them waiting for him.

"Good morning, Benae, Squire." He frowned, seeming to note the tension in the room. "What is amiss? Has someone died?" He smirked at his jest, looking first at Benae and then Ramón, sobering when neither spoke. "Well?"

Benae stepped forward. "Your Highness, I do have something to tell you. I don't quite know how to start."

The prince's eyes narrowed. "Something that involves the squire, no doubt?"

Benae inclined her head. "I'm ashamed to say I've broken my promise to you."

Prince Zialni froze, like a snake before a mongoose. "What promise do you speak of?"

"My betrothal."

Ramón would have spoken up if he thought it would help, but he knew it wouldn't. He would only speak if asked.

"How?" Jiseve's query came out strangled, jaw clenched, and eyes riveted to Benae's face.

Oh Goddess, I was right all along. He'll destroy us!

The silence stretched.

Benae finally broke it. "I have lain with the squire."

Ramón took a deep breath and met the prince's furious eyes.

"I placed my lady under your protection, and you betrayed me?" He turned to Benae. "And you, Lady, agreed to be my wife and bear my children, yet slept with the first man who happened by?"

"Jiseve, it wasn't like that," Benae said, wringing her hands. "When I agreed to wed you, I didn't know that I'd fall in love with Ramón."

"In love! Spare me." He strode to the fireplace and spun to face them. "Lady, you don't have the luxury to marry for love. I've just returned from caring for your people. They welcomed the bridegroom of their lady, were overjoyed when I left more soldiers to reinforce their military." His gaze cut through to Ramón. "You, Squire, I thought to *wed* to Alecia when she returned. I *hoped* you would find her for me. You could have been my *son-in-law!*"

Crushing pain hit Ramón's chest as each of the prince's words fired home. What Ramón had long hoped for had been about to come true; a union with Alecia. Finally, he had won the respect of his employer, only to lose it.

The old Ramón within, wilted beneath Jiseve's contemptuous gaze, but the Ramón who loved Benae squared his shoulders. "I love Lady Benae and she loves me. I'm sorry I betrayed you. My feelings were too powerful to resist."

Fury was evident in every line of the prince's body. He snorted. "Lust! You both have been swayed by lust. It's not love you have for one another. Look at my betrothed, Squire. What man would not want to bed her? *Most* would be deterred by her betrothal. I thought I could trust you!"

"Jiseve, I wish to be released from our betrothal," Benae said quietly.

There was absolute silence in the room. Ramón held his breath. Prince Zialni glared at him and then at Benae. "Out of the question," he snapped.

Benae grabbed his arms. "I love him, Jiseve. You don't wish to marry a woman who loves another. You're too proud a man for that."

"What do you think it will do to my pride when the populace discovers my bride has rejected me for the *squire*," he sneered. "I will not hear of you breaking our engagement. The wedding goes ahead as planned. In one week's time, you will be my wife and you *will* produce an heir for the kingdom. That is all that matters. My daughter betrayed me and now you, Lady, have done the same, but no one will know of *your* betrayal. We will wed in one week, before the king."

Ramón's heart broke, not for himself, but for Benae, who clutched her stomach as if a fire seared her insides. She stared unblinking at her betrothed, eyes wide and spasms wracking her throat. He coughed. "You'll not wish me to continue in my role, Your Highness. I'll prepare to vacate the castle."

Prince Zialni's face tightened as fury swept over it. "Vacate the castle," he shouted. "I should kill you!" His hand moved to his sword.

Ramón prepared to fight for his life, though he was weaponless. It would be a poor contest.

The prince drew a deep breath and his hand dropped from his weapon. "You will stay and continue your duties as before. Perhaps I will still send you in search of Princess Alecia. Be in no doubt, you will suffer for what you have done." His glance took in Benae as well. "You will both suffer."

Benae's eyes watered as she stood with one hand over her mouth, the other on her stomach. "I won't do this, Jiseve. I can't be without him."

"Oh, you will see your squire, Lady. He will be under your nose night and day, but you will not touch each other. He will watch as I make a proper wife of you, as you bear my children, and he will *never* have you." He turned to Ramón. "You may go now, Squire."

Ramón looked to Benae, but she stood as before, only her eyes were closed. *How had it ever come to this?*

"Leave!" The prince's barked command brought him back to the moment. He bowed and left the breakfast room. He could check on Benae later. *All will be well, have faith.*

* * *

A tear slid down Benae's cheek as Joletta fastened the buttons down the back of her wedding gown. This should be the happiest day of her life and instead she felt ill. She hadn't slept properly in a week. When she did sleep, she was haunted by nightmares. She longed to talk with Ramón, to assuage the loneliness she felt. Even time with Flaire didn't banish the deep pit of despair inside her.

"You look beautiful, My Lady," Joletta said, as she fastened the last button.

Benae knew she was far from her best. The luster had gone from her hair and skin and, despite Joletta's skill with paints and powders, the dark smudges beneath her eyes were obvious. She sighed. It would have to do. She didn't care to be beautiful for Jiseve.

Her bridegroom had been cold with her all week. Would he punish her for the rest of their married life? She hadn't thought he had it in him to be cruel, but he had threatened to kill Ramón if she didn't hold to her word. She dared not tell Ramón of the threat. She feared he would respond by challenging Jiseve to a duel. No matter the outcome, Ramón would be doomed. She couldn't bear to lose the center of her universe.

So, she let Ramón believe she had agreed not to break the engagement in order to keep her word and to keep her people safe. Ramón understood sentiments such as those. He was a man of honor; he knew people mattered. Jiseve had her just where he needed her *and* keeping secrets from her lover. *What a muddle!* For his part, Ramón seemed to have returned to his old life, though he spent even more time at weapons practice than he had in the past. He had entered Brightcastle town on several occasions this past week. Perhaps he was planning to leave in search of Princess Alecia or just leave altogether.

Benae couldn't bear to imagine of him in the arms of another woman. Small chance it would be Alecia's arms. Jiseve would never allow it now. Yes, they had certainly burned all their bridges.

"I hear the music, Lady Benae. It's time we headed to the audience chamber." Joletta's voice intruded on Benae and she suppressed a stab of anger. The woman was a far cry from Merel. *Dear, sweet Merel…*

"Yes," Benae said, gathering her skirts, "Let's go." She swept from the room and down the hall, the maid trailing in her wake. Descending the stairs, Benae crossed the entry hall to the open doors of the audience chamber. The music altered to the bridal march as she stood at the threshold of the room and her new life. All eyes turned toward her, full of happiness, as they should be at this joy-filled occasion. She swallowed hard and squared her shoulders. Her attendant, Sofia, one of the Queen's ladies-in-waiting, stepped behind Benae to manage the five yards of lace that trailed.

Benae looked to the front of the chamber. Jiseve waited at the end of the carpet, before the priestess. A balding, blond man stood beside him; his nephew Piotr. The younger man had been asked to stand up for the prince, though, as next in line after Jiseve for the throne, there was no love lost between the two. King Beniel and Queen Adriana were seated on thrones on the dais. Benae felt the full weight of their stares as she stepped upon the carpet between the last row of guests. Ramón was there, at the rear of the room, his blue eyes shining at her. She cast only the briefest of glances in his direction for fear her resolve would fail and she'd run into his arms.

She couldn't. There was too much at stake. The secrets she held isolated her as thoroughly as if Jiseve had imprisoned her. She plastered a smile on her lips and slowly walked the twenty paces until she reached Jiseve's side. He was the epitome of the mature bridegroom; handsome, graying at the temples, a broad smile on his face and the jaunty air of the man who had never expected to be so blessed. Only his eyes gave him away. They were like chips of ice. Benae hid the shudder that wriggled up her spine at the thought of being intimate with him. She had made her choice many weeks ago when she embarked upon this rescue mission. She could give Jiseve what he desired and if she couldn't have what she most craved, well, she would have children to love and a nation to protect. The fear in her stomach settled and she smiled up at her prince.

* * *

Ramón punched the wood of the stable door, ignoring the sharp pain that flooded through his fingers. *I've lost her!* Benae now belonged to the prince. Who was he deceiving? She had always belonged to Jiseve Zialni. He'd have to stand by and watch while Benae gave herself to the kingdom, to Brightcastle. Soon there would be children and each child would bond her more firmly to her husband. How could she have gone through with it? Each of her steps upon that carpet had been agony for him, and with every one, he had expected her to falter, to turn, look at him and dash into his arms.

But she had walked steadily down the long runner and straight up to Jiseve Zialni, giving him such a beautiful smile on her arrival that all would believe she was just where she wanted to be. Perhaps she was. Perhaps Benae had come to terms with her choices, her promises. Honor dictated that she keep her vow to the prince and Benae was brave enough to make that sacrifice. She cared enough for her people to put her happiness aside.

Where did that leave him? Condemned to watch her with another man? Ramón couldn't stand by if the prince treated Benae with contempt. Equally, he couldn't bear to watch if their marriage succeeded. Today she had appeared a bride in love.

In that moment, he had his answer. He'd stay until he knew Benae was safe and happy then leave Brightcastle forever. He'd return to Wildecoast. It was where he should have stayed. Even if he must work his family farm forever, at least he wouldn't have to watch Benae with a clutch of Zialni children.

***

The wedding feast was over. Joletta prepared Benae for her first night with her husband. Benae had drunk too much but it was the only way she could forget the pain she had seen in Ramón's eyes. They danced briefly, and he had wished her well. It had sounded like goodbye. Her squire left the feast soon after and she had turned to the wine. Numb, she might make it through this night.

Once Joletta had dressed her in the flimsy, floaty night attire, Benae donned her dressing gown and left her rooms, heading for Jiseve's suite. Horrible, great, hairy moths battered her stomach. She wanted only Ramón's arms around her, but she must tolerate Jiseve's attentions or risk the life of her lover. She sighed and shook her head, imagining the weeks and months ahead.

She slipped through the door to Jiseve's suite, closed it behind her and crossed the sitting room to his bedroom. He stood by the window and turned as he heard her.

"I never thought this day would come," he said. "When I lost my first wife, it felt like my world was ending. I vowed never to replace her."

Benae crossed to him and stood gazing up into the shadows of his face. "Why did you change your mind?"

"I realized the kingdom was more important than my love for Iona. You are a beautiful woman. I thought we could forge a strong relationship together."

"I am sorry, Jiseve. I never meant to betray you."

"You thought you could use me to save your people."

A deep chill swept Benae. Would he renege on his promise? "What do you mean?"

"Oh, do not fear, *Princess*. I would not go back on my word. You have wed me and so I am bound to care for your estates and their inhabitants. They belong to me now. You need never fear for them as long as this marriage holds true. You will produce heirs for the kingdom and not a word of the scandal of your affair with Ramón Zorba will *ever* reach the ears of the populace."

Benae frowned. Wasn't it a little late for that? Perhaps Jiseve didn't know of the court gossip at Wildecoast. It would die down soon enough, and the memory of the lady and the squire would fade in time. Brightcastle might never hear much of it.

"I married you and here I am," she said.

His eyes flicked over her. Benae experienced the chilling certainty that she was now another of Jiseve Zialni's prized possessions. He drew her into his arms, his lips claiming hers. Benae imagined the mouth and arms of another as Jiseve claimed her.

* * *

Ramón woke in a sweat, the sheets tangled around his legs, heart pounding. The last vestiges of the nightmare clung to him. He had been watching the prince couple with Benae. Except it wasn't just a nightmare. Over in the west wing, Jiseve Zialni slept with his bride, with the woman Ramón loved. Already they were man and wife in the true sense of the word.

Ramón gained only fleeting satisfaction from knowing he had loved Benae first. How was he to live under the same roof while the prince made free with her body night after night? *His* body burned with the need to take her in his arms and join with her. They had danced tonight, briefly, and it had almost been beyond Ramón's ability to let her go. He had been swept by a mad impulse to run with her from the ballroom and into the night, but she had been so distant.

Perhaps she truly did want this marriage.

CHAPTER 17

TWO weeks had elapsed since the wedding and Benae's life had settled into a dull routine, broken only by her rides on Flaire. Jiseve never accompanied her, preferring to send two female soldiers he had specially trained as her bodyguards. Briette and Florenna were stiffly polite on their rides but they could not have been called friends or confidants. She had the feeling they disapproved of her.

Flaire had just been rubbed down by the groom, who had left to attend to another task. Benae's presence in the stables made the workers uncomfortable. They weren't used to royalty under their feet. She placed her forehead on Flaire's and inhaled his horsey scent, filling her mind with his joy. Flaire was always content after a run in the meadow. It took so little to make him happy. She wished she were like him.

Footsteps sounded behind her and she turned to find Ramón. He wore tan breeches and a deep-blue vest over a snowy shirt. The hem of a cobalt-blue cape swirled around his calves. The cloak accentuated the breadth of his shoulders and she suppressed a wild impulse to run her hands over them. His glorious eyes dulled a little when he saw her.

"Princess," he said, the formality of his words piercing her heart.

"Must you be so formal?" she replied quietly.

"I think it wise to keep a distance. You're a married woman." The muscles of his throat jerked. "How are you?"

"I'm well. Why haven't you visited?"

"You don't know how many nights I've lain awake thinking of you in his arms. I stay away because it's the only way I can endure this… marriage."

Benae's heart ached at the pain in his voice. She didn't wish to increase his distress, yet… "I miss you." The words burst from her, aching loneliness carrying them forth.

"I'm here now." He stepped closer and brushed her cheek with the back of his fingers. "You're not sleeping." His eyes darted around the stable, checking they were still alone.

Benae closed her eyes, his touch making her weak. Perhaps loneliness was preferable to this aching need she felt when he caressed her. She opened her eyes, focused on his words. "Jiseve pursues his husbandly privileges assiduously. It's nothing for us to couple three or four times a night."

Pain flashed across Ramón's face. "Does he hurt you?"

"Sometimes. It seems he is impatient for his heir."

Ramón shut his eyes as if the picture she painted were impossible to bear. When he opened them, he seemed determined. "I'll take you away from this."

Hope flared in her heart. She imagined Ramón whisking her from Jiseve's bed and them galloping across the countryside. No doubt pursued by dark elves. The hope quickly died. "You know it's pointless to fight this. I made a promise and we did the wrong thing. I love you and I always will, but I can't be with you." She gathered herself for the words that would set him free. "You must make a life for yourself."

Ramón drew her into his arms, gazing down at her as if she were a precious figurine that might crumble if he gripped her too firmly.

"There will be no one else for me," he said. "It's you and will always be you." His mouth lowered to hers and he kissed her as if for the last time, tenderly and then more demanding as she responded, her mouth opening, his tongue exploring. When he broke off, his breathing was ragged. He pushed past her and continued down the stable. Benae gave Flaire one last pat and left.

* * *

Ramón shoved two changes of clothes into his saddlebags. Seeing Benae in the stable this morning had confirmed one thing. He couldn't go on watching her married life. He could still feel her lips on his and his manhood stirred at the memory. She was an addiction he couldn't fight and so he must cut her from his world. She might not like her existence, but she had accepted it. He must accept it too, but he was not yet prepared to leave for Wildecoast. Better to resume the search for Alecia and Anton. If he could return Alecia to her father, perhaps some good would come of it. The kingdom needed her, and Anton must pay the price for his part in the affair. Ramón's insides turned queasy at the thought that he had allowed this sorry state of affairs to occur, first with Alecia's escape and then with Benae. When it came to the women in his life, his judgement left a lot to be desired.

He exited his chambers and headed for the central staircase. In the hallway opposite, he spied a light under Benae's door. Wanting to bid her farewell, he ghosted up the corridor, knocked and the door swung inward. Benae stood there. He caught a glimpse of her curves through the sheer fabric of the nightgown before she drew a heavier robe across her chest.

"Come in." Dark smudges lay beneath her eyes and her face had a gauntness that hadn't been there this morning. "You're leaving," she said, staring at the saddlebags slung over his shoulder. "I wish you wouldn't."

The pain of her words made him stagger. "You told me to make a life for myself. That's what I'm trying to do."

"That was before I …things have changed." She looked even more tired, sicker than she had been in the stable.

"What has changed?" Surely she couldn't expect him to stick around like some kind of extra leg.

"I'm pregnant."

Ramón's breath whooshed from his body and he staggered over to a nearby chair. *It cannot be!* His gaze flicked to her belly. "How do you know?"

Benae rolled her eyes. "I'm late for my monthly bleed and ill in the mornings. Today the sickness lasted all day. I've been suspicious for days and now must face the truth."

Ramón couldn't accept that another man's seed might have quickened inside his love. "You could just be late."

She stepped closer to him. Ramón fought the urge to fold her into his arms as her jasmine fragrance swirled around him. "It's too soon to be Jiseve's. This is your babe."

Ramón shook his head and turned away from Benae in the hope that distance might order his fuzzy mind. This could not be happening. One night of loving couldn't result in a child, couldn't alter their lives forever. He turned and walked back to her, grasping her upper arms. "I'm to be a father?"

Benae nodded, tears in her eyes.

"It couldn't be your husband's?"

"It's unlikely." She placed her hands on her stomach, rubbed it gently up and down, then reached for his hand and placed it beneath her own. "This is our child, Ramón."

He swallowed several times before he found his voice. "Our child." Wonder uncurled the tight fingers of dread that had wrapped around his heart since Benae's wedding. He was to be a father and he suddenly couldn't wait to cradle his new son or daughter. He emerged from his reverie to find Benae frowning up at him.

"You're right, beloved," he said, one hand on her belly and the other cupping her chin. "This does change everything."

"What will you do?"

The question from Benae puzzled him. What did she mean? And then he remembered he had been on the verge of leaving. Well, not now. Not when he had Benae and her child to care for. "I'll stay, of course. We'll face this together." The prince would be furious that a child had resulted from their affair. Suddenly Ramón was troubled. How would Zialni react?

"Does the prince know?"

"No, I'll not tell him for several weeks. He won't believe it's his if I tell him now."

"He won't believe…" Ramón swallowed hard and pulled his hands from Benae's body. "You can't mean to lie about this babe!" The dreaded fingers clutched his heart again, but now they squeezed so tightly, a red mist clouded his vision.

Benae clutched his elbows. "Think Ramón, the only way I can safeguard my life and that of the babe is to allow my husband to believe it's his. This way our safety is assured. I've thought long and hard on this."

"You've not discussed it with me." Ramón pulled from her grasp. "Goddess, Benae, I'm the father."

"Keep your voice down," she snapped.

He stared at her, not able to believe she could leave him out of this. "It seems you've thought of everything."

"You'll support my deception? I can't do this if you don't agree."

Ramón had never felt more trapped. The urge to flee returned. Perhaps with distance and another purpose would come clarity? "I'll hold your secret in my heart, but I won't stay to watch you grow large with my seed."

"My love, I would not have you suffer, but I can't bear this if you leave. You give me strength just knowing you're near. Please, please stay."

Ramón gazed down into her eyes, shining with tears, and the ache in his throat intensified. *Goddess this is so unfair!*

"I can't. You know I dread the thought of him on you at night." A sudden fear struck, making him cold. "You said he sometimes hurts you. Will he harm the babe in his frantic efforts to produce an heir?"

"I don't believe the child will be hurt and I can bear it for another two weeks, more if I have to."

Ramón's stomach was sick to think of it. Perhaps when she told the prince about the baby, he would leave her alone and Ramón could depart. If Benae could tolerate another two weeks of abuse, surely he could stay and support her. Couldn't he?

"I'll stay for now."

"For now, Ramón? This is *your* child."

"He'll have a father's love." Ramón gazed deep into Benae's eyes. "Just not mine." He'd never be able to acknowledge his child or have a future with Benae. Their wild dreams of a life together were just that; dreams.

Her eyes dropped. "That's how it must be. Only you and I will ever know."

"Better to walk away than to watch another man raise my son." He bowed to her and withdrew, his saddlebags slapping against his back as he returned to his room.

* * *

Despair engulfed Benae as Ramón departed. All she wished was to throw herself into his arms and forget about her farce of a marriage. *Oh Goddess, why did you send me this man to love?* Life would be easier if she had never met Ramón, never felt his arms around her, his lips on hers. But there was no point wishing. The babe inside her simplified yet complicated matters further. At least she would be able to give Jiseve a child. He'd be overjoyed when she told him. She prayed it would be a boy.

She had hurt Ramón and it was a hurt that she couldn't mend. She needed him so much and yet she couldn't bear to think of him tormented by watching her body bloom, knowing he'd never be a father to his child. Selfishly, she hoped he wouldn't be able to leave but what would come of that? More stolen moments in the stable? Sooner or later someone would discover them together.

Jiseve was still coldly angry with them. Benae had no choice but to comply with every one of her husband's demands. He threatened Ramón's life almost every night and rejoiced in describing the horrible death he'd inflict upon the squire should she deny him. She truly didn't know how much more rough treatment she could take. Two weeks —

that was all that was needed before she could announce her pregnancy. Ramón must remain ignorant of the full extent of Jiseve's attentions; must not discover the tortures he inflicted on her almost every night, nor suspect the wounds she sustained on his behalf. *Oh Goddess, I never imagined a man could be so cruel.*

The babe must live. She couldn't truly believe Jiseve would hurt that most precious part of her where he deposited his seed each night.

CHAPTER 18

A WEEK later, Ramón was finishing weapons practice as Benae returned from a ride. As he replaced his practice sword and shrugged into his shirt and tunic, he watched her dismount under Briette's watchful eye. She staggered and would have collapsed had Briette not steadied her. Floretta lead Flaire away and Briette helped Benae into the castle. A spike of fear sliced through Ramón. What had happened? Had she hurt herself on the ride? Fallen maybe? His heart leaped into a frantic drumming rhythm and he rushed from the practice yard, across the graveled drive and into the castle. Benae was just starting up the staircase with her guard.

He gripped her arm and Benae turned. The smudges beneath her eyes were even darker than they had been last week. His jaw clenched with the effort of controlling his anger at seeing her in this state.

"Leave us," he said to Briette, his voice harsh. "I'll attend the princess."

Briette hesitated then nodded and departed.

"What has happened, Benae? Did you fall from your horse?"

She staggered and as he threw his arm about her waist, she winced.

"Speak to me!"

"Take me to my room."

Slowly they ascended the stairs and limped to Benae's chamber. Once he had opened the door, Ramón swept her into his arms, crossed the sitting room and entered her bedchamber.

"Leave now. He must not see you here."

She trembled and turned her head into his shoulder. As Ramón deposited her gently upon the big four-poster bed, her riding costume hitched up and he spied a dark bruise on her ankle. His fingers caressed the damaged skin and Benae gasped.

"What's this?" he asked. "Is it the cause of the limp?

"Flaire bumped me against a tree," she said. "He can be clumsy."

Ramón glared at her. "Flaire wouldn't allow you to scrape your leg against anything, let alone a tree."

"It's the truth, Ramón." She didn't meet his eyes.

He examined the other ankle and found similar, though lesser bruising, there. "I suppose he bumped this leg as well?"

"It's nothing. Thank you for bringing me up. You must leave."

"I can't leave you injured. I'm calling the physician."

"If Jiseve finds out the physician has been called —"

"Why would the prince object to you receiving medical help?" Grabbing her arm, he pushed the sleeve of her dress to the elbow and gasped, fear for her almost stopping his heart. There was ugly bruising on her arm above the elbow. "He did this to you."

"I'm well, Ramón. Don't interfere."

"You're not well. Tell me how these marks came to be here, or I swear I'll find your husband and ask him myself."

Benae swallowed hard, glancing around the room as if seeking inspiration.

"Tell me the truth," he said, his voice barely a whisper.

Her eyes filled with tears as she gazed up at him. He sat on the edge of the bed and gripped both her hands.

"He ties me up to his bed most nights and I struggle. That's where the marks come from. He ties my arms by the elbows, so the bruises don't show."

"Why would he need to tie you up? You'd lie with him willingly, no?"

She nodded. "He hurts me. He ties me up to keep me still."

"What does he do, Benae?"

She closed her eyes as if gathering strength. "He bites me, especially on my breasts. He pushes a cloth in my mouth so I can't scream. The cruelty seems to arouse him, make him hard, and then he pounds into me. I've never felt so helpless."

Ramón stared at her in shock, imagining his lovely Benae being tortured. "You can't allow this to continue. He'll hurt you or the babe."

"He's angry with me. Once I tell him I'm with child, I'm sure he'll be gentler."

Ramón pushed off the bed and paced to the window and back. He was more than ready to rip the head off her husband. That he could do this to a woman…

"I'll find a way to get you out of this, Benae. You'll not put up with him for another night." He fled the room, ignoring her pleas for him to return.

Ramón found the house easily once he had asked directions of the locals. Alecia had trusted him enough to tell him some details of her friend Hetty, which allowed him to trace her to this district. The rest was easy. The princess had spoken of Hetty as a wise woman, but Ramón was a country boy and he knew the term "wise woman" was synonymous with witch. Hetty's help was just what he needed this night, just what Benae needed.

He had run long and hard after leaving Benae. His anger had settled to a stomach-churning acid burn instead of the raging bonfire it had been. He wouldn't act in anger as he once had. He could challenge the prince to his face but the outcome of that couldn't be assured. One of them would be the loser and if it were he, Benae would be left exposed. Better to get help from another quarter and leave himself free to observe and rescue Benae if needed. That was where Hetty came in.

He found the door and knocked. The hollow sound echoed in the quiet street and a dog barked nearby. The door opened a crack and an old woman peered through it. He couldn't see her face, merely her outline against the flickering light in the room behind.

"Hello, Hetty, I'm Squire Ramón Zorba and I need your help."

"I know who you are." She peered at him a few moments longer and he felt a prickle of something across his scalp. "Come in."

She stepped aside and Ramón squeezed through the gap she left in the doorway. She closed the door and bolted it behind him. "Follow me."

He trailed her to the kitchen where a pot bubbled over the fire. The stench was almost unbearable but when Ramón tried to take his mind off the smell by studying the old woman, he became even more disconcerted. Her eyes were almost black and seemed to look straight through him, to see all his secrets. He remembered the itch over his scalp at the front door and shivered. She seemed unafraid and Ramón wondered how powerful she really was. Her craggy old face was wreathed in wrinkles and her silver-gray hair spiked from her scalp in crazy, zigzag patterns that defied restraint.

"What help do you imagine an old woman such as I can give you?"

"You were a friend to Princess Alecia."

"Don't speak of her in the past tense. She'll return one day to claim her birthright."

"Do you know of her whereabouts?" Ramón didn't mean to snap out the question.

"Is that why you've come? To find the princess?"

Ramón frowned. "No. I come on another matter. I need help for Princess Benae."

"Ah, the prince's new wife? Is there trouble in paradise?"

"More trouble than you know."

"Why should I help you, or him?"

"You wouldn't be helping the prince, Hetty." Ramón paused, not sure how much to reveal.

"You're in love with Princess Benae?"

"This has nothing to do with how I feel. She's in danger. He ties her up and bites her and once he is aroused, he...She's defenseless against him."

"She's not defenseless. Why doesn't she refuse him?"

Ramón paused to consider Hetty's words. The old woman was right. Benae could refuse the prince. She was strong enough. Did he drug her or was he holding something over her, threatening her with worse if she didn't comply?

"It doesn't matter why. I must stop him. Will you help or not?"

Hetty's eyes narrowed. If she didn't have some miracle to offer, he'd be forced to act on his own.

"Princess Alecia would want me to offer what I could to a woman in trouble, even that perpetuated by her own father." Hetty considered for a moment longer. "You must buy an object for the prince. I believe his birthday is in two days. I'll enchant the item and you will give it to him as a birthday present."

"I'll buy him a signet ring. He was ever a fan of jewelry," Ramón said. "What will you do to the ring?"

"The spell I cast will make Prince Zialni impotent. His rod won't perform as long as he wears the ring."

"That will anger him. Benae could be more at risk."

"I know the prince. He'll be mortified. He may be angered at first but will soon run and hide. You may lurk outside the room in case the princess needs you, but I don't think it will be necessary, unless to untie your lady."

"Can it really work?

"All that's required is that your gift be sufficiently attractive to the prince for him to wear it. You know his taste."

Ramón nodded, his thoughts racing as he pieced the plot together. "I'll purchase the ring tomorrow and come straight to you. I don't want Benae to be tormented a night more than is necessary."

* * *

As Benae brushed her hair, her haunted eyes gazed back at her. She had not seen Ramón since yesterday when he told her he'd help. He hadn't helped and now she had endured another night of torture from her husband. Soon she must again meet him in his rooms. Where was

Ramón? Was he planning anything? She berated herself for relying on him, but a part of her wanted to be rescued. She sighed. Wasn't that how she came to be in this state? Seeking rescue from Prince Zialni for her people? *When will I ever learn?*

It was time to meet her husband. Benae checked her appearance and sighed again. No matter what she did, she couldn't banish the dark smudges beneath her eyes. Pulling on her thick dressing gown, she left her room and walked down the hall to Jiseve's chambers. He answered the door at her knock and drew her into his bedchamber, pushing her down on the bed.

"Can we not dispense with the straps tonight, Jiseve? I'm worried someone will see the bruises."

"You had better ensure no one notices your injuries." He pulled off her dressing gown and pushed the sleeves of her nightgown above the elbow. With practiced efficiency, he secured the leather straps and tightened them until they pinched her skin. She tried to suppress the whimper his rough treatment brought but she couldn't. Jiseve smiled at her distress. Once he had her arms tied, he moved onto her ankles and fastened them. Within seconds she lost all feeling in her feet.

"What present will you give me tomorrow, wife?" Jiseve asked. "The news that you are with child would be welcome."

Benae gasped. Had he guessed? He must not know yet. "It's too soon to know if I'm pregnant," Benae said through gritted teeth. Her arms burned and her fingers were going numb.

Jiseve pushed up her nightgown to reveal her naked lower body. She was so vulnerable like this, spread-eagled and trussed so she could barely move. "Your lover has already given me my birthday gift." He waggled his right hand at her. A signet ring with a ruby stone adorned his right ring finger. "Is it not handsome?"

Benae couldn't speak. She nodded because she had learned not to ignore her husband. Why had Ramón given Jiseve a gift? It was the last thing she would've expected. She didn't understand. Was he trying to lull Jiseve into a false sense of security?

Jiseve fell upon her bare chest and bit her nipple. A scream ripped through her, tears springing from her eyes. Damn her weakness. Now he'd gag her, and she hated being gagged. Sure enough, he pulled a square of cloth from his sleeve, stuffed it into her mouth then returned to alternately kissing and biting her breasts.

She was choking, saliva pooling in her throat, fear and tears making it difficult to get her breath. Was this it? Would she die in this moment, her child unborn? Benae writhed under him, her pelvis jerking as she tried to pull against her bonds. Through a mist of tears and a fog of semi consciousness she watched her husband drag his breeches from his hips, ready for the coupling that was a finale to his torture.

His rod freed, Jiseve knelt over her and plunged himself into her core, making her scream anew. Tonight, he was more frantic than before, thrusting harder and harder as if he were trying to burrow into her. Fear for her unborn child almost overcame her fear of asphyxia. Surely her babe couldn't withstand this treatment. She tried to think of a tranquil lake but the only picture that came to mind was a storm-tossed sea.

Suddenly he stiffened then collapsed upon her, his body trembling with his release. The first of several couplings for the evening was over. Benae tried to swallow the moisture that pooled in her throat, but it was nigh impossible with the rag in her mouth. She sobbed, wriggling under him, desperate for him to remove her gag. Surely, he would do that much?

Jiseve didn't move. His body relaxed, his weight pressed down upon her and a new panic gripped Benae. She wiggled and bucked but he couldn't be shifted no matter what she did. What was wrong? He wasn't moving. He wasn't breathing… Could Jiseve be dead? With the thought, that she was stuck under the body of her dead husband, came sheer mind-blowing panic. She thrashed about, trying to tip him off her, but his deadweight held him fast. In her struggles, her fist must have flown out to the side. The bedside lamp fell to the floor with a crash. Oil spilled and flame exploded along with it. The carpet beside the bed was alight in seconds, flame creeping toward the bedcovers. Once it reached the bed she'd be beyond help.

"Benae! Are you here?" Ramón's voice floated to her through the haze of her fear and she spied his face at the door of the bedroom. "Goddess!"

He charged over to the bedside, rolled the carpet over the fire to starve it of air then hurled a blanket across the top of it all. He pushed Jiseve's body off her and Benae flinched at the horror on his face. It was only there a split second before he dragged her nightdress down to cover her and pulled the gag from her mouth.

Benae drew a long, ragged breath once the cloth was removed. Her gaze found her husband's body. The startled expression on his face might have been funny in different circumstances. Ramón had the leather cuffs untied in mere moments and stood massaging the blood back into her lifeless extremities. He didn't speak. His eyes, hard as flint, made Benae hold her tongue. *What now?*

"Say something, Ramón," she said.

Instead, he gave her ankles another brisk rub and pulled her to a seated position on the bed, his eyes avoiding hers. Still silent, he retrieved her dressing gown and pulled it around her shoulders. He scooped her up and carried her from the room, down the hall to her chambers. Fire still warmed her sitting room and Ramón sat her gently in the chair that was drawn up to the hearth. "I'll return shortly," he said as he left.

Benae didn't know how to react. She couldn't rejoice in the death of another being, but it was an enormous relief to be free of his torment, to know she didn't have to endure another night of Jiseve's attentions. Her breasts throbbed with the injuries he had inflicted just moments ago, and she would carry the scars for weeks. She tried to slow her breathing, using the flames in the hearth to distract her from the image of her husband lying stiff upon her. She heard a noise and looked up. Ramón stood in the doorway.

"I've called the guard and the physician. I laid the prince out, covered him with a sheet and disposed of the leather cuffs. There's no need for others to know what torture you've suffered." Ramón looked like he had been tortured as well. His eyes darted around the room, not meeting her gaze and he pulled on his fringe hard enough to wrinkle his forehead.

"Are you well?" She loved him even more for protecting her in this moment, but her insides buckled when she thought of how he had found her.

"I should be asking you that, Benae," he snapped. "How could you allow him to treat you like that? You should've told me sooner." He pushed his hand through his blond locks. "Weeks and weeks of torture and I never knew. Why?" He stood before her, his fists bunched and his eyes desperate.

"Let's not talk of it now. It's over."

"We must talk. There will be questions. What happened?"

"Jiseve collapsed while in the act. It must have been too much for his heart to bear."

Ramón walked away, seeming to struggle with her words. When he faced her again, his gaze was even more troubled. "Tell me exactly what happened."

Benae shrank inside. "Must I?"

"Benae!"

She shook her head. "I can't do this now."

He looked as if he'd argue further but his face softened, and he nodded. "I'm sorry. You've had an ordeal this night. I'll meet the guard and the physician and speak on your behalf. In the morning, you may feel more able to endure these questions." He bent and kissed her cheek then pulled her up, lifted her and walked into the bedchamber. He laid her gently on the bed and pulled up the covers. "Rest now. I'll visit you later."

* * *

Ramón's mind boiled with questions that had no immediate answers. The prince was dead. *Dead.* The word left a flat, emptiness inside him. It might be his fault. What had Hetty done to that ring? Or was it coincidence? Should he tell Benae what he and Hetty had cooked up between them? *No!* Better to see what she had to say first and talk to the physician.

He paused outside the prince's chambers and drew in several slow, deep breaths. His racing heart calmed a little. He squared his shoulders and knocked on the door. It opened and two soldiers pushed past him, carrying the burned carpet. Lieutenant Vorasava stood, hands on hips, in the middle of the sitting room.

"Ah, Zorba, I believe you found the prince," he said, his dark eyes narrowing. "Come in."

Ramón stepped over the threshold. "Strictly speaking, Princess Benae found him. I arrived soon after."

Vorasava frowned. "Where is she now? I'll need to speak with her."

"I've escorted her to her chambers. She was distraught. I suggest you wait until morning."

"Perhaps. The Goddess knows there'll be enough here to keep me busy all night. This is an appalling mess."

Ramón held his tongue.

"How did you happen to be near these chambers?" Vorasava asked. He was no common soldier. Ramón knew he'd have to be careful or he'd dump himself in the swill.

"I usually do one last walk along the hallways before turning in. I smelled smoke and decided to investigate. I found the prince slumped upon his wife and flames licking at the bed covers. His Highness was already dead."

"What I don't understand is how the fire started."

"I believe that happened in the lady's struggle to get out from under the body of her husband," Ramón said.

Vorasava winced. "A grisly business."

The physician appeared in the doorway to the bedchamber. "You can remove the body to the cellar now, Lieutenant."

"What's the cause of death, Doctor?" Vorasava asked.

"It's too early to say. I've taken samples that may tell me more.

It could be a weak heart. I'll let you know when I've completed my investigations." The doctor nodded to them both and left.

Vorasava shuddered again. "Physicians set my teeth on edge; poking about in other people's corporeal fluids and digging amongst dead bodies. Are you listening Zorba?"

Ramón was jerked into the present by Vorasava's sharp tone. "What? Oh yes, not a job for everyone I expect. If you'll excuse me, Lieutenant, I'll take some rest while I can." Ramón nodded and left before Vorasava could object.

* * *

Benae pushed herself from her bed, finally giving in to the reality that she wouldn't sleep. She hardly recognized the face she saw in the mirror. Haggard was the only word that fitted. Her mind shied away from the reason for her appearance; shied away from everything since her wedding. It had been a nightmare, only worsened by last night. If she dwelled on it now, she'd become unhinged. Better to keep looking forward, to concentrate on what might be. She need no longer fear her nights with Jiseve and her babe would be safe in her womb.

There was a quiet knock at the door and Joletta arrived. Seeing Benae, she paused inside the door and curtsied. Her gaze held uncertainty and fear.

"Come in, Joletta." Benae hurried on before the maid could speak. "Let's not talk of the events of last night." Joletta was sure to have heard of Jiseve's death. "Instead please do your best to make me presentable for the day ahead,"

"Of course, Your Highness." Joletta's eyes traveled over Benae and she immediately called for the bath to be filled. While they waited for the water, Joletta sat Benae in a chair and massaged her shoulders and temples, her skilled fingers easing away some of the tension that made Benae's head throb. *Perhaps she will make a suitable lady's maid after all?*

The bath prepared, Joletta washed Benae's hair. For precious moments, she relaxed as the maid's fingers massaged her scalp. All too soon, the pampering was over, and the soap washed from her hair. Still,

Joletta's attentions had worked their magic. The woman who emerged looked almost her normal self. Benae was even able to raise a smile in thanks as Joletta left.

Clothed in her only black dress, a gown that fitted to just below her breasts then fell into a full skirt with a short train, Benae made her way to the breakfast room.

Ramón was already there, looking just as tired as she felt. She longed to run into his arms so he could make her forget the events of the night.

He turned as she entered, and it was as if she were seeing him for the first time; his golden locks tied back from his face, his favorite blue shirt tucked into dark-gray breeches, his feet encased in soft black leather boots. But his eyes had changed from their first meeting. They were no longer those of a young man but of one who had experienced life; weary eyes.

"You never cease to amaze me, Lady," he said. "Even after the horror of last night, you're beautiful."

"And you, Ramón, are kind." She smiled and the effort lifted her heart. All would be well. She and Ramón would be together—somehow. She placed her hand on her abdomen and the movement attracted his attention.

"Are you well?" he asked, anxiety flaring in his gaze.

She nodded and crossed to the table to pour herself a cup of steaming tea. Ramón drew a chair from the table, and she sat. He piled fresh rolls onto a plate and began breaking them into pieces and spreading them with butter and honey.

"You spoil me."

"You need cherishing. I've failed you and so has your husband."

Benae frowned. "You have no cause to blame yourself for my predicament. You've done everything in your power to protect me. Is there any news of what killed Jiseve?"

Ramón shook his head. "None."

A spike of pain and nerves stabbed her stomach as she contemplated the changes her husband's demise might bring. The passing of a prince of the realm wouldn't go without consequences. The king would want to find a reason for the death of his brother, someone to blame. The power vacuum in Brightcastle would concern him as well. Benae didn't know how much responsibility, if any, would now fall upon her shoulders as Jiseve's widow. Would Jiseve's nephew, Piotr, move into the castle and, if he did, where would that leave her?

Where did it leave her unborn child? When her pregnancy was revealed, she would be the mother of the heir to the throne, unless she told the truth. Would Ramón keep her secret or would his need to be acknowledged as the father interfere with her plans? Could she lie about her baby's parentage? And when the child was old enough to be told the truth, what then?

"Ramón, we need to talk about the future."

He stood and moved to pour himself another cup of tea. The door opened to admit Vorasava.

The lieutenant's eyes flicked from her to Ramón and back. "Princess, I must talk with you."

Ramón stepped forward. "Have a care, man," he hissed. "Princess Benae has had a harrowing night and is breaking her fast."

Vorasava frowned and cleared his throat. "Yes, a most difficult night. How do you fare this morning, Your Highness?"

"That's a hard question to answer, Lieutenant. I find I can't accept what has occurred, and yet I must." Benae's voice broke as a sob escaped.

"Quite so." Vorasava cleared his throat. "I'd like to ask you some questions if I may?"

"Have you come to tell me the cause of death, Lieutenant?"

He frowned again. "It's much too early for that. I am but a humble soldier and the physician must examine the body. It appears to be a failure of the heart."

Benae's thoughts fluttered in her head like moths around a flame. How could Jiseve's heart have failed? He was a vital and energetic man. She felt her face heat. Lately he had been too energetic. She raised her gaze to Vorasava and found him watching her, his eyes intense.

"Can you tell me anything that might explain your husband's death, Princess? Had he complained of any ill health?"

"I can't think of anything that would point to a health problem. His death has shocked me."

"The squire tells me the prince died in the act of coupling with you. Is that correct?"

Benae drew in a deep breath. Images of the night before flashed through her head and her chest constricted. *Oh Goddess, let this day be over!*

"Yes, that's the truth. I don't wish to discuss it further."

"But we must, Your Highness. The prince is dead, and you're the last person to see him alive. Perhaps I should be more direct. Did you contribute in any way to your husband's untimely demise?"

"Lieutenant, you're out of order!" Ramón leapt forward, his face in Vorasava's.

"You're rather too quick to come to the lady's defense, Zorba."

The two men glared at each other.

Benae felt the need to escape from both. "Ramón, I thank you but there's no need to defend me." She turned to Vorasava. "Lieutenant, I know no way in which I contributed to my husband's death. Please leave me, both of you."

Benae could see neither man wanted to depart but, in the end, both did, leaving her blessedly alone. She sank into a chair and wondered how she would survive the day.

* * *

Guilt gnawed at Ramón's gut. What had he done? What had Hetty done? That signet ring he had given the prince was only supposed to cause impotence, not to kill. Should he see Hetty and ask her? She was hardly going to come out and say she had cursed the man who had once tried to kill her. At least Benae was now spared her nightly torture, but what if the physician or the king decided she was responsible? King Beniel had been summoned. In the end, it would be his decision. Perhaps it had been a natural death as it seemed, but the coincidence of the ring wasn't to be overlooked. How could he tell Benae he might be responsible? The thought of keeping another secret from a woman he cared about tied his stomach in knots. *Enough secrets!* He had to tell her and face the consequences.

* * *

Benae sat before her fire, the flames crackling and popping in the hearth, drawing her favorite brush through her hair. It was barely a full day since Jiseve's death but felt like a week. She should have been in bed long ago, but if she delayed retiring until exhausted, perhaps she wouldn't dream of dead limbs suffocating her.

A grinding noise signaled the opening of the secret passage in her wall and she turned to find Ramón there. She stared at him for long moments, the fire making his blond hair bronze, his blue shirt matching his eyes perfectly, black tunic accentuating the broadness of his shoulders. She so wanted him and now perhaps she would never have him. Everything depended on the physician's verdict and the King's decree. She was an outsider. If the king wanted to blame someone for his brother's death, he hardly needed to look further than her.

She stood, dropping the brush to the floor. Ramón hurried to her and drew her into his arms.

"My love, I'm sorry," he said, his eyes clouded with dread and guilt.

His fear scared Benae more than her situation. She held him at arm's length. "None of this is your fault, Ramón. There's no need to apologize."

"There may be more need than you imagine."

He wasn't making any sense to her. "What do you mean? However much you wished Jiseve dead, this had nothing to do with you."

He clutched her fingers. Hard. "I never did wish him dead. You have to believe that."

Benae heaved a sigh of relief. "I know you wouldn't wish him harm, not truly. You're a good man, and I love you for it."

Her words seemed to distress him even more.

"What is it, Ramón?"

"There's something I must tell you. I've kept enough secrets in my life to know I can't hide this from you."

"Tell me," she snapped. "You're making me afraid."

He drew a deep breath. "I went to a witch for help."

"Tell me you didn't have anything to do with Jiseve's sudden collapse."

Ramón walked away from her and stood staring at the flames. She strode up to him, grabbed him and spun him to face her. "Tell me, Ramón!"

"I can't."

Benae gasped. A shudder ripped through her body and she clutched his arms for support. She stared, desperate to find some sign he jested. His eyes held only guilt and self-loathing. "Are you telling me your actions led to Jiseve's death?"

"Goddess, Benae, I don't know." He tore himself from her grasp and began to pace back and forth across the small chamber. "I couldn't stand to see you injured, to know he pounded at you night after night and with my babe at risk. I went to Hetty for help. All I asked for was something to stop him abusing you."

Horror flooded Benae. She panted, unable to take a proper breath. Her head spun and she clutched the back of an armchair. "What did she do?"

"She might not even be a witch, beloved."

"Tell me," she ground out.

"She bade me purchase a gift for his birthday."

"The signet ring!"

"Yes. She enchanted it so he couldn't complete the act. Or so I thought."

"And the very first night he wore it, he died." Benae's throat closed over and dark spots danced before her eyes. She staggered around the chair and sat. Ramón poured a glass of dark-red wine and placed it in her hands.

"Drink, it will ease your fright."

"How could you meddle like this?"

"You asked for help. What did you expect?"

"Certainly not this!"

"A man doesn't stand by and watch his lady abused. His pregnant lady. I was desperate!"

"That much is quite clear!" Benae tried to sort through her jumbled thoughts. In her weakness she had relied on Ramón and this was what it had come to. Where was his judgement, not to mention hers? She couldn't deal with him now, had to have time to process the revelation. Her lover might have killed her husband. "Leave me. I don't wish to see you until I call for you."

"What will you do?"

"I must wait on the physician's verdict. My pregnancy may save me if his judgment goes against me. I'll say the babe is Jiseve's." She stared at the man who had been her most precious gift. "No one will say otherwise." She watched his eyes harden and steeled her heart to stop it breaking.

"If that's what you wish."

"It is." A dozen questions lined up in her mind, but she didn't know how to give voice to them. Ramón was not the man she had fallen in love with. She felt she had never really known him.

"Then I will take your leave." He bowed and left through the secret passage without a backward glance. The wall closed with a dull thud that echoed in her heart, but all that mattered now was her babe. Ramón had interfered and in so doing he might have risked everything; his life, their babe's and hers. Jiseve was dead and nothing could change that, but his death might change everything.

Chapter 19

BENAE cleared her throat for what seemed the hundredth time since being ushered into Brightcastle's small audience chamber by the King's chamberlain. Beniel Zialni had arrived the day before, with a small attachment of his own staff, and taken over the running of the castle. Benae's stomach churned so much she hadn't been able to eat breakfast. Now she regretted the lack of food in her stomach. Her head spun whenever she rose too quickly, and the high neck of her black satin mourning gown seemed to choke her.

She stood carefully, made her way over to the tea tray and poured herself a cup. Underlying her terror of the future, was annoyance that the king had assumed control without as much as a by-your-leave. The queen hadn't come with him; a sure sign this wasn't a visit to support grieving relatives, but a monarch tending to the business of the kingdom. It didn't bode well, and neither did Beniel's cold attitude toward her. He hadn't mentioned Jiseve, hadn't offered his sympathy. He blamed her, suspected her and probably hated her.

The door opened and Benae steeled herself to greet the king, but it was Ramón who entered. He froze when he saw her.

"What are you doing here?" she asked, hating the tension in her voice. She inhaled deeply to regain her composure.

"I was asked to attend the king."

"I hardly think he would have meant you to present yourself at this hour. I have an audience with him now."

"Think what you like, Princess."

How far things had deteriorated between them. Four days ago, Benae could never have imagined feeling betrayed by Ramón, would not have believed he could speak to her with such indifference. But that had been before she learned of Hetty and the ring, before she knew he might be partly responsible for placing her life and her child's in this position, before she told him that she would declare Jiseve the father. She must do what she could to safeguard her babe.

"Can I trust in your discretion when I inform His Majesty of my pregnancy?" She gripped the handle of her teacup so tightly it was a miracle the fragile china didn't break.

A muscle tensed in his jaw. She focused on that rather than meet his accusing azure gaze. It was not *her* fault that Jiseve was dead. He had meddled and now she must deal with the king.

"I'll hold my silence," Ramón said, "but it's a bitter pill to swallow."

She chose to ignore the second part of his answer. "Thank you." The words were drawn from her almost against her will.

The door opened and King Beniel swept in. Benae shivered at the chill in his sharp blue eyes. The look he gave her, and then Ramón, spoke volumes.

Forgetting her infirm body, Benae swept a curtsy and staggered against Ramón. He grasped her arm to steady her and she cried out in pain at the pressure of his hand against her bruises. *Goddess, would her shame be exposed for the kingdom to judge?*

King Beniel's eyes bored into her as he took a seat on the small throne on the dais. "It pains me to visit under these circumstances," he said. "There are questions that need asking and decisions to make. I did not imagine, mere weeks ago, that your wedding was the last time I would see my brother alive."

Benae's breath caught at the pain in his voice. She mustn't forget he loved Jiseve.

"I couldn't have anticipated this sorry circumstance either, Your Majesty. Your brother was a fit man and had everything to look forward to."

"And yet, I've just seen his corpse. I can't help but suspect foul play. Did you have anything to do with my brother's death, Princess?"

Benae wanted to cringe, to close her eyes and run from the room. Instead, she clenched her teeth and met his gaze. "I did not, Your Majesty, except that he died in the act of love. I was of course present."

Beniel frowned, his eyes running over her. He rose and stepped off the dais to stand before her. "What ails you?"

Terror gripped Benae's gut and she felt the blood drain from her face. "I am perfectly well, Sire."

"You are ill. You nearly fell a moment ago and then cried in pain when the squire gripped your arm. Why?"

"It's just grief, Your Majesty. I've not been eating well."

"Raise your sleeve," he said, his voice as cold as the mountain passes.

Benae's fists clenched, instinct rebelling against the order. *I have no choice. I must do as he says.* Slowly, she pulled the sleeve up to reveal her black and swollen elbow.

Beniel's eyes bulged. "How did you come by your injury?"

She remained quiet, unsure how to tell the king his brother had abused her. Would he even believe?

"I will not repeat my question," Beniel roared, making Benae jump. Her heart skittered like a mouse in fear of the kitchen cat.

"Jiseve," she said.

"What do you mean, Jiseve?"

Benae squared her shoulders and met the king's hostile gaze. "Jiseve did this. He tied me to his bed and tortured me during our coupling." She pulled her other sleeve up and then bared her ankles. "There are more I can't show you."

It was clear Beniel didn't accept what he saw. "Tortured? Why would he need to torture you? You are his wife. There must be some other explanation, punishment for some infidelity?" He turned to Ramón. "I seem to remember rumors of impropriety involving you and the lady when you visited Wildecoast."

Benae stepped forward. "Don't blame Ramón for Jiseve's cruelty. I'm sorry if I destroy your good feelings toward your brother, but you must understand."

"That's exactly what I'm trying to do."

"Just listen, please." Benae quashed the guilt that reared at keeping the whole truth from her brother-in-law. "Jiseve's abuse started on our marriage night. We never made love without the straps. He would bite me, especially on the breasts, then he gagged me when I cried out. I believe the torture excited him, helped him complete the act; at least that's what I told myself."

Beniel was quiet for a long time. When he raised his eyes to her, she saw hate in them. *He will take Jiseve's side then.*

"*If* my brother tortured you, you had ample reason to want him dead."

"I didn't kill Jiseve, Your Majesty, you must believe me."

"The squire then." He turned to Ramón. "I would hazard a guess you knew about these marital problems. You wouldn't stand by and allow a woman to be thus abused. Is there anything you wish to tell me?"

Now Benae bit the inside of her lip. How would Ramón avoid incriminating himself? Or would he admit his actions? She couldn't bear to lose him too, despite the animosity that now stood between them.

"Yes, I knew, and I wanted to help, but I didn't wish the prince to die. He was my patron and I owed him much."

"You made free with his lady!"

Benae couldn't help her gasp of surprise but Ramón stood calm in the face of the accusation.

"Rumor only, Your Majesty," Ramón said.

"What occurred in the hut that night of the storm?"

"We took refuge. We did nothing wrong."

Benae had to admire Ramón's composure. She hated being in this position; feeling her way through these questions.

The king turned to Benae. "Something upset Jiseve before his marriage to you, Lady. He was a changed man when I visited for the ceremony." His sharp gaze wandered from her to Ramón and back.

Benae went on the attack. "Did you ask my husband what was wrong, Your Majesty?"

Beniel paused, frowning. "I did. He declined to answer. He assured me all was well. But I know my brother." He cleared his throat. "Rather, I knew my brother, and he was hiding something. I can't help feeling it is linked to his death." He fell silent and his mind appeared to wander.

"We will know more when the physician finishes his examination," the king said. "He has assured me he will present his findings late this afternoon." Beniel's throat moved as though something were stuck in it. He cleared it again. "I will summon you when the findings are handed down, Princess Benae. Until then, I would like you both to stay in your chambers." Beniel stood and walked from the room without another glance in her direction.

Benae didn't know what to think.

"Why didn't you tell him about your pregnancy?" Ramón asked.

"It wasn't the right time. I wish to hear the report before I tell the king. Perhaps if the news is favorable, he will more readily accept the babe as Jiseve's, and if not, it won't hurt that the news was delayed."

Ramón stiffened. "I forget how practiced you are in *dealing* with people."

"*I* am practiced?" she snapped. "You avoided answering the king's question quite expertly, I noticed." She wondered if they really knew each other, if they could ever have made each other happy.

"I will take my leave until this afternoon." He turned and left.

The chamberlain appeared in the doorway and Benae sighed as she moved to join him. She was little more than a prisoner in her own home, but a future still might be salvaged, depending on that report.

The summons came almost at the dinner hour and Benae cursed the timing. She needed sustenance if she was to face bad news, but the king's man had arrived to escort her, and she dared not argue. She ground her teeth at being treated like a criminal but, for her babe's sake, she must be meek, must guard her tongue. She had never thought pregnancy would make her so vulnerable.

The king awaited her in the grand audience chamber. The formality of the hall made her hands clammy and she forced herself not to wipe them on her black skirts. She was announced and paused just inside the open doors. Taking a deep breath, she scanned the room. A dozen chairs were drawn up and in them sat Lieutenant Vorasava, Ramón, the physician Damald Monive and Beniel's nephew, Piotr Zialni. The masters of the guilds were also in attendance. A spasm hit Benae's stomach and she swallowed, now glad she hadn't eaten.

King Beniel stood and pointed to a chair to the left of his on the dais. "Please be seated, Princess Benae." He resumed his throne, stony-faced.

Benae approached and sat, casting her gaze at the men gathered before her. It felt like a trial, but she reminded herself it wasn't one. She was familiar with what that entailed and knew she would have notice if she were expected to defend herself. Ramón appeared composed but the slight tremor of his fingers betrayed deeper emotions. He didn't meet her gaze.

Damald Monive was a gaunt, balding man. He smothered a yawn as if bored with the proceedings already. Vorasava frowned at her as if he no longer knew how to treat his mistress. Piotr stared at her, quirking one eyebrow. He had an unruly shock of sandy-colored hair and was roughly her age. His protruding stomach and lacy collar proclaimed him to have lived a privileged life. What did Piotr's presence mean? Was the king ready to hand control of Brightcastle to his nephew? After this morning, that could well be the case. She was brought back to the matter at hand by the king.

"I have gathered you all to hear the report of our court physician, Damald Monive. He has been charged with finding a cause of death for our beloved brother, Jiseve Zialni, the master of this castle and its lands… and my heir." Beniel's voice broke and Benae found his burning gaze upon her. Oh yes, he blamed her.

Beniel cleared his throat three times before he continued. "I had not thought to be in this position. We bury our dear brother tomorrow with the succession of our throne in question." The silence following his words was absolute and Benae's jaw clenched with the strain.

Without Princess Alecia, Piotr Zialni was next in line to the throne of Thorius. By the smirk on his face, Piotr fully expected to be given control of Brightcastle.

"Let us address the matter at hand. Doctor Monive, please present your findings."

The physician stood and strode to the center of the dais, black robes swirling above his soft green slippers. He consulted the sheaf of papers in his hands and then met the eye of every person in the room.

"I am grieved that I had to examine the reasons for my prince's untimely death. I can confirm his demise occurred in the marital bed."

At his words, all eyes swept to Benae. She raised her head and focused her attention on the physician.

"External physical examination revealed nothing," Monive said.

Absolute quiet cloaked the hall as the physician paused. Benae's heart raced, causing an ache in her breastbone. All would be well, she just had to believe that.

"With nothing obvious externally, I explored beneath the skin." At this, the king cleared his throat, glaring at the doctor. Benae forced her mind away from the thought of the surgeon slicing into her husband.

"Yes, well," Monive said, wiping a hand across his forehead. "to continue, Prince Zialni's heart was discolored and the inside structure destroyed, leading me to conclude that this organ failed. You will all no doubt be stunned to hear this, considering the prince was a fit man and, some would argue, in his prime."

Damald Monive paused for effect and Benae swallowed hard on the fear that threatened to choke her. She clung to the fact that she had done nothing wrong, at least not since her marriage. She had been a faithful wife, fulfilling her duty each night, enduring Jiseve's abuse. It had been a nightmare, but she hadn't been responsible for his death. She stared at Ramón and his gaze met hers. For a moment, fear and desperation stood clear in his eyes before he looked away. If she knew him at all, those emotions would be for her, not for him. She hoped he didn't speak up before all was resolved. Much could be salvaged if the Goddess favored them.

The physician continued. "Since the prince's heart bore such damage, I have performed various tests on the bodily fluids, looking for poisons, bad humors and other substances. I also examined a wine glass, found in his chambers, which contained a curious sediment."

At this, the king surged to his feet. "Doctor Monive!" he roared. "We grow tired of this. Your investigations are no doubt fascinating for one of your field, but may I remind you… you discuss our brother and I do not appreciate your lack of sensitivity."

Monive's face flushed. "Of course, Your Majesty, forgive me. I will be brief."

The king sat. "If you could, Doctor."

"In the body —"

The king shifted and glared at the physician. Benae squared her shoulders, pity for Beniel sweeping through her. Curse Monive for dragging this out! Didn't he know how this affected them all?

Monive cleared his throat and went on. "The stomach contained wine and fragments of belladonna, toadstools and crow's foot. This matched the dregs in the wine glass."

There was a buzz in the room as the news was delivered. Benae clutched her throat, uncertain what this might mean. This time when she sought Ramón, she found him staring at her, shock written large on his face. When she turned back to the doctor, she saw the king glowering at her.

Beniel clapped his hands and quiet descended.

"So, Doctor, what have you concurred? That my brother was poisoned? Those sound dangerous substances to have in your nightly drink."

"In deed, my Liege, but there may be another reason for their presence." The doctor turned to the assemblage. "On further searching of the prince's chambers, I discovered the decanter which housed the wine was similarly contaminated. I searched the kitchens and found in the pantry, a small stash of herbs, mainly ginseng, belladonna and red sage, along with powdered toadstools, which the cook said she used to brew the prince's nightly drink. The woman had been shown how to concoct the brew by the prince himself."

"Are you saying our brother poisoned himself?" the king asked, his hands clenched on the arms of his chair. The icy fingers that had squeezed Benae's heart loosened their grip, if only a little.

"We may perhaps never know, Your Highness. All I can say is that the materials found, while being poisonous to a greater or lesser degree, are also aphrodisiacs of one sort or another. For example, red sage helps with penile erection."

The king's eyes were wide as the implications became clear. He slumped on his throne, staring into space, while the doctor allowed the full import of his findings to register. Deep fatigue swept over Benae and she also reclined in her chair, eyes closed, taking deep breaths to steady her swirling head. Did this mean that Ramón was blameless, and she would be exonerated?

"Your Majesty, Princess Benae, assembled guests," Damald Monive said, "please be advised that Prince Jiseve Zialni died of a failure of the heart brought on by excessive exertion, and aided by the presence of the aforementioned substances. It appears he must have known and approved of the substances in his wine and that he was consuming them in the belief that they would help secure an heir. I find it impossible to apportion any other blame in this instance."

The king stood. "Thank you, Doctor Monive. You have put our mind at rest. Nothing can ease the sadness of our loss, but knowing he was not murdered does make his passing somewhat easier to bear. The funeral of our dear brother will be held tomorrow and then his body will travel to Wildecoast to be entombed in the family crypt. Please reassemble at dusk tomorrow."

Benae rose to leave with the others and Beniel halted her. "I would ask your company at dinner, Princess."

Benae curtsied, her heart beating a staccato. "I would welcome that, Your Majesty." All she really wanted was to escape and process the news the physician had delivered.

The king escorted her to the dining room where candles burned at one end of the long table. He seated her to his left and took the chair at the end of the table in front of the fireplace, below the painting of himself.

Servants set another place for Benae, brought a thick broth and bread, then departed.

"It seems an apology is in order," Beniel said, once he had given the blessing. "I am sorry I blamed you for Jiseve's death."

"You are forgiven, Your Majesty. I'm grateful that matters are becoming clearer."

"Call me Beniel in private, if you please."

Benae inclined her head. "You'll miss him."

"I will indeed and his passing leaves so much uncertainty."

"Perhaps I can ease some of that."

Beniel's eyes narrowed and he leaned closer. "Oh?"

"I didn't want to say anything earlier, given the situation. I didn't want to influence proceedings."

"Get to the point, Benae."

She nodded again. "I am with child."

Beniel's body jerked and he gasped, tears welling. She quashed the remorse she immediately felt at lying to him.

"I hoped but dared not count on an early pregnancy. This means so much for the kingdom. Let us pray it's a boy. Did Jiseve know?"

She shook her head. "I've only just found out myself."

"All is well?"

"I believe so."

"If only he could have known before he passed. A child was so important to him."

"It was the reason for this marriage."

"Not the only reason, I hope."

Benae thought of her people, safe in the protection of the kingdom. "No, not the only reason."

"There was tension between you on your wedding day. I saw it with my own eyes. It was the reason I blamed you for his death. Can you tell me about it?"

Benae longed to confide in someone, to explain the torture of the last few weeks, but Jiseve's brother was not the person for that. "The path of love is never a smooth one, but I need you to know I honored my wedding vows and tried to be the wife Jiseve wanted."

"That is all one can ask." Beniel's face was troubled. "I cannot help wishing you had confided Jiseve's abuse to me. I could have helped. Perhaps your suffering and his death could have been avoided."

Benae closed her eyes and took a deep breath. Steadying herself, she faced the king. "It wasn't easy to admit to anyone the abuse I endured. Jiseve would've been furious if I had told you. I could not have known how dire the consequences would be."

"We are all wise in hindsight," Beniel said, nodding.

Quiet descended as they finished their broth and slices of venison pie were served.

Benae stewed on the next question she must broach. "Can I ask your plans for Brightcastle and for me? I need to know the people will be secure."

Beniel paused. "I will give it some thought. I cannot see a problem with you running the principality on behalf of your unborn child, as long as you get the required help with the task."

"What of Piotr?"

"My conniving nephew will need watching. I did not expect him to be here today but somehow, he heard of Jiseve's death. I do not trust him."

"Jiseve wasn't trusting of him, either. My husband feared his nephew had an eye on your throne."

"Yes, my dear. Piotr will not be best pleased to learn that Jiseve fathered a child, but will he act on that knowledge? Perhaps it would be best we kept the news to ourselves for a time."

"There's no telling what he might do," Benae said, her hand rubbing her abdomen.

Her actions were not lost on the king.

"Do not fear. Your child will be our highest priority, as will finding Princess Alecia. She must be located and told of her father's death."

"Would Piotr try to harm Princess Alecia if he found her?

"As to that, who can know?"

"Where is your nephew at this moment?"

"He had some business in the town. I have two of my men keeping an eye on him. He has requested an audience with me tomorrow, no doubt to suggest he manage Brightcastle as heir apparent to my throne."

A shiver ran down Benae's spine and she took a gulp of her watered wine.

Beniel gripped her wrist. "I will not allow him to hurt you. I will see you are closely guarded."

"Can you be sure that Piotr hasn't had a hand in Jiseve's death? Perhaps that's how he knew of it in time to travel here so quickly."

Beniel's eyes narrowed. "Yes, I see that now. Without evidence, I can do nothing."

"Nothing but watch him and keep him at a distance." Benae said.

"You can be sure I will do exactly that."

"If you will allow me to take my leave, Beniel?" she stood.

The king followed. "Let me escort you to your room."

"Oh, but you must stay and finish your meal."

"Like you, I have lost my appetite. I have work to do if I am to stay one step ahead of my nephew."

* * *

Ramón watched King Beniel accompany Benae to her room as he lurked in the shadows at the end of his wing. She leaned on the king for support, shoulders slumped, and his anger with her cooled a little. Benae needed his help not his rage. It was just intolerable to be prevented from acknowledging your own child.

The monarch departed and Ramón slipped along his corridor to Benae's room, knocking quietly on her chamber door.

She answered and stood with the door partly open, her beautiful face pale against her dark mourning dress. "I was preparing for rest, Ramón."

"May I come in, just for a moment?"

She sighed and stepped back, allowing him through and closing the door quietly behind him. He wondered where his fiery Benae had disappeared to. This pale, tired woman was surely an imposter.

"I want to know where we stand, where I stand," Ramón said, pushing his hands through his hair because he didn't know what else to do with them. What he needed was a weapons session, or a good long run or …an evening with Benae.

She frowned. "I don't know how I feel about you. Your actions were careless in involving Hetty. Jiseve is dead and the cursed ring could well be the cause. The old woman has her own agenda."

"We'll never know, will we? Can't we put this behind us and seek a life together? I want to raise my child."

"This child is mine and I'll decide how his life shall be, with the help of the king."

Fear swirled through Ramón like a chill wind. "What do you mean?"

"I told Beniel about the babe and he believes it's Jiseve's. He's overjoyed."

"So, I'm still shut out?"

"I wish you wouldn't see my actions like that. I must find a balance that safeguards my child, my people and the kingdom. How would declaring you the father do that?"

Ramón considered her words. It didn't sit well, but he saw Benae was right. "Still, I can't like it."

Benae seemed to relax at his grudging acceptance of her decision. "The king is concerned about his nephew Piotr; that he might interfere for his own purposes."

"I spoke to Piotr after the doctor's report. He asked many questions, about you, his cousin Alecia, even Vard Anton. He seemed well informed for a man who lives so far away. I told him as little as I could, but the king is right to be concerned."

"Beniel told me he was surprised when Piotr arrived. He wondered how he knew of Jiseve's death; how he arrived so quickly. *I* wonder if Piotr had something to do with Jiseve's demise."

"Ha, so the nephew comes under suspicion and I'm off the hook?"

"I can't forget what you did," Benae hissed. "I'll forever wonder if you contributed to his death and that's not the way I wish to think of the man I love."

"You still love me?"

She tried to look stern, but a smile tickled the corners of her mouth. "I can't help it. I love you from your gorgeous blond hair right down to your boots. Still, I'm not sure of the way forward for us."

A spark of hope shot through him. "What does the king say about your position here?"

"He thinks I can run the principality, for my child, with help. And he's concerned for the princess if Piotr finds her before we do."

"I'll find Alecia and bring her home. That was the plan all along."

Benae stamped her foot. "Didn't you hear me, Ramón? Beniel wants me to run Brightcastle and surrounds. I'll need help and I thought, perhaps, you might be that support."

All thoughts of finding Alecia flew from his mind at the idea of a partnership with Benae. "Has the king agreed?"

"I've not suggested it yet. It would be better if it were his idea."

"How are we to achieve that?"

"Ramón! I can't think of every solution. That's up to you."

"I'll have competition. That devil Vorasava has been shadowing the king since his arrival. He likely intends to profit from the prince's death."

"You know things that the lieutenant does not, beloved. Put him out of your mind and concentrate on aiding the king."

Benae's words cleared Ramón's mind of the clutter that had been there for so long. Suddenly his path was clear. "The funeral is tomorrow. If there was ever a moment for Piotr to strike it's then." He took her hand and kissed her fingers. "I must go. The security plans for tomorrow need reviewing."

He took his leave, energized by the task before him despite the late hour.

CHAPTER 20

DARKNESS gathered in the grand hall, along with the guests come to farewell Jiseve Zialni, Prince of Thorius. Ramón stood at the rear, his eyes everywhere at once. The dim lighting from candles didn't aid his task. Shadows flickered at the corner of his vision, pushing his nerves to the limit. Benae sat beside Vorasava who had been appointed her escort for the event. The flickering candlelight accentuated her beauty and fragility this night and disguised the dark smudges beneath her eyes. He needed to be with her, to love and protect her, and to watch his child grow. Nothing had ever meant so much, not his parents, his sisters or Alecia. Ramón had never imagined the intensity of love he now experienced. He pushed his feelings aside, determined not to be distracted.

Stepping away from the wall, he began a patrol of the perimeter of the room, opening doors to peer into the halls surrounding the venue. Painstakingly, he pulled each hanging away from the wall, looked beneath seats, behind pillars and cast his gaze to the ceiling. There were two small galleries, one on either side at the rear of the hall. They were accessed by narrow stairs, the doors to which had been locked yesterday. Vorasava had assured him this morning that no one could enter these high galleries.

Ramón exited the hall at the back and checked both doors, finding them locked as the lieutenant had reported. Worry gnawed at his gut. He just couldn't rid himself of the certainty that disaster was a hair's breadth away. He had approached King Beniel the night before and asked to help with security, convincing the monarch to include him based on his knowledge of the castle and the guests who would attend. He had scrutinized the castle maps during the hours of dark and was convinced he had thought of all possibilities. Only he knew of the secret passages. He had uncovered them the night Alecia left, exploring them in the weeks after her departure. None of the passages exited in the hall, but they were a risk for the guest and family rooms if their existence was discovered.

This hall was secure; he was convinced of that. So why did he still have this feeling? He took one last turn around the walls, repeating the checks he had just performed. As he approached the first row of seats on the right, his gaze met Benae's and she smiled. His breath caught and he swallowed the upwelling of desire that echoed the emotion in her eyes. Her vulnerability ate at him, awakened his protective instinct. Nothing could happen to her this day or ever. He would sacrifice himself before he would allow her to be hurt in any way.

Ramón completed his last check, Vorasava's eyes upon him, a smirk on the lieutenant's lips. He didn't care how much or how little respect Vorasava had for him. The soldier was convinced Benae wasn't a target. News of her pregnancy hadn't been released. Only the king, Ramón and Vorasava knew of the impending birth, so Benae shouldn't be at risk this day. *Should* not.

A blare of horns announced the arrival of the king and his chamberlain, closely followed by the priestess who would officiate at the funeral service. Ramón cast his eye over the assembled mourners. Black was the order of the day with an occasional dark gray and midnight blue to relieve the lack of color. Ramón wore a charcoal-gray tunic and breeches over a light-gray shirt. His sword hung in its scabbard on his left hip and a small crossbow swung from his right hip. Daggers nestled in each boot. He was as prepared as he could be.

The king, chamberlain and religious celebrants took their places on the dais and the assemblage stood and sang a hymn to the Goddess. Ramón did not sing but examined the crowd, his task made nigh impossible by the standing mourners.

He sighed with relief when they sat, and the king moved forward.

"Welcome one and all to this most sad of days." Beniel wore unrelieved black and his head was bare of the crown he usually wore for these occasions. "I stand before you bared, mourning, desolate, and bereft of a precious brother. I thank you for helping me remember and farewell him."

The king returned to his throne and the priestess moved forward.

"Be joyful people, for though we farewell Prince Jiseve Zialni from this world, he has his reward in the next. We remember a joyful life, a life of service, and celebrate all he has left behind. I cannot be sorrowful for I know the rewards the Goddess has prepared for our beloved prince and brother, and I know that Jiseve Zialni has left us a legacy…" There was a pause and Ramón wondered why. "A legacy in the form of a child."

Shock and fear crashed through Ramón and he froze as the assembled citizens gave a collective gasp. Someone stood and cheered and then everyone was upon their feet, hats in the air, a great rolling wave of excitement and chatter spreading throughout the hall. Ramón's eyes found Benae, briefly glimpsed between the people in the row behind her. She sat with head forward and he imagined she stared straight at the king.

Beniel gave a brief shake of his head, stood and moved forward. He raised his hands in the air and waited. The people gradually fell silent.

"We had planned this announcement for a later date."

Even from the rear of the hall, Ramón saw the wave of anger that swept across his face. The priestess stood just behind him, oblivious to the displeasure of her monarch.

"My people, it is true. My brother fathered a child before he departed this world. The Princess Benae is expecting a babe."

The crowd rose again and clapped as Benae stood and joined the king. Ramón's shoulders stiffened further at seeing his lady so exposed. She was now a real target for any assassins working for Piotr. His eyes scanned the hall frantically. All he saw were smiling faces, except for Piotr who looked anything but pleased. Nothing moved along the walls or in the galleries. He forced himself to relax, releasing his grip on the crossbow, finger by finger.

"Sit down, Benae, just sit," he muttered.

All returned to their seats except the priestess and her assistants, who continued with the ceremony. The king, Piotr and the head of the guilds spoke about Jiseve in turn, paying tribute to different aspects of his life. Ramón barely heard, so engrossed was he in scouring the walls, his senses tuned to the perils that might threaten Benae and his king.

When the service was over, the guild masters moved forward to raise the coffin upon their shoulders. Vorasava stood, first to trail the coffin. Benae and the king followed. Slowly, they moved down the center aisle of the hall and toward the back doors.

Ramón saw movement from the corner of his eye and glanced at the galleries. A figure stood high in the left gallery, crossbow trained on the exiting party. Ramón's bow was unclipped and raised in a flash. He let off his dart, taking the would-be assassin in the right eye. The man toppled over the rail, landing with a sickening thud, just missing the wife of the master jeweler.

"Get down!" Ramón yelled, as he pushed his way to Benae's side. The procession paused, all confused as to what had just happened.

Vorasava pulled Benae down to the tiles and Ramón dragged the king down beside her. The coffin bearers remained standing, their eyes darting around the hall, trying to find the source of the threat.

"Pall bearers! Stay where you are," Ramón said. "You form protection for the king and princess. Your Majesty, Princess Benae, please stay down while I investigate."

Ramón stood and moved through the frightened, milling guests to reach the fallen body. He gently guided the shocked jeweler's wife into a chair. Another lady attended her. The assassin's form was unremarkable. He wore nondescript black clothing and a black cap; his features were bland, ordinary. Of course, it was always difficult to identify a man who had a crossbow bolt protruding from his eye socket.

He knelt to examine the body and check for signs of life.

"Good shooting, Zorba," Vorasava said from beside him. "I'll take it from here."

Ramón spun and glared at the lieutenant. Perhaps Vorasava thought the danger was past but Ramón wasn't so sure. The niggling sense of peril remained. He strode to Benae and the king, who both stood up. He drew Benae against his chest, not caring any longer who saw. She trembled and he held her tighter.

"We owe you a great debt, Squire, perhaps greater than we can ever repay," King Beniel said.

"Time for that later, Your Majesty, when the danger is past. For now, we must complete this ceremony and remove you from the threat." He looked to the pallbearers. "Continue the procession."

The coffin advanced, the king's attendants clustered around him, while Ramón kept Benae tight against his side. Soon they would pass through the doors and enter relative safety. Perhaps he would escort Benae to her chambers thus removing her from harm. Curse the priestess who had placed her life in jeopardy like this.

A searing agony ripped through his ribs and he looked down at the bolt protruding from his chest, bright blood already seeping into his tunic. His legs buckled and Benae tried to catch him as he slid toward the floor. Darkness joined the pain.

CHAPTER 21

BENAE knew true despair as she watched the agonizing rise and fall of Ramón's bandage-swathed chest. He was so pale. In two days, there had been no change. She'd done all she could, as had the physician. Removing the bolt had almost killed him. Thank the Goddess the weapon had been so small, it created less destruction in Ramón's body than a normal bolt would have. She flinched as she recalled the sound of the metal tearing through his flesh and the surprise on his face as he collapsed.

The bolt had been meant for her, she was convinced; meant to wipe out her child before he had a chance to draw breath, leaving one person as heir to the throne: Piotr. The king's nephew had departed the day after the funeral, but his dirty plans had left their mark. King Beniel remained, determined to see the end of Ramón's battle for good or ill.

Benae swallowed the lump that rose to her throat and blinked away tears. She wouldn't cry again.

Someone coughed at the door. Seeing Beniel standing there, she rose from her chair. He waved her back down.

"How is he?"

"No change."

"And you? I worry you are not getting enough rest."

"I'm not the one lying on my deathbed." Benae couldn't hide the anger in her voice.

Beniel nodded. "Still, you carry a precious cargo." He fell silent for a time. "The squire was a good man."

"*Is* a good man."

"Of course, I only meant —"

"I know, Your Majesty, and I agree. He is the best of men."

"You love him." It wasn't a question and Benae wouldn't deny it.

She nodded. "I love him even more since this. He would truly give me everything."

"Is there a chance he will survive? The physician says his death is but a matter of time, but I have seen you tend him. I think there is something special in your care."

Benae met his eyes, wondering if he had divined the true nature of her healing. "There's always a chance while there's life. It's part of the reason I sit here. I talk with him and hope he can hear how much he has to live for."

"I am sure that will help. Send me word the moment there is any change."

The king left and Benae resumed her vigil. She had never hoped for anything so much as this; Ramón's survival. What he had done with Hetty didn't matter. He loved her and their child. He was a good man who had been manipulated by a crafty old woman. That was the worst of it. The best was the possibility that Jiseve had indeed died from the damage the herbs had done to his heart. Only Jiseve was to blame for that. There was every chance she'd never know the truth, and she wouldn't live the rest of her life without this man. She couldn't condemn him for seeking help from Hetty. If he lived, she'd tell him she forgave him, and wanted to spend the rest of her life loving him.

The decision made, Benae felt her eyelids grow heavy. Suddenly she couldn't stay awake. "I love you and forgive you, Ramón. Come back to us…"

* * *

Ramón fought his way up a long dark corridor toward the shining light at the end. A familiar voice called to him, speaking words of love and forgiveness. It was the voice of his beloved Benae. A great sadness filled him as the memories of the preceding weeks slowly returned. He had lost her and let her down. Again, and again, his impatience had led to impetuousness that resulted in disaster.

Except for this last time. He had put himself aside and acted for the good of another and for the good of the kingdom. He had placed himself in the firing line, been responsible, and that action had saved Benae. One assassin lay dead, and he had taken the dart from the other. He recalled the agony in his chest and the terror on Benae's face as his vision faded.

What had happened afterwards? He had to know. He forced his way to that shining light and the pain doubled, almost sending him back down the tunnel. He held on as the pain faded enough for him to open his eyes. At first none of the images made sense. The room was too bright, and his eyes had been closed for so long. As he adjusted to the glare, he saw Benae asleep in a chair beside the bed, her face exquisite in repose. His heart lurched at the sight. The agony in his chest nearly made him pass out. She was well, tired but well. He could only pray the king had also survived. Ramón was so weak he couldn't lift his head from the pillow. He opened his mouth to speak but nothing came out.

He tried again. "Benae..."

She opened her eyes and stared at him as if the picture she saw confused her. Then she sat up straight. "Ramón! Beloved!" She rose and leaned over him, her gaze sweeping his face.

Why doesn't she touch me? Is it truly too late for us?

"How do you feel?" The fear in her voice told him more than words could. She hadn't expected him to survive, perhaps still didn't.

"My chest is on fire. How is the king?"

"His Majesty is well. The second assassin was found dead in the gallery. He took poison rather than be captured."

"So, we're no closer to knowing who sent them?"

She shook her head. "Piotr has gone but Beniel believes it was he. He knew too much of Jiseve's death." She peered at him. "I must examine you."

Gently Benae pulled down the covers and peeled open the bandages swathing his chest. The wound he saw there made his head swim. How he had survived a bolt that had entered the center of his chest, he couldn't imagine. The thought of the hard steel slicing through his flesh…He pushed the image from his mind.

"Don't look. The wound is serious, but the bolt didn't destroy anything important. Despite this, we nearly lost you. The battle against the wound poisoning goes on. I think we're winning." She laid her hands upon his chest and closed her eyes.

At last! Ramón gloried in the touch of her skin against his, but then realized Benae touched him as healer, not lover. His chest warmed beneath her hands and his breathing eased.

She opened her eyes, and despite her tiredness, there was a renewed spark in her gaze. "All will be well, praise the Goddess. You'll heal. I've removed the last traces of the poison that coated the dart."

"Poison!"

"We nearly lost you. You've lain for two days, hanging between life and death. I couldn't do more until your body gained strength."

Ramón found he was strong enough to sit up against the pillows. Benae helped make him comfortable.

"I'll send for food. That and rest are all you need now."

"There's one thing more I need," he said, drawing her down and taking her hands in his. "I need you. I need to know there's still hope for us."

She looked at him as if weighing the good and the bad. Ramón squirmed as he had in past years, when his mother held him to account. But he was a man now and had given everything for her. If that wasn't enough, he had to face the fact that he'd never be enough.

"When I found out what you planned with Hetty, I thought it had destroyed us. I always believed any ill you did another man would come in combat, not in stealth."

Ramón flinched at her words. If only she knew what he was capable of; the secrets he held close to his heart. He couldn't hold them forever, but he'd not tell her now.

"I placed you on a pedestal," she said. "Now I know I was wrong to do so. You let me down when you went to Hetty, but your actions since have made me realize that you're a brave and good man who made a mistake. You risked your life at the funeral, and I believe you would have been glad to die for the kingdom, for me and for our child. I can't turn my back on you or be angry with you. If there is a way for us to be together in this new world, I wish it so."

Ramón drew her close, inhaling the heady jasmine scent of her hair and ignoring the pain as her body pushed against his chest. Benae pulled away and cupped his cheek with her hand. Her lips met his, soft and warm, stirring desire he had tried to ignore for too long. He needed her, body, mind and soul.

"I love you," she said, releasing him at last.

"I love you with everything in me, Benae. I never want to lose you."

"I must leave you for a time. I'll return with food."

He wanted to beg her to stay by his side, but she brushed her hand across his forehead and sleep claimed him.

CHAPTER 22

BENAE settled Ramón into a chair in the intimate confines of the small audience chamber. She couldn't help the tremor that shook her at the thought of what might pass when the king arrived. Her future was very much in Beniel's hands. He had indicated that she might manage Brightcastle, but no formal decision had been made. Monarchs could be fickle.

It was unlikely he'd banish her to her estates when he thought she carried the future heir, but he could place someone else in Brightcastle to oversee the principality until her child was born. And what when her babe entered this world? Would she be allowed to raise him?

She didn't know what the king might do. One thing was sure; he'd try to act in the best interests of the kingdom of Thorius, and the succession. Her child held the key to her future. Where Ramón would fit in, she had no idea, but he had been summoned along with her and Beniel knew how Benae felt about the man who had risked his life for Thorius.

Ramón was still very weak but had insisted on dressing for the occasion. He smiled at her and squeezed her hand as she took the seat beside him.

"All will be well," he said, wincing as he drew breath to speak. "Have faith."

"It's difficult to have faith when so much has gone wrong lately. Sometimes I fear my life, and that of those around me, has been cursed."

"You saved me, beloved. You need no longer doubt your gift. If you remember, you've saved me twice now, and let's not forget what you did for Flaire. His leg is now full strength."

She smiled. "He yearns for the day when I can race him across the upper meadow once again."

"I still can't believe you can communicate with him."

She nodded. "We share a special bond."

The door opened and Beniel entered. Benae stood and curtsied while Ramón nodded.

"I see you continue to heal, Squire, and I am glad. I feared we would have a hero's funeral to conduct."

Ramón smiled. "No one is gladder than I, Your Majesty."

The king took a seat and Benae resumed hers.

"I feel the need to reward you in some way, Ramón Zorba, and I have thought long and hard about how I might achieve this."

"Your Majesty, there's no need. I'm glad I could provide this service to you and to the kingdom. Your safety and Benae's is all I require."

"I am sure you are genuine in that sentiment."

Benae realized she was grinding her teeth and deliberately relaxed each muscle in her face one by one. The king's gaze rested upon her for a moment. She took one deep breath and then another.

"I know you both realize the precariousness of the kingdom of Thorius and the importance of Brightcastle within that. The child Benae carries is my immediate heir, if it's a boy. I hope and pray that is the case. To add to the difficulty, Princess Alecia is still absent. I have no one to administer this principality. That cannot be allowed to continue. Piotr waits to move into the void that circumstance has created. This part of my kingdom must remain stable and protected. To achieve that, I need a strong leader here. Benae, I believe you can run the principality. I will grant you the official title of 'Princess' to aid you in your task. From now on you are a princess in your own right, not just as wife of Jiseve."

Benae gasped and flew to her feet. "Thank you, Your Majesty."

"Princess Benae, have I not requested you call me Beniel in private?"

"Thank you, Beniel."

The frown on the king's face didn't fade. "As much as I respect your ability to run the kingdom, Benae, you will need help. You will need a man behind you to order the army and help you deal with those who will not heed a woman's word. I gave this much thought." His eyes fell upon Ramón. "Squire, you have proven yourself loyal and brave. Additionally, you have the cunning to anticipate danger and problems. You did not relax your vigilance, even when Vorasava mocked you for your attention to detail. If not for your actions, one or both of us might well be dead, giving Piotr the kingdom. I wish you to aid Princess Benae in her task of administering Brightcastle and raising my nephew when he is born."

Benae couldn't believe her ears and Ramón's mouth had dropped open, his blue eyes wide.

"Ramón Zorba," King Beniel said, his voice ringing in the small room, "will you accept this task?"

Ramón snapped his mouth shut and Benae stared at her beloved, hardly believing they had the king's permission to be together.

"I'll give everything I have to ensure the health of the kingdom, of Princess Benae and her child. No one will ever sacrifice more."

"Ramón Zorba," the king said, drawing his sword. "I name you Guardian of Brightcastle and Knight of the Realm." He touched his sword to each of Ramón's shoulders.

Ramón stared, his mouth slightly open, as Beniel placed a golden chain of office around his neck. "You honor me far above what I deserve, Your Majesty."

Beniel waved away his words. "Do not be deceived," he said. "This task will not be easy, and you must both be vigilant. Guard yourselves, for you will continue to be targets. I will leave soldiers to help and you must train more. Vorasava can handle those details. Benae, your female guards are an excellent idea, but their numbers need expanding. Intelligence must be stepped up, so we are made aware of threats. I will send my best people to help with this."

The king stood and so did Benae. "I leave for Wildecoast at first light with the body of my brother. These territories are in good hands."

Benae curtsied and Beniel pulled her up and kissed both her cheeks. "Farewell, sister-in-law. Let there always be friendship between us." He turned to go, then stopped and faced Ramón. "Find my niece, Zorba. That is almost as important as keeping Benae safe."

"I'll do my best, Your Majesty."

The king strode from the room and Benae knelt in front of Ramón. They gazed at each other for long moments, Benae basking in a warm wave of contentment. Finally, she could love Ramón without guilt and subterfuge.

He broke the silence. "I love you." He leaned forward and she met him halfway. Their lips touched and Benae's stomach fluttered. This man thrilled her so!

She pulled away and smiled. "You give me everything I need. You're so much more than other men and now the king has set his seal of approval upon you. You never lost faith, even though I turned my back, even when circumstances kept us apart. Many times, you could have ridden away. You didn't."

Ramón's handsome face creased in a rueful smile. "I thought of it often, but I could never take that step. You held me near you. I couldn't leave you alone to fend for yourself."

"You will never know how glad I am that you didn't."

"I have some idea. When will I be healed enough to show you how I feel?"

Benae shook her head. "Incorrigible rogue! It will be at least a week until such a time, but there are many pleasures we can indulge in before then."

He drew her to him, his warm lips capturing hers, turning more demanding as she responded. She threw her arms around his neck and he gasped in pain. Benae pulled back.

"I promise an evening you'll never forget," she said, her mind already exploring the possibilities, "when you're well enough."

Ramón frowned and Benae had to restrain a giggle at his grumpy expression. Wasn't *she* the impatient one?

"I need you," he said
She smiled. "You'll never know how much I need you too."
"You have me, now and forever."
Benae smiled. "Now and forever."

EPILOGUE

LL was in readiness. Benae stood outside the doors to Brightcastle's grand hall, her attendant, Queen Adriana, by her side. She thought she might burst with joy. How a mere two months had changed everything! Today was her wedding day. Eight weeks ago, she had pledged herself to Jiseve. Now she prepared to walk down the aisle to Ramón Zorba, Steward of Brightcastle.

King Beniel Zialni awaited inside with Ramón, having offered his services as best man. Benae still couldn't believe the turnaround in her fortunes, nay *their* fortunes. A month ago, she had imagined her life over, her husband dead and suspicion upon her shoulders. But Jiseve was declared dead by natural causes and his brother, the king, had named she and Ramón guardians of Brightcastle.

She lay her hand over her belly and allowed herself to dream of a future where she and her husband would raise their children. They'd be happy, as would all the denizens of Brightcastle. She and Ramón could make it fact and turn back the clock to the time before Jiseve Zialni wreaked such fear amongst his people.

Perhaps this was the real purpose behind her failed arranged marriage? It had been the stepping stone to the life she sought when she left Tylevia. The support of the king and queen were evidence she had made the right choice in seeking a marriage of convenience with Jiseve Zialni. She would have been a loyal wife, but he didn't deserve her. And today, after weeks of abuse at Jiseve's hands, she would marry the man who rescued her.

Each time guilt rose to threaten her happiness, she pushed it aside, dwelt on the man who had saved her and would stand by her as she had this child. Her fortunes had changed for the better. Now all that remained was for her and her groom to commit to their future, together.

Queen Adriana fussed with the train of her emerald and gold bridal gown, as Benae wondered when the music would start. She smoothed her hair and checked her appearance in the large, gilt-framed mirror. Even now, she worried that something would spoil her happiness.

She listed potential hurdles, determined to reassure herself. Ramón was well, recovered from the assassin's dart meant for her or the king. He was as healthy as ever and she couldn't wait for them to be one again.

Over the last four weeks, she had met with Brightcastle's merchants and heads of guilds. All had been, if not effusive, supportive of her stewardship of the principality. King Beniel's support counted in her favor. If a threat should come, the business community would not be the source.

There had been many raised eyebrows among the nobility of the region, but again, royal support had silenced them. While she enjoyed Beniel's visible backing, no challenge would come from the court.

Unless Princess Alecia is found. The thought hit her stomach like a lead weight. The princess was out there somewhere, Benae was certain. She would be devastated when she learned of her father's death; distraught and furious. Benae only had to contemplate for seconds to realize she would be the target of Alecia's rage.

The first notes of the bridal march sounded, and she came back to the moment. Adriana caught her hand and gave it a squeeze, before handing her a posy of red and white winter roses. The queen smiled and nodded as the doors opened.

Benae caught her first glimpse of Ramón as he turned, his bearing proud, his gaze joyful. All thought of Alecia flew from her mind as she took the first steps toward her bridegroom, and the future.

THE END

GLOSSARY

Places

Kingdom of Thorius (Thor- ee- us) -the kingdom of men which encompasses the King's seat of Wildecoast and the Prince's seat of Brightcastle, along with other smaller towns

Wildecoast (Will – dee – coast) -the capital city perched on the top of a cliff overlooking the sea on the east coast of Thorius; climate is mild but windy

Brightcastle - large inland town surrounded by forests and farms, three to four days ride west of Wildecoast

Tylevia (Tie-lee-veeah) – a kingdom to the northwest of Thorius; home of Benae Branasar and Princess Avalin

Issia (Iss-ee-ah) – a kingdom to the west of Thorius; home of Princess Marey

Brevisten (Brev-is-ten) – a kingdom to the southwest of Thorius; home of Princess Lella

Amitania (Am – it – ay – nia) or *Elvandang* (Elle – van – dang) in elvish - the deserted city north of the Usetar Mountain Range in northern Thorius; once a thriving city; disputed ownership between elves and man

Usetar Range (You – set – ar) -the mountain range running across the northern parts of Thorius

People

Lenweri (Len – weir – ee) -the elven people who are tall and elegant with black skin and pointed ears and mainly dark hair; live in mountainous forests north and west of Thorius, in places encroaching onto Kingdom lands; also known as dark elves

Sis Lenweri - the faction of dark elves that wishes to take the kingdom of Thorius back from men

Defender - a race of shapeshifters who are created to defend those in danger; they sense those in need of their help; a Defender can shift into animal form and the ability is inherited through family lines

Characters

Princess Alecia Zialni (Al – ee – sha Zee – al – nee)) - the King's niece and daughter of Prince Jiseve Zialni who rules the principality of Brightcastle and is next in line to the throne. Alecia's story begins in **Princess Avenger** and continues in **Princess in Exile**.

Vard Anton - a shapeshifting Defender; army captain of Brightcastle in **Princess Avenger;** holder of many secrets; his story continues in **Princess in Exile**

Prince Jiseve Zialni (Jiss – eve Zee – al – nee) - next in line to the throne of Thorius, younger brother of the King, a widower; father of Alecia Zialni

Lady Benae Branasar (Ben-ay Bran-a-sar) – noble lady with an estate in Tylevia; heroine of **The Lady's Choice**; healer

*Ramón Zorba (*Rah – mon Zor – bah) - Lord of Wildecoast and squire to Prince Jiseve Zialni; his family have an estate south of Wildecoast; hero of **The Lady's Choice**

Merel (Mare-elle) – maid to Benae; more like a sister

Joletta (Joal-etta) - maid to Benae after Merel

Princess Avalin (Av-ar-lyn) – daughter of the king of Tylevia

Princess Marey (Mary) – daughter of the king of Issia

Princess Lella - daughter of the king of Brevisten

Hetty – mysterious ancient woman with magical powers; once Alecia's governess and nanny; declared a witch by Prince Jiseve and sentenced to death but rescued by Alecia

King Beniel Zialni (Ben – ee – elle Zee – al – nee) - King of Thorius; lives in Wildecoast; older brother of Jiseve Zialni and uncle of Alecia Zialni; married to Adriana

Queen Adriana - wife of the King; lives in Wildecoast; Alecia's aunt

Josef Formosa – Lieutenant in the Wildecoast army; cousin to Ramón Zorba

Elinor Zorba – Ramon's twin sister; dead in childbirth

Alique Zorba (Ah-leek) – sister to Ramón, younger by three years; lady-in-waiting to Queen Adriana

Nyon Zorba (Nie-on) – sister to Ramón, older by one year; wed to ship builder in Wildecoast.

Jacques Vorasava - Lieutenant in the Brightcastle army

Lord Giornan Finus (Jor – nan Fie – nus) – recently come to Brightcastle from a neighboring kingdom; Jiseve Zialni's advisor

Jorge Andra (George Andra) – previous squire to Prince Jiseve and close friend to Alecia; killed by mercenaries who were trying to collect money from his parents

Piotr Zialni (Peter Zialni) – son of Beniel and Jiseve Zialni's younger brother; next in line to the throne of Thorius (his father is dead) unless the King, Prince or Alecia have a son.

Izebel (Is – zee – belle) – a previous warrior Queen of Thorius from centuries ago, when females could rule; Alecia's idol.

Alvan Branasar – Benae's dead brother; killed by the dark elves

The Orards – farming couple east of Brightcastle; daughter called Elin who is ten years old

Damald Monive – physician to Prince Zialni

ABOUT THE AUTHOR

Bernadette Rowley is a lover of epic fantasy who is a veterinarian by day and an author by night. She is currently published in the genre of high fantasy romance with eight books, all set in her fantasy world of Thorius.

When she was a young teenager, an aunt gave her a copy of The Sword of Shannara by Terry Brooks and Bernadette has lived in various fantasy worlds ever since. It's no surprise that her chosen genre when writing romance is fantasy.

"I can see these settings so vibrantly in my mind and hope my readers can too."

But Bernadette has no desire to spoon-feed her readers by laboriously describing her fantasy settings. She would rather the reader use their own imagination.

Along with sword and sorcery, dashing heroes and stunning heroines, this author includes strong healing themes in many of her books- an element central to her everyday job.

"When I started writing the Queenmakers Saga, I never imagined my day job would force its way into my stories as it has."

And of course, there are animals, especially Bernadette's beloved horses.

Bernadette lives in Brisbane, Australia, with the four heroes in her life- her husband Michael and three grown sons.

241

Connect with the Author

Website: www.bernadetterowley.com
Facebook: www.facebook.com/bernadetterowleyfantasy
Twitter: www.twitter.com/bt_rowley